To VENTUR, the Subs were a nuisance. All the underworld's billions were fed and housed: under the stern, loving care of VENTUR's great machine systems. No one could deny the benefits of VENTURan organisation, VENTURan welfare. Of all the cultures, only the Subs refused to be grateful and humble.

ALIC was an innocent tourist, a retired games conceiver; drawn to the Subcontinent in the hope of a little old-fashioned excitement. Then she met Millie Mohun, who invited her to play a game that would beat any other she had ever tried . . .

And then ALIC fell into the depths, into the churning peopled void . . . Her whole existence became a desperate attempt to escape, while around her a great, ancient culture was surging towards violent revolution.

This powerful futuristic novel is the new book by the author of the critically acclaimed DIVINE ENDURANCE. It is the chilling and convincing portrait of a world ruled by all-embracing technology and an arrogant oligarchy, a world in need of hopes and dreams.

# Escape Plans
## —GwyneTH Jones—

'from the body of this death'

Romans 7:24

London
**UNWIN PAPERBACKS**
Boston          Sydney

First published in Great Britain by Unwin Paperbacks 1986
This book is copyright under the Berne Convention. No reproduction
without permission. All rights reserved.

**UNWIN® PAPERBACKS**
**40 Museum Street, London WC1A 1LU, UK**

Unwin Paperbacks
Park Lane, Hemel Hempstead, Herts HP2 4TE, UK

Allen & Unwin Australia Pty Ltd
8 Napier Street, North Sydney, NSW 2060, Australia

Unwin Paperbacks with the
Port Nicholson Press
PO Box 11-838 Wellington, New Zealand

## 01459527

**British Library Cataloguing in Publication Data**

Jones, Gwyneth
  Escape plans.
  I. Title
  823'.914[F]   PR6060.051/

  ISBN 0-04-823344-7

Set in 10 on 12 Point Times Roman by A.J. Latham Ltd, Dunstable
Printed and bound in
Great Britain by
Hazell, Watson & Viney Limited,
Member of the BPCC Group,
Aylesbury, Bucks.

for Peter

# Contents

# Acknowledgements

Thanks to Karen Hart, Dinah Clarke and Peter Gwilliam.
And also to Brighton ROC — for inspiration and support.

# Escape Plans

# Et in Arcadia Ego

# 1

*My heart pounded, my mouth hauled air. Across my shoulders a line of terrific tension knit my muscles, engaging in force with those other muscles, thrusting pistons of bone wrapped in blood and glistening hide. The pack surrounded me in thunder and bodily heat, little cold gouts of animal spittle hit my cheeks I felt the thighs — my thighs — clench in a compulsion more violent than any amorous climax; and an enormous surge under me. I bowed my cheek against grey flesh running with a hot gloss of sweat, making myself light as air, standing on my toes, floating, no longer tense . . . Everything slowed.*

Ah. Good one.

I slipped my vicset down around my neck and parted from the throbbing animals. The scented breath of deodar and pine, filtered into our conditioned air, returned to me. It seemed I could have reached out and touched green branches. I was standing on a wide deck of golden (simulated) natural wood that floated unsupported in the middle of a grove of majestic trees. In the distance a massive bank of monitors gibbered at me brightly. Soft sighs and little stirrings fluttered through the crowd of stylishly dressed locals as we all came down. I blinked at a streak of rainbow sheen caught in the cedars, betraying the presence of a bubble canopy between us and the world outside: and felt a little lost. Where was the race?

I was in the Enabled Pavilion at Subcontinental Area Command: SHACTI, to its friends, attending a glittering underworld social occasion. Everyone was talking about the bizarre execution in the Presidential Palace, a story which had just been allowed on line. It had a rich assortment of compelling features —

starships, rebellious basics: vile orgies. Briefly, a basic number had taken to leading little mobs out of SHACTI's number accommodation to watch for starships (a pan-galactic emissary, you see, was about to arrive). The Sub President had her arrested: and then murdered — as live entertainment at a dinner party.

The days of savagery had passed. There were no more secret agents sneaking down to earth to rescue precious genotypes. The underworld was tamed and organised. In the official phrase, successfully librated — all its destructive forces balanced in an ever-changing, never failing equipoise. There was peace plenty and tourism over all the ancient mother-planet. The Subcontinent, however, was still showing a little fight. It was the smallest of CHTHON's 7 administrative units and the latest to enter the libration. The Subs had a culture of their own, instead of a bland pastiche of life in Space. They were yet able to make life difficult for their Rangers, and interesting for travellers.

Still tingling with the pleasure of that borrowed adrenalin, I made my way through the between-races surge of muttering and fluttering to join my Ranger friend SETI. The enabled fondly imagined that they were affecting the manners of elegant VENTURan society. Alas, the presence of so many bodies in one space almost made this VENTURan physically sick, the first time she met it. I was over that now. After all, I'd come down here expressly for the strange, alien experiences.

SETI was in uniform. I had put on a suit myself: visitors were directed to dress formally whenever in public. She inclined her sleek head as I approached. On the Subcontinent men went bare headed while women grew their hair: whereas CHTHON personnel always depilated. Sub Rangers bore the confusion with dignity.

SETI wasn't here voluntarily, and couldn't imagine why I bothered.

'If you tourists like 'em so much,' she said. 'Why don't you stay in their funxing hotels? They're forever grizzling about your lack of economic input.'

'I tried it SETI. Couldn't stand the bugs.'

'ALIC!'

14

'It's true. I couldn't even get my door to open. And the bathroom kept pelting me with grapefruit juice.'

We were speaking acronymic, so there was no risk of offending anyone.

SETI grinned, while her eyes perused the crowd with a spurious expression of deep and Ranger-like attention.

She was blind. She'd been blind from conception, the result of one of those odd bargains our executive lines make with PRENAT. She wore a prosthesis, invisible and efficient. Executive pride wouldn't allow her to go back on her parent(s) bargain and have a nerve graft. But knowing SETI's opinion of this kind of duty, I was sure it was in her sleeve.

'Commander's pulling frightful faces at you,' I suggested meanly.

'Oh, funx off ALIC. She isn't even here.'

'Isn't she? Why not?'

SETI's blind eyes narrowed in reproof.

'Can't talk about it ALIC, sorry.'

I had been meaning to tease her, and see if I could elicit more of the execution story: the details too gross to be committed to decent circuitry. I changed my mind. She was in her Ranger mood, and I had better be humble.

On the breast patch of her spruce blue suit SETI wore 2 stripes, one silver, one red as blood. I could wear the silver myself. It merely stated that she was a PIONER — an adult passenger/ inhabitant of a neo environment rotation. In other words, a citizen of the Space communities collectively known as VENTUR. The red stripe said she was a menarch, trained and able to give birth to a live child. The gene-lines (or families, as they would say on the underworld) who preserved abilities of that kind came near to being our ruling class. SETI traced her menarch ancestry back to officers of the first carousels. In theory our most select executives are always ready to abandon the machines and set about wresting life from the raw elements of an unknown planet. And though we know they will never be required to do so, we have to respect the principle. It is essence of VENTUR.

The menarchs never managed to become Rulers of the

Universe. VENTUR is a democracy. So they have to be content with serving as underworld Rangers. After passing through the ranks of CHTHON at something approaching the speed of light, SETI would proceed straight to the plenum Secretariat; so long as she didn't catch pernicious leukemia somewhere on the way. But by that time — VENTUR hoped — she would have worked out her empire-building urges where she couldn't do any harm.

Thi SETI and I had been at school together once. My desk had captured her name on the Sub Area Command list when it was planning my trip: and we had resumed a half-forgotten friendship. I neither envied nor resented Thi SETI's status. In Space, as they say, no one's on top. Down here it was slightly different. She was accustomed to dealing with numbers: I had to humour her a little.

Now, in the middle of the deck, Pavilion threw up a cage of light, which sang a warning to stray racegoers who had wandered on to the stage. In the cage appeared the galloping horses, a soundless overwhelming presence. The bars of light disappeared and we were left with the replay. It was my race. I recognised the iron grey and felt an answering beat of excitement in my blood. There was no attempt, naturally, to reproduce the whole race. This was art; and very good too, for the underworld. Beyond the light stage a jockey had been brought in, to be petted and praised. She rode My Sorrow, exclaimed my dangling vicset band. The grey, by Gay Sorrow out of My Mountain . . . Note the phenomenally low pulse rate of this superb athlete. Sporting enabled slipped their hands inside the girl's clothes to feel if it were true.

'I do hope,' muttered SETI bitterly, 'they aren't going to bring in the horse.'

If there must be crowds, high ranking Subs made a pretty show. The Subcontinent was famous for its head-woven textile – *gengra* they called it. There was a strong cultural prohibition against nakedness, so when they wanted to look like us they wore body-hugging gengra from head to toe. Forked fragments of stars and sunsets, herds of zebra; flowers growing, rippled around the jockey. Gengra feeds off any nearby power: it would be a warm

16

day on Titan where your pretty clothes refused to run. But as I remarked to SETI, the vicsets looked peculiar. At a games stadium at home, we'd be wearing sweaty trackstraps or nothing.

The underworld 'vicarious experience games' were nothing like vic games we played in Space. There was no subjective scenario in them, no physical; no role play. In the actual stadium trained basics competed against each other, sometimes with the help of other animals. Next door, the enabled were standing around in their best clothes, with twinkling vicset bands around their temples. Each participant chose a player from the programme — and experienced something of what happened to her or him. The trance was so light it was perfectly possible to reselect if your choice seemed to be having a hard time (an unsporting option that really shocked me when I first came across it).

I had a professional interest in the phenomenon of underworld vic. I had once been a games conceiver myself.

'Did you know,' I said to SETI. 'According to their cultural prax the Subs are forbidden to use vicarious experience equipment.'

As far away from the jockey as they could be, a group of heavily clothed figures stood together. Their hair hung to their shoulders, their heads were together in earnest conclave. To SETI they were trouble, to me they were unspoiled, valuable survivors. In a rush of post-vic benignity I wished I could bring the 2 together.

'I've been taking a burst course,' I announced. 'From their University. It's fascinating —'

SETI looked bored.

'Most tourists,' she remarked gloomily, 'come for the scenery. Capt you later ALIC. I'm on duty — have to circulate.'

I had spotted an enabled acquaintance of mine — a woman called Yolande Tectonics. I strolled across the deck to network a little.

The enabled families of the underworld all had inherited rights of access to our facilities. But Yolande was a special case. Her grandmother or great grandmother had been raised to the silver stripe. She was immensely proud of her PIONER status, though of course she was never likely to leave earth.

Her friends melted away. They belonged to the overdressed and hairy contingent. I hoped they might come back when they saw I was not a Ranger. Yolande herself wore a close approximation of a formal VENTURan sheer; on the breast a broad gleaming band.

'Do you think this woman should have been terminated?'

'Oh, certainly Pioneer Aeleysi. What are you thinking of? Don't you recognise anti-VENTURan agitation when you see it?'

She treated me like a child. It was the same with every enabled I had encountered. They must know better, but without the Ranger blues and bare head they looked at your face and couldn't help themselves. It was clever of her to pronounce my name correctly. I had been called 'Alice' over my screen occasionally — a somewhat startling intimacy. Yolande knew acronymic, at least a little of its etiquette. She would not ellide my personal ID unless I suggested she should. But she still said 'pioneer', which set my teeth on edge.

A group of extremely gaudy enabled passed by, in the centre of it one of the Sub President's nephews. It might have been the decadent young man who had been closely involved in the live execution. Those beautiful people, the Sub Presidents, were a CHTHON institution. I was surprised it had not noticed they were the wrong crew for the serious-minded Sub. Possibly there were other considerations. All systems are a little corrupt, after all: that's why we need the libration.

Yolande scowled balefully after the giggling rainbow. Her vicset was round her neck, dead and dull because she had not keyed it to her wristfax. Nobody could accuse her of joining in the 'brain orgy'.

'People like that ought to have their heads burned off,' she growled. I did not ask if she was still talking about the rebellious basic.

We had not met in-person before, only over the screen in the University net. I was impressed by the alien being in front of me: half savage, half Space-veneered sophisticate. Yolande, however, seemed perfectly at ease.

'It's strange,' I said. 'As I learn about your culture, I'm amazed at how close it is to VENTUR.'

'Huh?'

'Well. Yolande, we have "SERVE" and you have your "Function" —'

Every other culture on the underworld recognised an array of systems much like the VENTURan array. When CHTHON took over, it was easy enough to patch 'the money machine', or whatever it was called, into our FUNDS. And so on through each area. On the Subcontinent there was no such arrangement. They had one system, known as Function. They refused to admit it could be divided. CHTHON patched them in anyway, but the disjoint caused endless problems.

'You know what SERVE is Yolande. Zero Variation Process Control. It's our oversystem: the one that keeps all the others running as they should, here and in Space. SERVE's the thing that stops my shuttle booking from interfering with your toilet pump.'

I laughed, to show her that was meant to be funny.

'Don't you see? Function and SERVE are really exactly the same thing.'

The rest of the numbers found the Sub attitude to systems intelligence offensive. Most of them personified their arrays to some degree, and they didn't like to see the friendly ghosts so brutally dumped out of the machines. CHTHON personnel, who ought to know better, were not free of this hostility. But I had come to the Sub as a traveller; my mind was open. I saw at once the identity between this 'single oversystem' and SERVE. So much goes on in the lightlines, such fertile connections between this and that. The process of keeping it in balance becomes the most important process, if not the only process . . .

Yolande gazed at me solemnly out of her little greenish eyes. I noticed suddenly that I could see the furtive outline of some cultural undergarment, peeping through her sheer just above the generous 'pioneer' stripe. I had to bite my lip, and lost the thread of my argument.

'You are wrong,' said Yolande.

'What?'

'SERVE is not identical with Function,' she explained.

She looked around the deck, perhaps hoping her friends would come back and support her. I saw her CHTHON tag winking in her ear: but also another glint of metal, in a less acceptable location.

The Subs had a relationship with their 'Function' which could only be called symbiotic. The characteristic way they grew their hair, with a shorn crown and a thick fringe dangling over their temples, only seemed to emphasise what it was trying to hide. Yolande had two holes there burned through flesh and bone, wired up with gold and never allowed to heal. Every time I accidentally caught a glimpse of the arrangement on any Sub, I couldn't seem to help imagining myself *touching* (Augh!) one of those open sores. The real burns were inside, in the brain itself. Yolande's family was in the construction business. They made mobile domes. Yolande was hard-wired. She was a walking plastics process, you just had to plug her in.

It was no use. Having remembered the holes, I could not continue a serious conversation.

'Come on Yolande,' I cried bravely, gesturing towards a sunken furniture nest with a games console in it. 'Let's play something together. We can use hand controls.'

Yolande T politely excused herself. 'I'm afraid I don't *play* with machines. Pioneer Aeleysi.'

A slight emphasis on the word 'play' put me firmly in my place.

There were basic servants dotted about, bearing trays of weird delicacies. Enabled underworlders liked to cannibalise their basics. It was not an economy, the collars were expensive. They just preferred personal service. The prospect of being surrounded by human domestic appliances dissuaded many people from visiting the underworld: it was more of a deterrent than the fearsome gravity well. I took a canapé with practised ease. I was used to them now, I could see the girls and boys as pretty, in their nice tight little sheers. They stood in decorative groups, waking up when the collars round their necks called them. They could be petted too, but I wasn't quite brave enough for that.

I didn't want to take another race. The excellent win on My Sorrow had left me pleasantly high. But I felt rather aimless now that I'd exhausted my contacts. There were no other tourists about. The Sub was not a popular resort, and also people were nervous about in-person mixing. It was a pity there were no men around. Rangers were not encouraged to bring partners of either sex on tour. SETI complained about it bitterly. I had less use for the other sex than she, but a nice hearty companion would have been useful for this occasion. A Ranger's partner, interested in the local culture. Exec men, in my opinion, were generally brighter than the women.

I wandered over to the monitor bank and stared at the other underworld games: some realtime and some recorded, tiny and far away. Little voices jabbered on my vicset as I came into view: I keyed them out. I had no wish to dump income on the Southern2 ice soccer. In a larger screen in the centre of the bank lay SHACTI racetrack, under a perfect blue sky.

The stands were packed with basics. It was odd to see them. In this Pavilion and on the shiny enabled mall I had been more in-person with hordes of unknown numbers than ever with my closest friends at home. But just when I'd decided the crowding was quite bearable, I always saw or heard something to remind me of the truth. The enabled were nothing, absolutely nothing. The real underworld was down there: and I would never understand it. But who would want to? I gazed, slightly vertiginous, at the wriggling seething mass. Could one vic it? I wondered. No one would dare.

I looked for SETI after that. I found her but she seemed abstracted. Perhaps she still had her eyes in her sleeve.

'Oh ALIC,' she said. 'I forgot. It'll be on your desk by now. We've had to turn down your access to go and shoot snow leopards.'

There was a recreation preserve north of SHACTI, on the alt wall. Only Rangers were allowed to go in and record the animals in-person, but SETI had promised me that she could ax it.

'Things are a bit funxing wobbly at present. There's a study centre up there, so it all has to go closed.'

I had been counting on that trip.

'What's so special about a study centre?' I wailed. 'Trust me SETI, I'm not going to sell my story —'

21

Mistake! CHTHON personnel were so sensitive about those places. I shouldn't have protested at all.

'Capt your later —' said Thi SETI coldly, as she walked away.

I'd been wondering ever since the replay came up, what would happen to you if you walked around the horses. I walked around them. It's bad manners anyway, to go through a light stage; spoiling everybody's illusion.

What happened was that I was sat down in a furniture nest. My mood had broken. SETI was a real live Ranger and she had a lovely body: copper bright through her sheers with UV protection. And she didn't mind a little old fashioned space-love to while away a tiresome tour without her partner. I had been too grateful, too admiring. She repaid me by treating me like one of her enabled. There probably wasn't any prohibition. She just didn't feel like doing me a favour.

And what an idiot I must have looked chatting to Yolande T. The poor woman didn't seem to understand a word I said.

I stared at the golden floor between my bare feet. I was irritated with myself and ready to leave.

I looked up. I saw the jockey from the race I had vic'd sitting under the monitor bank. She was quietly eating canapés from a napkin in her lap. She had a straight back and good shoulders, neatly muscled but not at all masculine. Good breasts. She was wearing a pale blue sheer cut off at mid thigh. It had the SHACTI stadium logo on it. She wore a collar round her neck but it didn't seem to have lobotomised her. There she sat, neatly eating. The vic-players had forgotten her. The self-respecting Subs wished that she didn't exist. She smiled at me.

It was a wonderful smile, a subtle and promising smile. My momentary depression lifted.

There are probably 16 of her, I thought. Maybe you can take one home. Then I remembered human cloning wasn't allowed down here. The stadium could seed its horses, but not its jockeys. The problem we have with numbers isn't that they are hard to produce. What made me think of seeding? Clones always have a certain air, as if they pity the rest of us for our haphazard origins.

Games players were chosen out of the mass from their early MEDIC assessments. They were *biels,* bonded labour: owned by the stadium. That gave my jockey a rather dubious status in local society. In theory, Sub orthoprax prohibited the buying and selling of basics. Part of the extreme distaste for vic games was the fact that they involved intimate contact with biels.

She was the rider of My Sorrow, I remembered; and checked my programme. Millie Mohun, the famous hill girl, whispered the vicset band against my collarbone. She had been brought in from the surface and was doing very well on the Sub stadium circuit. All of them were famous, but I was obscurely pleased to find she was one of the wild ones. I wondered if she was enabled to smile at me like that? Perhaps no one could use her except for the vic. I might have checked with tourist information but I felt a slight embarrassment. It's always the silliest things you commit to circuitry that come back and haunt you. I didn't want to become the object of Ranger hilarity in a monitor room.

The races were over. I did not notice SETI leave, Yolande was lost in the crowd. I let a plump doll help me into my boots and suit and took the little used gravity lift down from the Pavilion foyer to the ground.

+

Among the girders of the Pavilion's permanent mooring, garishly coloured aircars shuffled on the parking lot, being channelled to their owners inside the underbelly of the lustrous egg. One by one they popped up into the mouth there, popped out again and sailed away on the grid. Collared domestic servants, pets and drivers squatted beside the rows and hopped and jumped to get inside when the cars started moving. The floor was fused dirt. Everything had the rough uneasy air of a place that isn't meant to be seen. I patted the parking attendant reassuringly. Hello friend, it whispered. Hello ALIC. It was uneasy because I didn't ask for any service. I had to speak sharply to stop it following me about.

At the back of the lot there was a tunnel leading directly to the physical stadium. I could see in, through the rather murky quadrant of heavy plastic, to a vague grey area with dispensers on the walls and a few numbers loitering about. From the underside of the Pavilion a fat stem reached down to the ground, opposite the tunnel lock. It was the servants' exit. The path between stem and tunnel was marked with slender rods about 3 standard feet high. They didn't carry the restricted access field, they were just a reminder so the domestics didn't accidentally step out and get a jolt.

I had not realised I would be so conspicuous. I had imagined bustle of the kind I'd met on cultural walkways, eye contact as she passed, and then − whatever.

The catering domestics suddenly appeared. They were no longer wearing their matching sheers, they must have a locker room somewhere. I saw them each stand docile while the gate took their collars off, and out they came: scurrying past me in a sudden burst of chattering and giggles. I thought I'd have to wait for my jockey, then I realised she was there, in the last group. She had changed like the rest into shapeless opaque pyjamas. I would not have known her, so disembodied, except for the set of her shoulders; a nice look of working muscle among the juicy girls and boys. She didn't see me. She wasn't wearing a collar any more and I didn't know her number, so how could I attract her attention? I was just about to step forward and make myself known somehow, when something happened. The loiterers must have been watching the exit too. As Millie went through into the grey area, they all rushed forward and she was surrounded. They were all male, bareheaded and they didn't look very respectable.

The domestics quickly hurried on and disappeared. The male surplus problem! I was always hearing of it, from the Rangers. But perhaps these were fans, perhaps they were the famous jockey's bodyguard. They'd rather spoiled my discreet encounter, anyway. Oh well, I thought. It wasn't important.

I was turning away, when Millie glanced over her shoulder. She knew I was there after all. Her eyes looked straight into mine.

I had no idea how the numbers were policed. I did not know what to call, or how long it would take whatever process there was to operate. I stood for a second, my hand on my wristfax − but the men had already bundled her out of sight. I went through the Reac: forgetting as always that there was no need to push and

24

nearly falling over nothing. I started to run after them down the tunnel.

It seemed cold in there under the permanent lights. My clumping gallop echoed around the hard scuffed walls. I ran downhill. Almost at once I saw ahead a moving parti-coloured mass and came bursting out into open space. In front of me was a surging crowd of numbers, seething like lava towards the stadium gates.

Subcontinental SHACTI occupied the top of a ridge. The basic accommodation was sealed on to its southern face. The stadium was to the north, in a partly natural valley hanging over one of the region's sudden gorges. I saw that the masses must have tunnels through the ridge: I glimpsed grey archways into the hill, beyond that heaving flow of life.

It was bewildering. So many — how could anyone imagine there might be so many? And the sky was wrong. It was blurred by the field that kept these masses from oozing out into the landscape. I had not realised how much the image on the Pavilion monitor was edited. The shadows of dark hills rose round me. All SHACTI life was on the heights, it was strange to feel enclosed.

But I was only disoriented for a moment. I saw that the bare terrace on which I was standing was covered with trickles from the main lava flow: little rills and puddles of number. The men who had ambushed Millie had her up against a wall. Nobody was taking any notice. I shouted 'Hoi!' or something and charged forward. But they had already vanished when I reached her. I suppose the suit was enough for them, without further inquiry.

That part was easy, a reversion to my long ago space-cadet days. Always break up a fight, fights are dangerous. Now I didn't know what to do.

'Are you hurt?' I said. 'Did they take anything?'

She was not unusually pretty after all. She was small and wiry as a jockey must be, with a healthy mid-brown complexion, and the ubiquitous Sub fringe. She had a look — a brightness, that I couldn't pin down to any feature. Perhaps it was just that she was young. VENTURans live long, and we do not grow old very easily. We look good. Our faces do not wrinkle, nor does the flesh fall away in that depressing fashion from cheek-bones and

25

eye-sockets and under the jaw. Not until we are ready to retreat to fractional gravity and a quiet end. However, there is a price. In a sense human tissues starts ageing the moment the cells begin to divide. For all practical purposes though, the end of adolescence is the beginning of senescence, so that is where it must be arrested. I looked at Millie Mohun, who was no adolescent, and saw what perfect young maturity was meant to be. For a moment, I felt blighted.

3 years, I thought, or 4, and it will be all over with that face. What a pity. What a pity for all of us. Time's relative.

'I saw you in the Pavilion,' I said. 'You smiled at me, do you remember? You ought to tell the stadium about those louts. Or I will.'

'No, don't do that.'

There was something wrong. She was too calm, considering she had been rescued from an unpleasant attack. I remembered that when the men first jumped her she had neither struggled nor protested. She did not cry out, except to me, with her eyes. It had been almost as if she was expecting them.

'Millie, are you in trouble? What did the bullies want?'

'It isn't important. There are things they want me to do and I have to disappoint them, that's all.'

I thought I understood. At home gambling on the vic was a personal affair and had little to do with FUNDS. If you wanted to play those games there was always the Interplanetary Futures Exchange. But the underworlders maintained bizarre controls to preserve a random element in their simple sports. They did not race horses, as one might imagine, to strive for better time over distance. A lot of disposable income moved around the stadium circuit: and the Subs, despite the inevitable cultural prohibitions, were as keen as the rest. None of Millie's sensors controlled the way she played her race. Who wants to experience being a puppet? Therefore she was vulnerable to unscrupulous persons who wanted her to 'do things'.

'Why are you protecting them Millie? Are they blackmailing you in some way?'

A single vic rush doesn't last long but perhaps it was still enhancing the world a little. I thought I had stumbled into an exciting adventure. I saw myself tracking down a gang of number criminals, to general applause.

Or perhaps, it could be, I didn't quite like the way Millie Mohun was standing there. She was only a number, the first centre-living basic number I'd ever met. I didn't think they were supposed to be like this. I felt it had been a mistake to come chasing after her. With a desire I would not have admitted, to gently reinstate the distance between us, I reached out, smiling kindly, for the tag in her ear. The little silver shield came away easily. It lay on my palm, warm and bright.

After a moment I let it go. The metallic thread retracted, the shield nestled into place again. I had intended to check it through my fax, to find out what was going on here. There was no point. I knew it was not Millie's. The tags the numbers wore were made of a responsive NA alloy, sensitised to each individual's tissue ID. Every little piece of metal was effectively unique. On the right skin contact they shone silver bright and warmed to blood heat. Detached they turned black and cold, very rapidly. There was no need to look any further for Millie's trouble.

If we were to keep the numbers fed and clothed and breathing we must know how many there were, what state they were in and where. Even the most enabled had their tags — though with a 'PIONER' like Yolande T you wouldn't just read her on your wrist, not without showing good reason.

Millie's tag had 2 functions. It held her serial number and a summary of her current status: information which I could read on my wristfax; which anyone could reach, so long as the inquirer understood the codes or had a reader sophisticated enough to translate. More importantly for Millie, the tag was her access to the systems. The parking grub under the Pavilion recognised me as a unique physical index called On ALIC R4, because I was a PIONER and written into the great VENTURan memory of which that grub was a tiny remote part. Equally, underworld machinery recognised a number's tag. She needed it to access food, to move about. It was the way SHACTI centre kept track of her, and constantly updated the body of information that was *Millie* and no one else.

Even the wild numbers on the surface knew they must bring

their babies to be accounted. They knew CHTHON and all SERVE's monitors would pursue them unforgivingly if they did not.

Millie stood waiting, calm and composed. I wondered what she thought I was going to do to her.

She had been wearing a collar in the Pavilion, which would have protected her from immediate discovery. Enabled IDs could be added to the recognition lists of a place like the Pavilion, but we didn't do that with basics. The collars biels wore not only carried restraint and instructions, they also blocked the tiny tag emission. So the Pavilion didn't get upset about the presence of unlisted numbers, security was preserved and everyone was happy.

I suddenly wondered, did it upset Millie to be collared? Almost certainly not. She was probably delighted to be a gamesplayer on any terms. Even on the Sub there must be glory in it: something for her to remember when she was turned off. She might not, of course, survive her physical peak. Underworld games facilities were designed for excitement, not the safety of vic-fodder. I had a flash of that eastern turn: banked so fiendishly, the drop into the gorge under my heel. I wanted to explain to her that at home I had done things just as dangerous: subjectively, at least. I wanted to say *I was with you*. But it didn't mean anything. Probably everyone in the Pavilion had been backing the favourite.

'You shouldn't wear a forged tag,' I told her abruptly. 'That's very serious. Who gave it to you? It was wicked of them.'

'It was well meant.'

Again that uncanny composure. I couldn't decide if it was a number's natural fatalism, or a sign of unusually low intelligence. She did not look stupid . . . Millie recalled me to myself by telling me that she had to go. 'My Sorrow is waiting for me,' she said. It took me a moment to recollect that this was the name of a horse. I was flustered. I told her: 'I'll see you again. I want to help you Millie —'

She was already walking away. She looked back, smiled and nodded; then the crowd swallowed her.

28

# 2

The world turned, the sun glided towards a black-green horizon. Crest on crest of forested hills; brilliant valleys between, reflected in their glow and shadow the changes of a painted sky. Away to the north-east a jagged line of snow peaks slowly drifted from crimson into apricot. Sub Continental Area Command (SHACTI) lay and glittered along the Ridge like the misplaced tongue of a glacier. Not as spectacular as Mars, nor as pure as Maria or Farside, but stranger, much stranger than either: the rich-textured mother planet.

Down in the depths the underworld belonged to the numbers. But in the secret agent days, Rangers had fixed their bases in high country. The air pressure at 5000 standard feet was near enough to Space level: and there were plenty of places in reasonable latitudes, even at earth's worst, where mountains remained thinly populated. Life on the 'Threshold' had become a CHTHON tradition. Now no one went down into the soup in-person, except on Mission duty. And if it meant the underworlders had to look up to see VENTUR, it couldn't do them any harm.

It was hard to believe, looking at SHACTI, that there were ABOOO basic numbers stowed away inside. Not to mention the enabled level with its elaborate shopping malls, bars and hotels. But that was the CHTHON miracle. Even in the depths the numbers were all contained, mostly in massive underground objects or 'centres' housing several millions each. Forests were growing again, seas and rivers had been restored to life.

For generations, the people of Space knew that things were going badly with the world below. It was the drawn out end of a collapse begun long before. That must have been when we developed our strong image of ourselves as a band of fugitives. We had escaped from the burning wreck, we didn't dare look back. The underworld Rangers began life as commercial salvage workers. It wasn't for the good of the natives that they came down. They were looking for mice and butterflies and other odd fragments, obscurely needed for our new web of life.

Responsibility came later when other things had changed, and by then it was almost too late. But we cleared them off the dying surface. We honeycombed the planet like an asteroid with light lines and transport tunnels. We deployed the MONSAT helix, so every cell of ground would be monitored as tenderly and minutely as the metal-glass shells of our own radials. I had spent some time exploring the high altitude desert beyond SHACTI. I had seen in-person the network of loc-points and beacons, sparkling over the most absolute wilderness. Nothing that happened on earth could escape CHTHON's attention, and every system was fully integrated. There could be no over production, no famine: no wars, no uncontained disasters.

And because of the tagging procedure we could let the numbers alone. In every case CHTHON customised the necessary restraints into local cultural prax and respect-for-systems. They could go anywhere, do anything in complete security, with the absolute minimum of active intervention.

Not all of them were grateful. The basics never complained, but resentful minor enabled often muttered. They said we had cleared the surface and 'imprisoned' their populations so we could use the planet for food plant. This was patently untrue. We'd never have survived the first 100 years in Space if we hadn't learned to feed ourselves. There was another ugly rumour, that we kept huge secret farms of basic numbers as live organ banks. CHTHON used a small number of basics in life-enhancing research. I felt a little uneasy about that myself, but it's hard to argue strongly against something that really saves lives. But as for the 'organ banks' — you could only deny the story calmly, concealing a natural reaction which might offend the accuser.

I sat under my favourite pines on a hillside opposite SHACTI, with my head bare and my suit unsealed. After the grapefuit pelting incident I persuaded SETI to access me a capin in LECM

(Local Environment Contained Modules). There was one of these annexes attached to every Area Command. It served as a resting place for CHTHON supernumeraries and a haven — for tourists — from the hurly-burly of serious travel experience. The units were capsule installations, individually landscaped and rooted to a buried centre stem. I might as well have been alone on LECM's hilltop, for all I saw of other visitors. It was very restful.

There was a permanent air grid over the immediate environs of SHACTI, carrying enabled cars lock to lock between their discreet homebases and the attractions of the Ridge. VENTURan tourists were requested not to acquire private transport: except hire-Rovers for the wildernesss. There was a taxi fleet, but I preferred to walk. I could do it like a Ranger now. I'd trained myself to tolerate the extra fraction of gravity, I had walked back from the Pavilion, alone in beauty. Here in the LECM grounds I was inside a restricted access field again, but the invisible barrier was a mere formality. The enabled, by a splendid CHTHON ordinance, were not supposed to set foot on open surface; and everything to do with basic numbers was hidden under it. CHTHON maintained a small surface population of 'wild' numbers on the Threshold in each bloc, for conservation purposes. But I'd never seen one near the Ridge. I wouldn't have minded that anyway. They were attractive creatures, innocent and shy as animals.

The long wet 'summer' was over. The air was crisp, the sky by day deep and clear. Several enabled had asked me *how do you like our blue sky?* It amazed me that they'd never bothered to find out that we had 'blue sky' at home. I had had to make an effort at first to believe I wasn't looking at an effect copied from my own radial's light dispersal. But I was hooked now. I was convinced. This is where we started . . .

In Space we traced our prerecorded history back to an otherwise forgotten Roman emperor, who decided that he wanted 'the whole world to be measured'. Caesar's geometers proved once and for all, for that empire anyway, that the world is round and not flat. Thus began what we call the 'Age of Unlimited Expansion'; which finally gave birth to VENTUR.

I sighed. It was lucky for the underworlders that the expansion turned out to have its limits. Clearly we would have been fools to watch the only living gene pool go down the toilet and do nothing about it. But they needed us far more than we needed them.

Whenever I was out on the surface I felt much more sympathetic towards the Rangers' callous lack of interest in enabled culture. At one point in the planning of CHTHON, there had been a serious proposition that we should save the planet but not the humans (or ex-humans, as they were sometimes called). That was the solution of maternity drive running wild. Me and mine, says the mother — and everything else goes out the airlock. As a plenum VENTUR could not consider it. Still, it was hard not to start dreaming, out here, about the way things might have been. It would be so delightful if the numbers just didn't exist and this was a genuine untouched, unknown planet.

The sky turned greenish gold, fingered over with deep, deep indigo. The uneasiness of that awkward little encounter at the physical stadium slipped away from me, as the last red limb of the sun dipped out of sight. There now — that was worth the shuttle fare.

My capin was a one-roomed bubble shack with a clear wrap front section looking out towards the Ridge. Trees, mist and scarlet-flowered rhododendrons were my neighbours, and in the mornings grey langur monkeys came and danced on the roof.

I stepped through the lock, shrugged off my suit into the clamps in the porch and asked housekeep if there was anything in the Jam that needed my attention. 'Nogo, Commander.' Housekeep attended to the capin's running needs in a smaller bubble on the side. I would have preferred to manage on my own, but Area Command had a policy of employing basics, in line with enabled prax, in all non-restricted areas. I had tried to stop her calling me 'Commander' but it seemed the recognition set of an LECM domestic contained only one type of VENTURan.

Pia was waiting for me inside the door. She gave me a smack, then scampered to a safe distance, and stood scowling, jutting her underlip bitterly.

'Oh Pia, that was naughty.'

32

'Didn't hurt you.'

'Yes you did, you *bad* girl.'

She looked so sweet and cross I could hardly keep from laughing. Darling Pia. I had leased her from a pet agency, out of scientific curiosity; now I dreamed of taking her home. I was alarmed at first to find she was only 16 years old (underworld reckoning) but was assured that in basic terms she was fully adult. I chose her out of the catalogue because her eyes were blue. We don't have blue eyes in Space. The 'genetic optimising' phase eliminated them as a design flaw. Alas, when she arrived in-person her eyes were hazel-grey, not unlike my own. And I was severely bruised in my tourist pride because I had not known blue eyes and dark skin was an unlikely combination. But I didn't send her back.

SETI disapproved of Pia. She didn't mind that I chose a girl, she tolerated my space-age ways. But she warned me severely against 'going cultural'. Making a house pet of a pretty biel was an enabled vice. To me leasing Pia was the same as sampling the strong flavours and peculiar textures of cultural food. Some of what I tasted might be rank and unwholesome, but I had to take the risk. I wanted to have the whole experience. Pia certainly didn't suffer. I did not treat her like one of those walking food trays at the Pavilion, or the dumb 'decorations' of the hologram catalogues on SHACTI mall. I had written her into the capin's recognition so she didn't need a collar. SETI was especially shocked at this. She pointed out that the enabled written into the Pavilion would not be exactly flattered by the comparison. Visitors must be careful! But I wanted my Pia to be her natural self.

A hotel room, a ship's berth, a rented unit can create or destroy any traveller's enjoyment. The Rangers called LECM capins the *pits* (personnel in transit) and hated them. They detested being hived off from the Command environment. But I was instantly happy in my peaceful bubble. It had no interior decoration, just smooth surfaces of grey-green heavy duty CHTHON plastic, same as on the outside. There was a shelf at the back for my bedroll; bathroom and galley suckered on to the walls. Pia and I sat up at the galley counter and ate our yeastie cake and veggies, the unimaginative Ranger cuisine a delightful respite from forays into cultural weirdness. There was a basic-food option for pets but she wouldn't touch it and I couldn't blame her. We acquired cushions and shawls and toys from the malls and littered the bare floor with cosy nests for two.

I was sometimes afraid Pia's next enabled user was going to track me down and sue me . . .

The only fixture in the capin besides bathroom and galley was a systems console, now occupied by my personal station. I let Pia indulge her sulk, sat down and looked at the local Jam (journal and messages). Housekeep was right, there was nothing my desk couldn't handle on its own.

Light patches begain to glow brighter in the walls and floor. I wanted something: a pleasure. I wasn't sure what kind.

SETI?

She came to the capin in-person, a gesture of considerable intimacy. But we did not make love that way, I might have been insulted by her reserve – however, in recent years I'd begun to feel in-person eroticism was a juvenile taste. One of those things you can't believe you'll grow out of, and then it's gone. We made fantasy clips and mixed them. I did the mixing. From the secretly respectful looks she gave me when I knew she'd been playing, I would bet she'd never had head-erotics from a LUDI conceiver before. I slipped the cliptube out of storage and into the decoder slot; and held the *deeby* band for a moment, pondering. Direct Brain Access (DB) is a wonderful thing. It was the possibility of creating a whole world in someone else's head – vicarious mindset – that first drew me to games conceiving . . .

We would have to junk the clips before I went home, that was accepted lovers' etiquette. It was not a lifetime attachment.

No. Not SETI.

I wasn't desperately upset at the way she'd snubbed me over the leopard shoot. Execs will be execs. But I wasn't in the mood for her company. I put the clip and set away.

Pia lay in the wrap, hip cocked defiantly. She looked over her shoulder, sensing my attention. What a sulky little bottom!

'Pia –'

The third time, she came over.  .

34

'You mustn't slap me Pia.'

'You left me alone.'

It happened too often. But I hated to have to put the restraint on her.

'It's true. I did. Will you forgive me?'

Pia looked down. She was naked. I kept the capin warm enough for my sheers and I didn't like her to wear clothes. I slid my hand down her smooth back and tried to make her sit on my knee. She resisted, but the sulky pout turned into a wary little smile. We could both see how her nipples rose and stiffened as I slipped my hand between her buttocks, rubbed into the soft crack. It was as harmless as stroking the fur of a kitten, and feeling the little back arch under your hand. So I told myself. But then Pia suddenly looked at me with helpless, bewildered eyes. She leaned forward and put her mouth on mine, clumsily.

*Thin fire runs through my veins.*

I got out of my sheer. I put my fingers into her; I could not stay outside her any more. She took my wrist and held me, her mouth fastened on my breast: we tumbled into the cushions nearest at hand. The enabled numbers all knew what a basic pet was 'for'. But I didn't intend this. When I accessed Pia, I thought I would keep her like an ornament, like a pretty kitten. I kept telling myself I mustn't do it again. Nobody knows, I thought. If anyone's watching, they can't *deeby*. They just see ALIC romping with her pet . . . And then thought nothing. When mind and body are one, where does mind go?

Afterwards, I always remembered with great relief that she was only leased, and it would end quite soon.

In that state — I said, when we were quiet again. In that state I seem to find a different ALIC, out of time and place. I don't see, I don't hear. I'm made of the same stuff as stars and darkness . . . I am. Is that the real ALIC? And if so, what happens to her the rest of the time?

I talked to Pia as if she could understand every word — but was honest enough to admit if she'd offered me an intelligent reply I'd probably have jumped up screaming. I wondered what she thought about the things we did together. She certainly enjoyed herself physically at the time, but she'd never yet come up to me

35

and asked for our pleasure to begin, of her own accord.

She nuzzled my breast. I stroked her head absently.

'Pia, why is it wrong for a Sub to be a biel?'

Silence. I tweaked her ear.

'It's because you can have a collar put on you. Then you haven't got a number. You're not a bit of Function any more.'

I felt a brute. My poor Pia was so embarrassed she wouldn't look at me. I hugged her fiercely, vowing never to use that horrible restraint again.

'Oh Pia. I nearly had a torrid affair today. But I was thrown over for a horse.'

'A horse?'

'It was Millie Mohun the jockey. Aren't you impressed?'

Pia sat up. She looked at me with big eyes and then took herself out of my arms. I thought I'd wounded her vanity. I followed her across the room, to the corner where lay 'Pia's nest' — a special heap of oddments that the capin was never allowed to tidy. She slept with me generally but I thought she needed somewhere of her own.

'Don't be silly Pia. I still love you best —'

Then I saw that she was showing me something. A face looked up at me, a rather wavery holo of Millie Mohun.

'Oh Pia, you're a fan. I didn't know.'

She nodded seriously. She seemed to expect something more, but I couldn't make out what. After a moment Millie went away again under a piece of blanket that had come with Pia from the agency. I was touched. I resolved to get her a better portrait.

+

Pia slept, her head nestled on my thigh. I watched the flat screen. Insomnia was a common tourists' complaint. VENTUR runs on a 20-hour day, and a year divided into A cycles of 30x20 hours. To achieve annual conformity the machines put chunks of leap hours on our days whenever they feel like it. We have no seasons, and only the most marginal concept of a general 'night' where all activity must cease. We thrive on this. We come down to the underworld, to the cycles that are supposedly printed in our chemistry: and grow fractious and sleepless and lose our appetites.

Originally I had programmed the flat screen in my capin to a nice landscape, and hung it on the wall in the living space. But a certain decadence crept in. I moved it back to the bedshelf and became mildly addicted to underworld mind-sweeties. This was the dregs that I was watching now: the Planetary Entertainment Continuum.

It was part of the basic numbers' life support package. It had no aesthetic content at all. PEC transmission consisted simply of non-sensitive surveillance footage from inside basic accommodation, chopped up and patched together at random. For variety, the true life drama was frequently interrupted by screens and screens of totally irrelevant SERVE code. There was a fatal attraction in the stuff — it was so quintessentially boring. I thought about Pia and decided I was imagining everything. We had a perfectly normal user/pet relationship. I studied a small lump in my armpit with my fingertips and wondered if it was a cancer. If it was, I ought to get it bombed.

Finally, I got up.

I remembered that my movement would have woken housekeep. She would scurry to her console and access me a light: that was the underworld notion of domestic convenience. I made a dash across the room and forestalled her, cursing the intimacy of all this; no less irritating because I rarely saw her.

Outside the wrap SHACTI lay moored against darkness, surrounded by a faint glimmering web of aircar grid. It was a clear night, I could see the moon in gibbous phase, and VENTUR 4 hours in its wake: a few geostationarys, the fuzzy stars. Down on the dark hills there were tiny scattered lights where the enabled had their living modules. They could park where they liked in the grid area, so long as it was discreet. They were no drain on SHACTI. The most desirable mods were entirely self contained: with luxury facilities such as recycled air and water, just like on a spaceship!

In leisure complexes over the alt wall, the richest enabled revelled in the knowledge that the environment outside was almost as hostile as if they were on Mars. It was all so sadly ironic.

The underworlders believed that the libration of earth's billions was VENTUR's proudest achievement. They imitated life in hard vacuum in envy and admiration, as if that was what we had set out to find. They were wrong on both counts. For us, saving the world was a consolation prize.

First there were the Tincans — cramped little carousels deployed in stable areas of the moon's orbit. Mining operations on the Moon came next: on Maria and on Farside, with small real populations. Then there was the Rift Valley on Mars, and eventually Trojan Camp — the first second generation project, with space-born founding personnel.

After Independence things were a lot easier. Exploration no longer had to fight for a budget. It became frankly our major preoccupation. The Star Probes went out, with CONMAG2 drive, to detected planetary systems within a 30Lyear radius. But the travelling jewellery sent ahead had lied a little: and the primitive CONMAGs did not stand up to test. Some of the Probes themselves were retrieved eventually, but there were no landfalls and no survivors. Meanwhile, our information about the neighbourhood was getting much better. We understood we'd have to go a lot farther. And slowly too, because 'faster than light' was a canard. Maria, Farside and the Tincans initiated the Vanguard2 Experiment in Navigable Travelling Urban Radials (the 'Travelling' was inset to make it 'VENTUR' — acronymic is a language devised by semi-literate romantics).

Martian Rift and the Trojans held off. The 'space babies' distrusted the Tincans because Carousel officers had once represented earth governments. But in the end everybody signed up.

It was unfair that we had to reach so far before we found out the truth. We had offered our most advanced machine systems the task of identifying and ranking target stars that possessed habitable planets. We knew from our utter failure to contact or detect other intelligences, that life was not so common as we had hoped. We expected the search to last 100 years. It was over almost at once. The system said: There are no other biospheres in this universe.

It was while they were at work on this enigmatic answer, that the early VENTURans stumbled on a strange and unwelcome conclusion. There is perhaps an infinite universe, supporting pangalactic empires of life. But not for us. The cosmos we inhabit, that we used to think so roomy, is actually a bubble-universe, a trapped region: possibly in the centre of the whole thing, if infinity has a centre. We've been here, if there was such an event, since the universe began. We are trapped, we are alone and we can never get out.

In the childhood of humanity we all believed that the world was run by arrays of great unseen presences called Death and Love and Chance and Harvest — personified but not controlled by us. There was another theory almost as universal. Human beings looked up at the deathless stars and decided that we would be immortal too, if we could get up there. For some cultures death was the way to the stars. The Subcontinent held the view that we had once possessed cosmic immortality but we lost it in some cataclysmic event in the distant past. But in one form or other the myth was everywhere. Its memory lingered on in the human psyche, undoubtedly; until people began to make models of multidimensional spacetime. And whether our myth shaped our physics or the other way round, the vision of eternal youth and unbounded freedom was buried somewhere in the drive to Space, and in the VENTUR project itself.

So that was the end of a very ancient hope, and also the end of exploration. There are sights to see within a few Lyears, but nothing worth spending half a lifetime on an in-person trip. We have plenty of materials, unlimited power. Our population is small so we don't need living space. Even the greening of Mars moves very slowly. Not that we really believed we were going to live forever 'out there'. But it has an insidious, enduring effect on morale to know you are living, more or less, inside a Black Hole.

I sat in the wrap with my little lacquer drug box beside me. The fumes of a gentle narcotic which I'd cracked and put in the holder stroked gently at my brain. We can't open our mouths without making dismal jokes about it, I thought. ALIC means something neutral about 'automated logic'. But SETI used to signify Search for ExtraTerrestrial Intelligence. Alas, there is one thing we can be sure of. If they exist, we'll never meet them. We can't go to them, and they won't come to us. *They wouldn't dare.* They can't even know we exist. It's problematic whether we do, for whatever's outside.

We looked back then, and saw that the aged parent had fallen into senile dementia. We came home, having failed to achieve anything, to nurse her in her old age. Our capital city is a linked formation of multigeneration starships, going nowhere forever. And the seed-corn that the brave venturers rescued from dying earth has been used to repopulate underworld wild life parks.

I sighed, snuffed my narcotic. On the whole, I agreed with the conservationists about Mars. That bare rock, the faint skin of ice and the black unbreathable air, is the truth. We are just a meaningless statistical anomaly.

The housegrub was trotting around quietly, clearing away Pia's toys. She was shockingly aquisitive. *What have you brought me?* was her usual greeting, when I didn't get a smack. I picked up a gengra scarf I had bought her: a process reject, but still very pretty. I would've liked to have some good gengra to take home, but someone had told me that the best was made by tiny children. I didn't know if I wanted to own something that had permanently deformed the brain of an 8yearold. Grub sensed me as it passed and stood at my elbow for a moment its small red sensors glowing dimly.

'*Hello friend. Hello ALIC.*'

'Hard at work? It's not my fault you know. None of this litter's mine.'

I gazed out of the wrap and thought of the darkness closing in, that no one can escape. I thought of my last lover and the miserable way we parted; of the years I spent as a conceiver, monitoring vic generation and occasionally getting a concept of my own accepted. It had seemed such a good idea to retire and have fun. Let's live, says the poet, and let's love, and count the censorious world worth not one bit . . . I had tried to follow that rule and here I was. 82 years old, middle age staring me in the face: without child, lover, work, anything.

For before us there is nothing but endless night . . .

ALIC! Route out of it!

I had noticed lately a tendency towards the cosmic glooms. It must be stopped. Thinking about death – I had heard of this disease. A kind of mind-cancer that poisons everything you do. I must not let it in. I had years of fun and excitement left, if only I could keep my head together.

Think of something more cheerful. Like how to help Millie Mohun.

Millie herself had probably forgotten our encounter by now, but it would be just too feeble and tourist-like for me to do the same. It would not be easy to help her. I couldn't ask SETI to intervene. I would become instantly the dreaded 'interfering tourist': and do no good to Millie. I could imagine the enabled authorities being very harsh over a case like this, and CHTHON would obviously back them up.

The blackmailers must have taken Millie's tag with an illegal cutting tool, and some physical force. Tags weren't meant to come off, and she wouldn't have been co-operating. No doubt they had supplied the forgery themselves. They didn't want to ruin her. They wanted her functioning, and frightened.

I wondered what it would cost to buy a gamesplayer. In VENTUR, people who 'work' outside the running of their own lives are awarded bonuses by the grateful populace. The populace generously ignores the fact that whoever benefits, nobody 'works' except for pleasure or greed. I used to be rich sometimes when I was with LUDI: the Leisure Universal Design Institute. Now I had only my basic PIONER income. It was a small fortune on the underworld. I might even be able to afford a famous jockey. But it seemed rather an extreme solution. Besides, her tag would be needed for the transaction.

If I already owned or leased her it would be simple. I'd have the appropriate local processes issue a new tag, without troubling the authorities. I had peeked at the inner workings of SHACTI out of curiosity. I knew I could manage that.

Thoughtfully, I turned and looked at the cabin console. My personal station, known as 'plaything', winked at me wisely from the contact plate. I never travelled without it. It had a LUDI screen, and the best *deeby* interface I could buy. The box looked like an ordinary personal processor of a rather old fashioned make and model. But it was customised inside: all my own work.

Updating plaything was the way I kept my old brain switching since I retired. Like any personal it ran on stored SERVE power and could perform its own range of tasks in isolation. By laying it on the contact plate, I turned plaything into my interface with the local systems.

What would happen if I tried to order Millie a new tag? There would be no problem getting in. CHTHON was a VENTURan organisation. As a PIONER, I had every right to go inside. Unfortunately Area Command had an equal right to watch me doing it. Plaything was being monitored, and though I was fairly good at playing hide and seek I was unlikely to get away with generating an unauthorised CHTHON tag, when I had no legal entry to the account involved.

With a start of pleasurable surprise, I noticed that I had discovered an interesting puzzle. And as I realised that a solution came to me – extravagant, outrageous, ridiculously satisfying.

There were basic numbers employed in the numbers' account section of SHACTI centre. They could not be suborned by me. They were plugged in, unconscious, and the information they processed vanished from their biological circuitry as soon as the shift was done. No conscious human mind could match the speed of the machines. Only the brain was necessary – on its own an excellent piece of firmware. At home we used SYNCOR: snythetic cortex. We could not improve on the design.

But the machines the numbers used were VENTURan machines. I had been on an in-person familiarisation tour that took in the processing halls. I'd seen our Ranger guide rotate one of the cataleptic bodies into the aisle. 'It's OK,' she said. 'Centre integration won't collapse at once.' She showed us how the actual interface was an old VENTURan station. Inert to the numbers, but still capable of waking up and answering a PIONER. Some of us were rather upset, and wished to take all the poor old processors home . . .

Housegrub had put itself away under the galley. All was still, the hollow empty stillness of an underworld night. I went to the console and sat down to talk to plaything. I was aware that Millie Mohun had upset me. Either her smile, or her predicament: or the combination. Perhaps she was partly responsible for the attack of cosmic glooms. If so, it was appropriate that she should fetch me out again. I remembered the heaving mass on the monitor in the Pavilion . . . and wondered if boring middle-aged ALIC still had the nerve to do something so downright silly.

+

I woke late, having slept wonderfully well. Pia was gone. I climbed into the bathroom, showered in stinging hot and then cold air. I did some response enhancer and detoxifier (for the lump) and then mirrored the wall to admire my well-grown head hair. I'd been working it for a while. I rather fancied myself as an earthling. I didn't have much of a fringe, but that would be expecting too much. We called the underworld geographical groups 'cultures' because the term 'nation' was irrelevant under CHTHON. Geographical division by race had been eroded before we came, by the process of history. The Subs were something of an exception to this rule. But I had brown skin, straight hair — sufficiently like the Sub majority to pass for a few hours.

Someone laughed as the door of housekeep's bubble opened for me. To my surprise I saw Pia sitting on the console worktop, wrapped in one of her gengra pieces. She slipped down and pattered back into the capin, just rubbing her cheek against my arm as she went by. I had never thought of them having active contact. I was startled.

'I hope she doesn't bother you.'

'She does not, Commander.'

My housekeep was a dour creature. She wasn't collared. She only belonged to me in a few restricted ways, she was really a processer, not a biel — still 'a bit of Function'. In case she suddenly decided to become a threat to my well-being, the doorway to the capin would not accept her entry. In fact, I was in a node of SHACTI basic accommodation when I stepped in here. I looked around me with interest I'd never felt before.

There was nothing in the room but the LECM console, a minute box for housekeep's hygiene and her cotbed in a corner with one neat synthetic quilt spread over it. She kept whatever

43

she owned in 2 small catering cartons underneath, but still always managed to be excruciatingly neat in shining white pyjamas. Beside the cotbed was the hatchway that was her exit. There was a tunnel down there, and transport back to SHACTI. I had thought about this, but it didn't quite suit my plans.

I was carrying my station. I moved her aside and contacted it to the LECM domestic. Plaything became an additional processor, doing my dirty work while I spoke innocently to LECM with my hands on housekeep's LR clusters. She could not know what I was doing. She only understood a very simple domestic routine. But to be on the safe side I used codes, not Natural English.

'Housekeep,' I said. 'Do you know where I could find a gamesplayer called Millie Mohun?'

SHACTI could have told me, but I was getting into the mindset of the game. I didn't want anything of mine even to mention that name, not even my wristfax. She knew. I was not surprised. I thought, perhaps, that all the basics were wired up at the back. But I was surprised — and remembered it later — at the change in her face. I decided with amusement that she must be another fan.

'Good.'

I had finished. I broke the contacts, feeling pleased and invigorated.

'Now then. Tell me what you would do if by any chance there was something wrong with your tag.'

Housekeep's unaccustomed smile vanished. She sat and looked at me, with a thoughtful, subdued expression.

# 3

Far down the gradient, deep within the maze of SHACTI centre a group of numbers stood waiting on a broad gloomy platform to be transported to their shift. In the world outside it was very early morning, local time, and here in imitation the lighting was low and the air was chill. The transport arrived behind a barrier that stretched the height and length of the hall. Then plastic shutters opened, and the passengers were checked on. Panels on the barrier winked occasionally with information that was repeated in a toneless chanting machine articulation, and the UBIQ monitors in the floor/ceiling glowed like little red eyes.

I was there. I had arrived like the rest, from the passageways. Now I watched the ones who stood alone and stood like them, tucking my hands under my arms and staring at the floor. The anhomogenous texture of my pyjamas felt rough against my skin. I shivered. But it was from excitement more than the cold. When the barrier announced my transport I shuffled cautiously forward with the rest, biting my lip to hold back a threat of helpless giggles. A back in front of me, breath behind me. I was shorter than some of the numbers . . . Does it take you by the throat? Do you have to stand in a special way? The woman in front of me was at the barrier. I saw her elbows go up. I was so earnestly trying to be invisible I didn't dare to peer round her shoulder. She was gone. I put my hands up blindly, pulled out the shield. I must have offered it: I heard a tiny clatter of metal on metal, felt a tug on my ear lobe — but for the vital seconds I think my eyes must have been shut.

Somebody caught my arm and steadied me. 'Hang on. Shit of a gate, nearly pulled you over —'

I was in the car. We were moving. I hardly noticed the number

45

who grabbed me, or the faces and bodies jostling and settling on the hard plastic benches. I've done it! I shouted silently, and felt an idiotic grin of triumph spreading over my face.

I had met Millie Mohun for the second time in a basic numbers' canteen. The first level of basic accommodation was easily accessible from the enabled mall. CHTHON personnel stayed out, as a matter of protocol. But although it wasn't meant to be a tourist attraction, there was nothing to stop me going down. I wore a suit of pyjamas I had bought to give someone at home as a souvenir, and carried a facepack against the smelly air.

Housekeep had told me Millie could be found in a place directly under one of the big cultural hotels. She was there often in her off shifts, or if not everybody knew her: someone would help me. I was dubious about accosting another basic, but luckily I saw Millie at once. She had a crowd around her — surplus males and troublemakers, Yolande T would have called them. I did not know much but I knew pets (not the exclusive hand-reared kind) and decorations were Sub lowlife. No wonder she gets into trouble, I thought, if she keeps such company. I was absurdly nervous, although I knew it was foolish to think UBIQ was interested in me. I told her what I meant to do, and showed her — with precaution — my number tag.

'Where did you get that?' she said gravely.

'From my housekeep. Don't worry. It's OK, I won't get into trouble. I'd have done it this way for you: but you see I don't own you.'

I told her she must look for me. I would come back to this canteen again when I had the replacement. It was up to her to get rid of the forgery.

'Then you'd better turn in those bullies, before they think of something else. You'll be quite safe, I won't leave any traces.'

In my session at housekeep's console I had reported that the guest in capin x had accidentally fuzzed up her domestic's tag, bringing it into contact with some powerful VENTURan gadget or other. LECM accessed number accounts. A few minutes later a replacement arrived in the solid mail delivery slot. I recorded that the damaged tag had been destroyed, and the new one was verified. Then I commanded LECM to forget about this transaction, and tell number accounts to do the same. It was easy.

I took plaything out with me and deposited it in a hotel. All sorts of alarms would start if someone tried to walk into basic accommodation carrying an independent processor. After meeting Millie I did not go back to LECM. I slept (not much) in the nondescript hotel I'd chosen, the kind that has no staff and where the guests never see each other. It was still 'night' when I began my final preparations, dressed in my souvenir disguise of dark red pyjamas and a pair of thick-soled local sandals.

It was a strange moment when the tiny metallic claws closed through my ear lobe. I felt nothing, no piercing sensation. I looked in the hotel room mirror and saw it, silver bright. As far as I knew no one had ever brought home a CHTHON tag as a souvenir, but that part was just a joke. What was so fine was that I had a tag that would run. Plaything had intervened in the trick I played on LECM. This shield had housekeep's records on it. But the tissue identity was mine.

With my tag in my ear I contacted plaything to the hotel console and made my way into SHACTI. I already knew exactly what had to be done. I worked quickly: found the list I wanted, deleted a number from it and added housekeep's number. There were security guards in SHACTI quite intelligent enough to make connections between this operation and some anomalous inquiries made previously by the same processor and the same PIONER. I had changed plaything's physical location, and put up a time barrier of several hours: simple tricks but surprisingly effective. I still had that interesting feeling − perhaps, as I sneaked about imagining myself invisible, someone somewhere was laughing heartily at my antics. My protection was that I was doing nothing detrimental to the libration. One more number, one less VENTURan, in Subcontinental SHACTI for a day. The Rangers might be outraged: but SHACTI security was more rational than human personnel, so the Rangers should never know.

Now for the last step. There was little point in leaving plaything behind and taking ALIC with me. I was recognised by all the VENTURan machinery on the underworld. It would be absurd if the screen on my accounts section console suddenly started flashing up HELLO FRIEND! I had attached my identity to housekeep's number. I would now destroy my other self (temporarily).

I felt regretful. I didn't often shoot amateur clips when I was travelling. The snow leopards would have been an honourable exception. If I wanted to review a trip, I could always retrieve myself out of MONSAT. But that search only worked for PIONERs, so I wouldn't be able to get hold of ALIC down among the basics. Never mind, I consoled myself. You'll be in SERVE somewhere. And grinned. It was our expression for permanently misplaced data.

HELLO SHACTI. I WANT YOU TO DELETE ME. DELETE ON ALIC R. PLEASE.

SHACTI looked blank, as well it might. Not a common request.

HELLO ALIC. ARE YOU SURE?

Y

ARE YOU REALLY SURE?

DON'T BABY ME SHACTI. I KNOW WHAT I'M DOING.

OK FRIEND. DELETE ON ALIC R.

There was no need, this time, to verify anything. My station went dead. I took my hands off the clusters and put them on again. Nothing happened. I said 'Hello?' Silence.

'ALIC is no more,' I whispered, fascinated. 'I've just killed myself.'

I had bought the room for a few days. It was cheaper than the hourly rate and I didn't know exactly when I would be back. I found some reds in my pyjama pocket and decided to take them with me in case I was tempted to sample the food. I locked my station, my wristfax and a small beam cutter in the room safe. When I was done, I would invalidate the hybrid creation I was wearing, and it should release me of its own accord. The cutter was insurance.

Then I went down the quiet mall and through the gate that led to Millie's canteen. There was no perceptible barrier. I resisted the temptation to turn round and try to go back. I had memorised the route to my platform on the internal transport but I still kept reaching to my wrist for a loc ref, and nervously desisting.

It did occur to me to wonder why I was going to all this trouble. But I had liked her smile, and it was no trouble. It was the most fun I'd had in my whole holiday. There was only one slight problem so far: which was that Millie had been unable to tell me her real serial number. Either she had never memorised it, or she was more frightened than she looked and was lying to me for some silly reason. I didn't want to bully her. The information I had should be quite enough to raise an account.

In the early days of Space the underworld went through (to add to its other problems) a traumatic change in its methods of production. Eventually it transpired that the arrival of a total automation system (ADAPT) need not mean the end of the human workforce, only a change from active to passive mode. In legend and in hindsight the Subs claimed the honour of having 'discovered' the possibilities of human firmware. They still regarded their gruesome version of the adaptation as a privilege and a glory. Other cultures used various non-invasive means — the Subs simply wouldn't believe that any milder form of connection with the system could be efficient. Theirs was the only route to Function. Every little girl had to be burned, whether she was in the workforce or not. As in other blocs, men weren't considered suitable for passive processing, so the little boys escaped.

The greater privilege of having a bit of your brain tissue permanently etched like photonic crystal was reserved for the enabled. Their conversion was called (reasonably enough) 'dedication'. It was very odd. At home, if someone said 'I'm a plastics processer' or 'I'm a metlas-welder' you would laugh. Unless other symptoms suggested actual delusion. But on the Sub such a remark could be simply true.

We had a different solution. We borrowed the idea to develop SYNCOR; otherwise we just let ADAPT get on with it. But our problems were not the same. CHTHON had never interfered with the passive processers. It used them in its own operations with good effect for number morale. Some underworld basics even managed to leave the planet as processers: recruited for projects where SYNCOR couldn't cope with the local conditions. Which was more than most enabled ever achieved.

I had never travelled on the emart before — the underground transport network. There was no safety harness, which rather shocked me. At home we say you trust in the systems, but you strap yourself in. There were only some worn lap belts. I noticed that other numbers didn't bother with them and surreptitiously undid mine. The cylinder shot upwards violently, with ominous crashing noises. We stopped, we jerked. Our car rose into the processing hall, inside a transparent barrier, until floor levels equalised. Outside, there were rows and rows of double consoles. Beyond and above them rose a neutral-coloured curving wall, tracked by floating lights and monitors. We were in the SAFE, the Systems Access Facility Enclosure. Ironically, I was outside the basics centre again, in a hemispherical blister that bulged out between the Mall canopy and Mission Command up on the peak of the Ridge. The enabled thought it was a horrid excrescence.

Through the SAFE, CHTHON sampled number processing 'to make sure the systems were being treated with proper respect'. Penetrating this place wasn't quite as daring as going right down to the numbers' number accounts hall. But I had decided if I did get caught it would be less embarrassing if I didn't have to deal with the Subs.

No one could get into this blister except CHTHON personnel and the numbers recorded on its lists. That suited me. It meant, classically, that there was less chance of being spotted once inside. A gate tried my tag again, checked me for contrabrand items and let me through. I stepped out cautiously, expecting a remote to lead me to my console, maybe a track on the floor. A human hand landed on my shoulder.

Oh, that confiding gesture, sliding up the tendon under your jaw: finding the shield with a thumb in muscle to keep you still, and flicking it out. She wore an opaque grey coverall with an ESB dangling at the belt. I eyed it and stood still.

Supervisors! How was I to know? I had noticed SAFE had an overplus of numbers who weren't identified as processers. I thought it was carrying spares. I had heard of 'supers'. I assumed it meant a special intelligent kind of basic. Not this one.

'You're new. What's your name?'

'ALIC,' said I, too flustered to think straight. She checked my tag on a large and impressive wristfax and examined the display studiously. It was obvious that she could not read a code of it. Holding me by the tag, she led me away. I had to remind myself firmly that it was only a game.

'OK Alice. Plug in.'

I was terrified, not of a touch of electric therapy but that she was going to destroy my plan. But when she'd put me in my console chair she left, apparently content to leave the rest to SAFE.

The burns were my major obstacle. I had not tried to fake them. I thought of it, but I remembered the first rule of sneaky work, on either side of the screen. Never lie unnecessarily, do as little as possible. I had seen (on the tour) opaque helmets. I knew from social contact that burns were generally kept hidden. No doubt the Subs were worried about making the rest of us jealous.

There was a restraining field to hold me upright and support my arms. It took control when the super was gone. The helmet was on the back of my seat. As in all underworld processing, everything had to be switched from photonics to weak electrical current and back again, to accommodate the firmware. On the Sub they made their own conversion fittings. The helmet came down over my head and I felt sensors hunting in my hair. This was the moment. Now I had to find out how to take over this station before SAFE decided there was something actionably wrong.

Long before CHTHON the young systems of Space took on the old systems of earth in a battle half commercial, half something more profound. Space won: and consequently all earth's machinery was actually VENTURan long before we came to impose the libration. We hardly had to use force at all. Because of that bloodless victory, I was sitting in front of a live VENTURan processor now. Some underworlders thought basics should not have even potential 'access'. But we don't make dummy stations. To produce them just for earth would have been like PRENAT deliberately creating a race of cripples.

On our familiarisation tour, people were surprised that the processers didn't use *deeby*. The Ranger guide explained patiently. Direct Brain Access is not what it claims to be. The brain does not receive the scenario: it is stimulated into

51

invention. The skill is in building up a signal that will switch the right switches; the details are the user's own. This is not a good way to handle practical information. Vocalisation would be equally useless at these speeds.

But talking is never really accurate. You tell your station – in acro with many ums and ahs – to do this and do that. All credit to the machine that manages to obey: none to the user. Power is not when the machine understands you. Power is when you understand the machine. And the clusters bring the 2 of you closer than any other interface. It exasperated me to hear VENTURans naively revealing they'd almost forgotten how to read and write. To me LR skills were essential. As vital in our relationship with the systems as marks on a sheet of pressed woodshavings in another age.

The LR clusters here were blank. Passive processers had no possible need for visible character set. I keyed the mode changer, invoking a standard alphanumeric, and it was touching to see how eagerly the old machine responded. I entered a current SHACTI handshake and the station was mine.

The screen above my board woke up and glowed deep bright navy blue with a silver YD function and its SAFE ID in base '12' code up in the top right corner. I commanded SAFE to take this processer's workload and redistribute it. On either side of me the 'work' the numbers were doing was already flickering endlessly up their screens, for the benefit of the UBIQ optical monitors. I arranged for mine to borrow display and leave me a window. Packed shining codes began to whip by but the bottom third of the screen cleared. And all was quiet on the floor. By the YD it was exactly 1 minute 40 seconds since the number in the coverall left me.

If ever I meet a machine that I can't talk to, may the great powerflow of the universe jump out and burn my hands off at the wrist.

SAFE sent micro impulses flicking through the numbers' fingers so their hands shook like an imperfect holo. I couldn't mimic that effect and I wasn't going to try. I didn't believe UBIQ would worry about the difference in the time I would be here, so long as there were no other signs of trouble.

The underworld handshakes were short numerical groups that would give you entry and (for the enabled) ranked access to facilities for the local area. They were readily available. Housekeep never saw them but they were written into the jam header when I accessed it on plaything. Periodically CHTHON would decide the handshakes had become insecure and change the lot. For the VENTURan tourist these crypts were just an inconvenience. But to me the H had suddenly become important. I was not On ALIC R at the moment. I was just a pair of hands with some facility in machine code. Like the merest enabled, I needed the handshake to get me in.

The revived station would readily understand acro or NATENG on its keys. I could even talk to it if I could get down and whisper to the sensor port. SAFE/SHACTI would have no perceptual problems either if I simply entered ‹GIVE MILLIE MOHUN A NEW TAG›. But I'd have trouble making it treat that as a legal instruction: and besides I must be invisible. The processes of a VENTURan personal talked to each other in a base 9 code, the machine common tongue; equivalent to acro. I must do the same.

In Space we had changed from decimal to base '12' because of its fertile relationships with what we called the innate codes. So far as it used a numerical base SERVE itself used 3, the most powerful of all. To my relief I found there was no nasty decimal conversion behind the screen here. I began to relax and enjoy myself. I had to find the codes that SHACTI used when talking to itself about such things, and use them. I had to generate a new CHTHON tag and have it delivered to a local solid mail address (my capin). I had to arrange my own exit, giving myself special permission to leave the basic accommodation. I must also call up VENTUR, recover myself from Radial4's memory and return myself to SHACTI on a time lapse. I didn't want to be ALIC until I was out of here, but neither did I want to be in the unpleasant position of having no identity at all, however briefly.

The supers walked up and down and leaned on the ends of the rows, swinging their batons idly. They must be related, I thought, to the *ulaux*, the underworld local auxiliaries: CHTHON's tiny number army. SETI had a squad of ulaux all of her own. They didn't have much to do except parade up and down in their barracks under Mission Command, roaring HELLO FRIEND! at a projection of SETI. These supers didn't seem to have much to do either. Perhaps they inspired respect. The SAFE itself existed only for that purpose. I wondered a little that CHTHON should need such a show. But it wasn't my business. All I wanted was access to SHACTI and to the greater processes beyond: from a point from which intelligent tampering would never be suspected.

Under my hands and before my eyes the commonplace transformation began. SAFE became SHACTI, SHACTI became CHTHON-in-the-Sub. Invoking these entities with my humble fingers would never be less than marvellous to me. And beyond and within them all was SERVE. Its rational light pulses flowed ceaselessly in the lightlines in this hall's flooring. The web was all around us, everywhere. SERVE was in the software that made the hardware and the hardware that made the software.

Far away in space, there was once a physical machine which 'ZERV' inhabited. That concept had become irrelevant long ago. SERVE was here in the Sub as much as it was in VENTUR. I understood that, just as I understood that the expressions we all used, of wires and circuitry, came from an age before the Space Communities. They had little relation to the physical integration of SERVE's photonic diaspora or the systems that received it. But there was still the irresistible temptation to think of SERVE as a Big Thing, located somewhere. I only lost it completely when I was deep into the codes . . . The processers stared and quivered. I stared too, and my fingers moved; almost as entranced as they. When my screen went suddenly blank I had a moment of pure panic. Then I realised that on either side of me numbers were coming to life. It was a break.

I followed the rest to a kind of locker room behind a partition, up against the curved wall of the blister. There was a row of stalls with half doors. I sat on the floor the way the others did and listened to a curious tinkling sound. When I realised what it was I was convulsed with silent giggles and glad of an efficient bladder. There was a dispenser on the wall. Some of them accessed snacks

54

or tubes of drink by putting their tags in a reader, or else, equally, posting hard currency into a slot. There was little conversation. No one took any notice of me.

The disadvantage of being a secret invader was that I wasn't able to pick up where I had left off. Everything was gone and I couldn't waste time finding out where SAFE had put it. But I knew what I was doing this time. I set up all my manoeuvres to go into action when I gave them the final trip; and leave no sign of interference. The delivery baffled me until I realised I was telling it to deliver the new tag to On ALIC R, who didn't exist at present. Changed it to my capin's address, and that seemed to work. At last I called up Millie Mohun, from number accounts, using the standard base 9 codes for alpha. I had left this to the last because it was the sensitive part and I was nervous, in spite of all precautions.

I was not greatly surprised when Millie failed to appear. If her account wasn't functioning completely normally that would explain why she hadn't been picked up already. I constructed a little search and sent it off to sift the Sub millions, giving all the information I had.

No Millie.

I wasted a few minutes staring, wondering what I was doing wrong. I had a feeling I was running out of shift. Without any concealment, I informed SHACTI it had lost an account. I gave it the details (I checked my codes). SHACTI thought about this and conferred, through CIITION, with its siblings all around the underworld. It told me after a slight but measurable interval — for it moved in time, not in SERVE's eternal instant — that there was no account in existence such as I had described.

Oh, no. It could not possibly need more information than I had given to make a match. Subcontinental. North-West Quadrant. Approx 20 – 26 years. Racial Sub type. Biel gamesplayer owned by SHACTI vic stadium. *Won a race on a horse called My Sorrow at the last meeting, in the heads of the whole Pavilion and full view of any amount of basics. Don't tell me she doesn't exist!*

On the fourth time of asking SHACTI replied with a pattern of whole and broken lines ⁝⁝⁝ in the middle of the screen. A dry message, straight from a VENTURan writer of long ago who had become immortal as the systems in this small way. MENG. The all stations interplanetary schematic for user, if you ask me that stupid question once more, I'm going to shut you down.

I had crashed.

I noticed, in a stunned interior silence, that the YD in the corner of my screen said 12:4A and some seconds and bits. I had begun my 8-hour shift at 06.00, SHACTI centre time. The field held me. Inside it every part of me leapt —.

But I did nothing. Pride kept me still. I hated to be defeated after promising so grandly that I could fix everything. After a moment I wiped my window off and sat looking at the borrowed codes. The next shift came in. Someone settled in the other place at the console and my screen went blank. All along the rows there was a luxurious ripple of stirring and murmuring and sighing.

I found myself on the grey platform again. It was no longer gloomy but bright and hot. I stood in a daze. One of the numbers walked up and said, 'Your name's Alice isn't it?'

'Cando. I mean — yes.'

'You haven't done our sort of Processing before, have you. Don't worry, you'll get used to it. Would you like me to walk you home?'

I had difficulty understanding her. Not only the language but the nature of this overture. Still, I told her the only name I knew. I hadn't left myself much option.

We walked out through an open gate into a bright passage. I wondered when we would reach the accommodation, then I saw we were already in it. On either side there were locks in the smooth walls. Where they stood open I glimpsed areas inside lined with other little doors. The passage stretched on with undeviating regularity — parallel, I thought, to the west-east flank of SHACTI ridge. The walls, and the floor/ceilings above and below where all the utilities were carried, were the same clear light grey. The centre was built, I knew, of agam: a multipurpose material processed out of permitted oil shales and factory waste. I touched the wall casing, found it unyielding and slightly warm. The passage was narrow: about a third the width of a residential gallery at home. The ceiling seemed low. It was a little like being on a ship. I imagined I could feel, as one can feel the subliminal presence of CONMAG, the mighty pressure of AB,000 numbers. Some of them passed us. Groups broke into single file or pressed themselves to the wall without breaking stride.

Up ramps and down ramps. The centre was too small for extensive internal transport. We passed through some minor concourses, formed by the simple expedient of omitting the corner blocks of an intersection. But there were no vistas, no gardens: nothing to break the regularity of the grid. I saw no greenery at all. Their air must be carbon filtered: it smelt like it.

My number chatted a little. I gathered that Millie Mohun lived in a 'well' in the outer stacks of level 6. She pointed out to me that the level number, and other loc inf, was displayed at each intersection on a wall plate. I did not trust myself to enter into conversation, but she seemed not to notice either my silence or my curious glances. She had shown no surprise when I mentioned the famous jockey – only smiled broadly. Maybe she was another fan. At an early intersection she paused, slipped the tag out of her ear and touched it to a reader; glanced at me enquiringly and then shrugged her shoulders. I thought afterwards perhaps I should have copied her. She often repeated the process, but my abstention didn't impede our progress. I decided not to risk it.

A well was one of the hollow squares behind the locks. 'Here you are,' said my guide. 'I have to access the overplus before it shuts, so I won't enter just now.' She left me at the open lock and trotted away. 'Millie Mohun? I said to a little number child sitting on the floor. She had her tag in her mouth, chewing. It dropped off her chin with a dribble of saliva. Millie? Yes.

Children appeared from nowhere and pressed around me. I had to push through them to get into the square. There was a collection of youths and men under the supports of a gallery that overhung the lowest cubicles. I looked at them with disapproval, remembering the gang at the stadium. But they said 'Millie!' too, and smiled and pointed. The walls above the gallery were three cubicles high, judging by the measure of the first row. Bright light came down from the distant floor/ceiling. I could hear blurred machine articulation far away, and PEC soundtrack close at hand. A door opened and there was Millie.

I couldn't decide if she looked the same or if the change in background changed her. I noticed again what I had seen in the Pavilion: something a little more, surely, than a good body well carried. She had presence. *She's been waiting for me*, I thought, surprised. In the room behind her I could see squatting figures turning away from a flat wall screen to stare.

'Hello Alice. So you've come to visit us.'

'It's like this,' I said. 'You know, the thing I'm doing. It's going to take a little longer than I thought. Can I stay here?'

'You should ask SHACTI, not me. But I'm sure it will be all right.'

I was conscious of a large audience. I felt ridiculous.

'You look tired Alice.'

She spoke to someone beside her and then sat down again. The other number came and led me through a doorway at the corner of the square. She took me up an angular arrangement of steps, helping me when I stumbled. I hadn't experienced this staircase business before except in vics of underworld ruins. She showed me a place at the end of a row of cubicles that she called the *per*. It looked primitive and unpleasantly social but I knew I was going to have to use it. Not even a space traveller's bladder will last forever. Then an empty cubicle. It was a box, containing a preformed cot with a quilt. Light came from a plate in the centre of the false ceiling, as strong as in the square. Under the cot I could see the outline of two shabby cartons.

She left me. I used the *per* and was deeply relieved to find an ordinary suction pan behind one of the half doors. I went back to my cubicle and sat on the cot.

The air was slightly fouled by nameless exudations from number bodies. The walls and bedbase had a few large ingrained stains and a furry look, as if the surface had been sucked too often by too many grub mouths. There was a YD function on the wall by the door. I glanced at it and realised I was stuck in here for 11 hours before I could get back to the SAFE and set myself free.

How bare this room was. A completely different minimum from the emptiness of my capin. The little scene below had been intriguing. It appeared that on her own level a Sub gamesplayer could be a person of some importance.

Millie was right. I was exhausted. It was a long time since I'd spent so many hours at a station for any reason. I found out that the bunkbed had a closure, that curved out of the wall and connected with the floor. But I couldn't sleep. With the closure down I would suffocate; up and the light was too hot and bright. I looked in the cartons — empty — and under the cot. I ran my hands over the walls. The door at least was still a door and moved out of the way when I stepped on the release bar. A young man was passing.

'Hey '

He turned. Quite a sweet dark face that looked oddly familiar.

'I know this sounds stupid. But — how does the light go down?'

'They don't,' he said.

# 4

I found that I could access a Sub biel named Pia with no trouble and without a number. I never knew it was such an obvious name, but my Pia was there on the list. So the difficulty was not that I didn't have enough information. Millie Mohun had been born, she told me, on a soft fruit plant under the alt wall north-west of SHACTI. I presumed she referred to a wild number settlement near an ADAPT installation. One of the under-world's roving talent spotters picked her out: 'bought her from SERVE' in the usual way and sold her to the SHACTI stadium. I asked no more. I didn't want to know about any evasive tactics she was using to survive without a tag. Nor did I want her to guess how little I had found out. She mustn't think she could get away with this indefinitely.

SHACTI number accounts had lost Millie. She couldn't have been destroyed. No system under SERVE ever erased anything. Sub SHACTI alone had enough disparate memory available to it to itemise the atoms in the sun. Unfortunately, the difference between *erased* and *terminally lost its label* will always be hazy. And SHACTI, in the pride of its heart, wouldn't believe me when I said it was in error. It menged me every time I tried to recover her from the underworld's back-up filing. No matter. She was there somewhere: her status the inner space analog of 'fallen down behind the furniture'. I would find her.

When I worked for LUDI, I spent much of my time exploring various alien environments. On one occasion on the planet Ozma, that little known satellite of Beta Hydri, my teammates and I got so annoyed with the sneaky chlorine breathing senti-ents that we called home for the secretaries' masers and sanitised the whole funxing planet. That was a bad scenario, the game never went on the market.

In those same years, when I was about 50, 56, my mother was finally dying. She was not my legal parent. She'd made her contribution to PRENAT and forgotten it, years before my father decided he wanted to be a daddy. But I'd always known that she was living; and that she took an interest in me. She was so old she remembered a time when every space inhabitant had to do regular hours of 'crew environment maintenance' — watching screen on screen of life support process. Holograms of the shell structure, chemical scans of suntube on suntube of rice and maize and tomatoes. First the visuals, then the codes. The zillions of tiny events that have to happen, exactly and in order, to keep the world running. Human attention to this process was non-functional even when my mother was young. But in her last days she started doing her siem again. She never explained why but I felt I partly understood. I networked with her in the sanatorium (since she seemed to like to see me). How patiently she watched the hynotic codes. As if her eyes were a necessary part of the whole . . .

I thought of my LUDI adventures frequently on this daring in-person foray. But as I sat at my SAFE console I was haunted strangely by images of my tiny huge-eyed mother, gazing at her bedside screen.

The curved wall in my cubicle was another bunk. Numbers all shared their rooms. I was lucky, I gathered, to have only one companion. The back of my 'shelf' was a sliding panel that allowed the grubs to enter for cleaning. I looked at it with misgiving. I had learned that if an old or sick number died in her shelf, the grubs would carry her away along with the rubbish. I had written myself into SHACTI's basic count when I wrote myself into the SAFE processer list. Sooner or later, the confusion between me and housekeep was bound to surface. But, in the meantime, so long as I was a well-behaved number and did not collide with the cultural authorities, no one was going to know there was anything wrong.

There was a bank of CHTHON dispensers in the well square where the numbers could use their tags to access basic necessities. In space we started fair, and never allowed life support to enter the market economy. CHTHON had imposed the same arrangement on the underworld. In the little concourses there were 'overplus' outlets where the local hard currency would buy cultural products. The enabled did not live on CHTHON welfare. The overplus was stocked with their reject consumables. They weren't allowed to handle bio materials because of the underworld's disgusting past performance. But here we had foods, drinks, furniture; clips of the stadium games and stale current affairs. It's amazing what you can do with mineral oil.

The hard currency was called 'slots'. I could have had my own issue, as a processer. We lined up at the end of shift and our allowance was punched out by a till at the transport barrier. I didn't notice this happening the first time. Subsequently, I generously decided to let the Sub economy keep my dividend. After all, I wasn't doing the work.

A serious responsible young number called Himem lived on the corridor at right angles to mine. She took me in charge and showed me around. We walked into the overplus booth in our neighbourhood concourse and admired the goodies, present in-person behind hard plastic wrap. There was a laundry for overplus clothes (dispenser pyjamas were meant to be replaced when soiled). There was a 'cult' booth which issued hard print-out instructions for basics, embossed with the tag signatures of their enabled authorities. The 'cults' were the number police.

She showed me the only directly VENTURan artefact I'd seen outside SAFE. It was the In-station — a genuine access to the Commanders' systems, where you could enter any question and get an answer. SETI had told me about these boxes. There was nothing inside but a multichoice clip, tripped by a few key phonemes. It doesn't matter, said SETI, when I expressed disbelief. They can't tell the difference. I looked at Himem, and tried to imagine the perceptions of a human being who couldn't tell the difference between accessing the systems and talking to a recorded message. It wasn't easy.

Himem had a sister, a partner and children, a mother (grandmother?) and a nephew (cousin?). They all lived together in one or maybe 2 of the little rooms. The wizened old grandmother gave Himem a lot of trouble. She was 73, and getting childish (this gave me a bit of a jolt!). I would wake up in my shelf to hear the old lady shouting defiantly and Himem almost tearful with embarrassment. When I looked out there would be a trail of puddles leading ominously to the per. Granny had been fetching water from the corridor fountain and pouring it down the suction toilet again. She had no excuse. This was a Commander designed centre with many thoughtful touches. On the door of each stall a small dedicated screen played constantly a really enchanting little animation about a happy smiling pyjama'd person: How to Use a Suction Toilet. I loved it. I could sit and watch it for hours.

I'd been very lucky. It turned out that Millie Mohun lived in a well almost entirely inhabited by *monozuke,* a division of the Sub basics considered highly significant by my burst course. The word meant 'mechanical connection', a NATENG borrowing from a prerecorded underworld language. Monozuke lived for nothing but their connection with Function. They would not use the overplus, the slots, the cultural hospitals, canteens, stadiums. They died on their shelves and were carried away by the grubs. And, the shiftmate who had brought me to Millie's well was a monozuke. That was why she 'transacted' with every tag reader we passed. If SHACTI required input, it would let you know by closing a physical or field gate in your path. But the monozuke didn't wait to be asked. They never missed an opportunity to interact with the system.

I asked Himem, who was also a monozuke, if it worried her that all the machinery involved belonged to the Commanders. 'Yes but you see Alice —' she answered. 'SERVE is behind it all, and at this point in the continuum, SERVE is identified with Function.' She had a delightful taste for long words, mispronounced with grave confidence. It was fun to be told I knew more about Sub culture than Yolande T. That was just what I tried to say to her at the race meeting. SERVE and Function are one and the same.'

Himem thought the Commanders looked after people very well. Only she wished someone would tell them to disband the ulaux. She didn't mind UBIQ. But the basic troops, those young men in collars and Commander suits, should not be turned loose whatever happened. I gathered she was terrified of being raped. I was puzzled at the horror the idea seemed to hold. We didn't do much raping at home (irrespective of gender). But I couldn't see it would hurt much more than a punch on the nose. The ulaux never did come down anyway. Their existence was just our gesture towards the underworld style of government.

I hardly saw Millie Mohun. She was always surrounded, if not by adult fans then by children. I had never seen so many larval specimens of humanity, in-person or otherwise. Gamesplayers did not have offspring. Perhaps Millie felt starved of this part of the basic life-experience. Himem and her sister, Dat, were devoted to Millie and often helped to organise and entertain her public. It was Dat who told me I mustn't use the terms number and basic. I had been trying to network with a group of fans in the square. They were a little surly: didn't seem to want to talk about racing. Dat put her hand on my sleeve as I gave up and moved away — a skinny dreamy girl with bad skin, a crooked nose and enormous eyes. (I still found it odd to be accosted by a disembodied head and a pair of hands.) I ought to say 'serial' she explained. We're serials and this is the seriate. Taken aback, I mumbled something about things being different in my former centre.

She wasn't a processer. Himem was older and had inherited the family privilege. Presumably this grieved Dat because monozuke longed for closer union with Function. She was brave about it. She spent much time quietly watching the communal flat screen with some older women. Overplus clips were not 'Functional' but PEC was. Even when the random flow came up with nothing but unintelligible codes they still sat there. Perhaps they liked the colours.

All through the daylight hours the men loafed around our well floor, idling and clowning; and playing with the ever-present junior Millie league. I watched them and thought about a joke we have in Space, the kind of joke that may be our form of folklore. Once upon a time there was a woman (in the dawning age of ADAPT) who noticed that men called all machines 'she'. If that's true, she decided, we've got them outnumbered now. In space women and men became truly equal, and perhaps it was partly because of the machines. On the underworld men became redundant.

The Sub, where to be functional was the only measure of value, was probably the worst place to be born male. No one much cared what they did, even though they were partners and fathers, and so they became the male surplus problem. Nobody cared about that either, so long as they broke each others' heads and left the light fittings alone. If vandalism reached a critical level Area Command would send DOGS down to help the cultural police. (Distance Order Generators: a heavy industrial grub converted for this purpose.) Then there would be flash burns, passages sealed, punishment collars issued: and quiet nights for a while.

Homosexual eroticism was once normal behaviour in space. People now called that a phase on the way to equality, but I was old fashioned. Apart from my father, the other sex meant very little to me. But my indifference was put to shame, somehow, by this happy, friendly scrapheap.

I tried to engage them in conversation. Fortunately, I was at home with NATENG. SETI would have hated it down here. She understood Natural English perfectly, but like most execs pretended it was terribly difficult.

The men jostled me, coated with Millie-midgets some too young even to walk. The children's mothers were in one of the well's screen rooms, listening to Mille describing how she approached a water jump (or something). What a collection of overgrown knees and elbows and larynxes! They didn't mean any harm, they were just being cheerful. They thrust forward a bashful youth with a nasty annealed stripe along his forearm.

'You ought to get that MEDICed,' I said kindly.

He stared, with a glazed expression.

HE DOESN'T SPEAK ENGLISH!

'Not speak Nateng? Don't tell me he speaks acro. Where on earth did he learn it?'

HE SPEAKS SIND!

'What? Oh, you mean Synthetic Neo-Dravidian. I thought that didn't catch on.'

It was a generated language, the recreation of a former Sub Commander who had attempted to start a precultural revival.

They dragged the burned young man away, and returned to their favourite game of trying to push each other into the waste disposal. But I thought about him afterwards. I was sure I had seen his face before.

I was more puzzled than alarmed. I cornered Ram, Himem's cousin (or nephew). He muttered, 'They are crazy boys' and would not meet my eyes.

'Do these crazy boys bother Millie?'

'Don't worry, Alice. She will teach them better.'

Ram was the boy who had told me I couldn't adjust the centre's lighting. I had been right to find his face familiar. He was an agency-reared pet, who had been returned to the masses in a stock reduction. As only one of Sub SHACTI's pet agencies was select enough to keep its 'stock' in reserved accommodation, Ram almost certainly shared pedigree with my Pia.

He lowered his plentiful supply of lashes coquettishly (he had some pet-like mannerisms) and sneaked away. I dismissed the incident. It made sense that the blackmailers should be monitoring their victim. And Millie couldn't do anything to keep such unsavoury intruders out of her well. She was only a basic in trouble . . .

But that was almost the end of my innocence.

My encounter with the men was after my third shift. I went to sleep, pleasantly exhausted. When I woke up the well was strangely quiet. It had been a rest day for a lot of processers. Something significant was happening on the local calendar. I didn't get a rest because I belonged to CHTHON. I sat in the screen room nearest to my shelf. Each floor had one of these networking rooms. The shelves had no illumination after dark; and the dispenser allowance of nightlights was rather meagre.

PEC flickered on the grey wall like a world glimpsed through a doorway. Occasionally a burst of green alphanumeric spattered across it. These were messages from the cultural authorities or SHACTI itself: sometimes general, sometimes specific. Numbers who couldn't read quickly enough could catch up on the concourse print-outs. Because we were monozuke there was little furniture, only a few shabby and peculiar plastic bolsters which must have come with the centre package. Himem's granny (mother) and another old woman were squatting by the heating element, provided for the synthetic chill of late-season night. They had put some food cartons on the plate and were happily poking at the contents. The cartons, naturally, were melting. I wondered, did they do these things just to annoy Himem, or was it genuine reversion? They peered at me, daring me to intervene.

My mother looked bad but she never looked like that. It was as if their faces (I was glad I was spared the rest) were being eaten away by some horrible incurable disease.

The doors flew open and Dat rushed in, with Input, Himem's eldest child.

'Come on Alice!' exclaimed the little girl. 'We're going to the Housing!'

I was thrilled. Every centre on the underworld had its symbolic access locations. There would be a suite of rooms appropriately decorated, presided over by the projection of a lovely gentleman or lady. Sometimes there would be little symbals everywhere, sometimes only one for each member of the array. The whole idea was an anachronism, a race-memory of Birth and Health and Food Production as incalculable Persons, to be placated with every mark of respect. But even in VENTUR the symbals were maintained. Everybody had a sneaking fear that if they were dismantled something dreadful would happen.

A Sub Housing was something different. No non-Sub was allowed access. The Subs went so berserk at the threat of intrusion that even UBIQ did not enter the inner precinct.

We were late, we ran half the way up to level 1. We passed through a double lock out of the normal seriate passage and entered a humming space of darkness

I had seen the enabled Housing (from a distance). Here was the lower half of the installation. I saw a huge gloomy concourse 10 or 20 times the size of the usual opened-out intersection. Strangely, so much unaccustomed space made the floor/ceiling look even closer. A square block in the middle, pushing 2 floors apart, was lit but the light did not seem to radiate outward. I felt I was walking into a big shadowy production chamber where human presence was not needed or expected. The hum of the machine was almost palpable.

'This is not the Housing,' said Dat softly. 'There is only one Housing, in our capital, where the connection between Function and the Sub is real. This is a remote node of that place.'

The hum was not machinery, it was people. The walls of the concourse were lined with booths. People were waiting at the doors, milling about; gathering in groups between the concourse support pillars. There seemed to be 1000s of them.

We found Himem and the others. There was an exchange of glances that made me think it had been Dat's idea to bring the stranger along: and I wasn't entirely welcome. I started to make a little speech, thanking Himem for this great privilege – then remembered awkwardly I was not supposed to be a tourist. But no one noticed. They were preoccupied: by the visit to their systems, I thought.

Suddenly, the milling crowd was aligned in one direction. A new surge of people was coming into the concourse. They were all young men, as far as I could see. They were laughing, clowning; staring about them brashly. The crowd gave a roar and began throwing things. Some of the stuff landed on me from the rows behind. It was coloured print-out, torn into ribbons. I had seen numbers picking it up from our concourse – I thought they were trying to help the cleaning grubs.

What a mess!

'It is deblocking time,' explained Himem, beside me. 'All these young men are going to be married, so they're coming to the Housing to have their fertility returned.'

CHTHON implanted a long-term contraceptive as part of the tagging procedure: either for boys or girls or both – the cultures made their own rules. Our surveillance would pick up any unlibrated pregnancy, so it was safe to allow them this freedom.

I noticed again that Himem seemed constrained. The young men disappeared into a particularly large booth: MEDIC's location, I supposed. I slipped away discreetly.

VENTURan symbals irritated me. Even if it were possible to *flatter* a machine construct, everyone knows there is no temporal/physical location for a system. EROA, the law, exists where and when it is accessed. The paradigm between times is in SERVE's memory, nowhere else.

On the underworld there was more excuse for the institution. The enabled had limited personal access to facilities; the basics had none. What I most missed in Millie's well was the console that should have been in every room. (Now I didn't have one, I appreciated the almost acronymic freight of direct meaning in that word. The piece of furniture that supports and interfaces your station is a source of comfort: and it *consolidates* the systems into unity . . . ). Basics had to come to the Housing in-person to make their requests. Like all cultures, the Sub used ax to fax as social control. In each of these booths an enabled Sub called a 'functionary' would be doing business over a screen; reading tags and allowing access only if the account was a record of good behaviour.

I tried to identify my old friends PORT and FUNDS and LUDI. I didn't have much success. I saw And, my shiftmate from SAFE, strolling along with a dazed-looking young man who had a piece of blue print-out hanging over one ear. She grinned and blushed, embarrassed at being caught with her deb.

The Subs buzzed around me, some carrying fluorescent globalls that bobbed mysteriously like little greenish suns. The deblocking was just an excuse. What they wanted was an illogical reassurance: that the air and food and water would keep on coming; and the bright light by day and the dim light by night. Even VENTURans need the same, occasionally.

There were figures going in and out of the central block, but I did not approach it. In the very centre would be the most curious feature of a Sub symbal: an empty space. That was Function. The Subs symbolically located their one system not in the access booths but in a cube of empty air. Even in my impenetrable disguise I decided to stay away. There would be a *frightful* fuss if they caught a non-Sub looking at their Nothing.

We laughed at the Subs. But it was not quite 'nothing'. If it was a cube of interstellar plasma it still wouldn't be that. All the zillions of tiny events, ceaseless and all-pervasive . . .

Is that what 'Function' is?

The support pillars were etched with little diagrams of the logic

69

gates: obviously copied from an older institution. I stood looking at one, feeling slightly disoriented. My adventure was having strange effects. Perhaps I'd better leave. If I stayed in this Housing much longer, I might find I wasn't a sightseer any more.

Millie Mohun walked past me, deep in conversation with another number. Naturally I turned and followed her. She had not been with the family group when I arrived: I hadn't seen her all day, I joined a small blot of number gathered in a niche between two access booths. And from SAFE suddenly appeared again, without her deb.

'Oh Alice!' she cried. 'Have you heard?'

'What?'

'Dat is dead!'

*'Dat!'*

The Dat I knew was in front of me, with Millie Mohun's arm round her shoulders. I had already noticed this, and was feeling jealous.

'The President terminated her. It's terrible. What did she do wrong? She only took us outside. So we could see the sky −'

I realised she was talking about the rebellious basic, whose startling end had been current gossip at SHACTI Pavilion 4 days ago. I had heard of it before that because I had access to a Ranger; and they knew all the Palace secrets. Apparently the news had just arrived in the seriate. An item in one of those green bursts on their screens had verified the death. I looked from And, to Millie Mohun, to the distressed and angry faces around her. I had a horrible feeling that for the past 3 days I had been very, very stupid.

The blot dispersed nervously. Millie kissed young Dat, who seemed especially distressed, and dismissed her. She stood with her fists up against the wall and her face pressed against them. I think she was crying. She turned her head, as once before, and saw me: with my mouth hanging open, no doubt. She knew I knew. She wiped her eyes a little and smiled.

'D'you like playing games Alice? I could show you a game more worth playing than anything you've ever tried.'

Something alarming happened to me as we were leaving the Housing. Dat and Millie, they said, would be staying longer. The gate at the double lock wouldn't let me pass. I entered my tag again, trying not to feel self conscious. The gate stayed shut. I froze. *Non-Subs are not allowed in a Sub Housing!* I was going to be the cause of an underworld incident!

Himem behind me, said, 'Don't worry Alice. It's just puzzled about something.' She leaned around me, took my tag out of the reader and put in her own. Spoke clearly and carefully: 'Hello SHACTI. The previous serial is well known to me, and a long time resident of this centre . . .'

The gate let me through. The men and children trotted on.

'Himem — why did you do that?'

She had 'known' me for 3 days. Talking to a tag reader was pure monozuke fantasy. But lying to a machine was unthinkable. She stared at me: confused, defiant? I could not translate.

'The centre was made for people,' she said abruptly. 'Not people for the centre.'

She hurried after her family, her 4 shadows bobbing dimly at her heels under the passage lights. The centre was made for people — I wondered where she'd got that from.

+

I caught Millie in the square floor screen room, on the day after the restday. She had Himem's child, Input, with her. I looked at the 2 of them with suspicion. Suddenly, Millie's interest in children seemed distinctly sinister. What had she been telling the little girl? Input scooted off. I wished I could lock the door. But the seriate locked its own doors, for its own reasons and not otherwise. On the wall screen a crowd of serials poured along a broad passageway. It might have been somewhere in the Sub, it might have been anywhere.

'So many,' I said. 'How could anyone imagine so many?'

'There's only one of each kind,' remarked Millie mildly.

She was holding a clip tube, fanmail from somebody on a higher level who didn't know any better. The overplus sold dedicated clip decoders for seriate screens. But you wouldn't find one in a monozuke well. With a rueful smile she tossed the scroll into a carton of litter that was waiting to be taken out to the waste disposal. I glimpsed, as she leaned forward, a glint of metal. She was burned, like any other Sub.

I still felt her attraction. She still had the lovely well-designed look that had made me think once of a VENTURan clone: a genetic mix so successful that people want exact copies. It was not pure altruism, or pure adventure that had brought me chasing down into numberworld. All my life I looked for love, because there was something in that phenomenon that took me out of myself, set me free. Millie could have done that, I was sure of it. Which was strange because none of the others seemed even on the same level as my Pia. But it was no use. There would be no encounter now.

'It is taking longer than I'd planned, Millie —' I began, in what was supposed to be an ominous tone.

'But I don't mind. I'm doing this for myself as much as for you. It's a new experience —'

This was not at all what I meant to say. I broke off, frustrated.

'I know you are.'

'What?'

'I know you're doing this for yourself. I ought to tell you, Alice. I won't always be here. I may have to go away.'

The coolness of Millie! I had never had a single word of gratitude from her. Not from the moment I first chased the louts away. She wasn't even looking at me now. She was watching PEC on the screen. Why couldn't I make myself confront her — with what I knew and guessed?

'We do our best, you know. This way, every human being on earth has enough to eat, clothes to wear, somewhere to sleep. Don't you know that's never been done before, ever?'

Millie glanced at me with an expression compounded of kindness and amusement.

She said, 'Who's blaming you, Alice?'

+

The microclimate of SHACTI centre mimicked the outside world, without going to extremes. Like our synthetic light and darkness, this was supposed to preserve the numbers' natural rhythms. Already it was colder on the platform than the morning I arrived. But that was partly because SAFE kept VENTURan time. A long day was due in space; and meanwhile my shift was slipping backwards into the night. Red UBIQ eyes looked down – Uncontrolled Behaviour Incident Quanitifier. Every time I noticed those eyes I was tempted to wave my arms and legs about and gibber. The numbers would just stare at me glumly. One thing they definitely lacked was a sense of humour.

I hoped the capin was taking care of Pia. She must be very lonely. I would certainly get a smack for this! I was slightly worried about housekeep. But she would be fine as long as she stayed put. I was fairly sure LECM domestics didn't need the tag to get their rations: and anyway she surely had some 'slots'. But her tag was my tag too. If she was in trouble I would soon know about it. UBIQ would get me, and I'd be stuck with my ear pinned to the wall when the embarrassed cultural police appeared. A lively thought! I might offer this game to LUDI, when I'd polished it up a bit.

I had made up my mind I was going to stay the whole winter. MEDIC would nag: ARE YOU GETTING YOUR RADS?? YOU'LL CATCH RANGER'S SYNDROME –. But 4 days away from Pia, had shown me I couldn't leave her yet. And I knew I'd always been kind to her but there were things I wanted to change, now I'd been with the basics on their own terms.

I need not have worried that first morning. Everyone had their own style of presenting the tag. Some just stuck up their chins and let the reader suck it in. To pull the shield out and offer it showed a special willingness to be accounted. Because I did that, and declined my slots, my shift all reckoned I was a monozuke.

Headshell on. H in. On my second shift I had sneaked my way into the stadium. It had seemed the obvious solution. But the stored racing events gave me no route to Millie. Accounts was supposed to interface with stadium over its biels and capture anything of lasting significance. The fact that it wasn't doing so in this case should have shown up. But would not – because SHACTI just decided there was nothing to copy.

I looked for Millie Mohun, and all I found was a series of little

73

holes in the machine, as if something hot had just dropped through it. It was uncanny.

The processers must have been surprised when I appeared. Numbers usually kept their places until they failed a MEDICal and were taken out of service: and generally the replacement was a younger member of the same family group. I had not noticed this when I was making my substitution. I only thought about convincing the machinery, not its biological parts. However, it didn't seem to matter. There was never any curiosity in the locker room, only a lumpish silence. The numbers in Millie's well went into giggles over my funny pyjamas. My sandals caused such excitement I had to hide them, and access myself a pair of plastic slippers (pressies) from the dispenser. At SAFE no one looked at me twice. I would have thought CHTHON had a policy of employing only unusually stupid basics. But And the monozuke was lively enough away from her work.

The funniest incident was when little Input stood at my open shelf and solemnly handed me a dispenser comb. Without a regular bathroom to look after me, I'd forgotten such niceties. There weren't many mirrors about. No, the funniest thing was the underwear that appeared on my cot, so tactfully. I had forgotten all about that too!

I was used to the lack of greenery and variation now. My eyes accepted the undeviating grid of corridors. It was clean: it was in keeping with the severe, uncompromising vision of all life as tributary to the inhuman processes of Function.

It was not so easy to grow accustomed to the human freak show. CHTHON's PRENAT package included a pregnancy implant that weeded out the kind of viable deviations (like congenital blindness) that would only cause misery on the underworld. Unfortunately, that control didn't do anything about their faces. But the old grandmothers and grandfathers were the worst. What must it be like for Himem − to see that face still uncannily like her own; collapsing so hideously into decay?

The old woman had a little song she like to sing. There were other songs and chants I had heard in our well or coming over the centre's PA, but this one appealed to me.

The tears on our faces
Run in channels burned
By the Design
The child in my arms was accounted
Before the stars

There was more, a catalogue so obscure the song might be older than Space — although effects like that can always be generated.

'But why the tears, granny?' I asked. 'Why put tears in there? Wouldn't it be nicer to have happy words?'

She patted me on the cheek. Her fingertips were hard and dry as agam.

'Ah. Alice you're young. You'll find out one day. The sad things are the real things.'

Then she pulled my short hair and cackled. 'You modern girls. If you knew what you looked like —!'

Poor granny. The Sad Thing had her in its grip. One must be realistic. For a number old 73 years was a long life. But what I found so poignant was that *they knew*. *'Tears in the nature of things, minds touched by the shadow of mortality . . . '* I had not expected to find such consciousness down here.

When CHTHON arrived, it must do business with someone. The tiny fraction of the underworlders then 'in power' became our enabled. We were aware, CHTHON was aware, that the division was arbitrary. We decided it didn't matter. If we sifted them for merit, it would be all the same in a generation: their history had proved that so often. It was a pity though, that a number like Himem couldn't advance herself. *She could not.* There was no route by which a processer could leave the seriate.

I was tired. It was difficult to sleep in that stuffy shelf. I was beginning to wonder if the night gangs were always so indefatigably rowdy.

And I was unwilling to face the discovery I had made.

Millie Mohun was not an innocent victim of number crime. Helping her was not an illegal but harmless amusement.

I had realised almost at once that Millie's wellmates had to be aware of her predicament. They must be sharing their rations with

75

her, unless she was living entirely on canapés. I was prepared to look the other way. I had accepted, at first, the eager fans. But how could a biel gamesplayer have devoted admirers among the monozuke? It didn't make sense. Dat and Himem never went near the stadium. The very idea of such unconnected behaviour would shock them to the core.

The scene in the Housing had finally opened my eyes. She was an agitator: closely connected with the woman who died, and probably far more dangerous. An anti-VENTURan agitator with a considerable secret following. What I had stumbled on in the stadium car park had been a falling out between criminals. Now I remembered the succession of slips Himem had made, and understood that the basics knew I was a stranger to the Sub seriate. I was horribly afraid they might even know I was a Commander — apparently condoning their plot.

I ought to report to Area Command. But I could not do so without reporting myself as a complete idiot — and I did not relish that. Besides, I had no proof. I hadn't heard a word of anti-VENTURan sentiment from Millie. The fans showed nothing but respect for SERVE/Function. Everything suspicious could be explained away: Millie probably wasn't the only number to cry about the fate of Dat the star gazer.

The best move would be to leave. Say nothing, and let UBIQ look after her if she was dangerous. But I didn't want my adventure to end.

I was trying to trace Millie's birth. Mohun was the cultural name for a north-western fruit growing area, which tallied with her story. I must insinuate myself into CHTHON's records of wild number populations out on the surface. My suspicions didn't make me any less eager to find Millie's account. Once I managed to trace it, I would know the truth.

It was not easy to sit immobile for hours, only alive from the wrists down. I was pleased with myself for standing up to test. The support field helped, and also a background in some rougher varieties of space travel. The basics were lucky, they didn't know anything about it. I wondered what they were experiencing. It was union with Function, according to their prax. Perhaps they knew something I didn't — beyond base 3, base 9; the groups and route-branches and all the rest of our mindset hardware . . .

Bright codes gathered, vanished and reformed. I fell deeper in, absorbed in the great game. I relaxed. But something pursued me. Before I saw the seriate, I thought it reasonable that Millie did not know her number. It couldn't be read on a tag — not by the human eye. I knew better now. Why wouldn't she tell me? What did she have against the number that CHTHON gave her, which ought to be her most precious possession? Her only real possession. It made no difference. If she was accounted, I must be able to retrieve her

If she was accounted . . .

# 5

It was dark, long past light change. The door of the screen room was wedged open, partly so we could keep an eye on the men and partly to give them light. From the top floor came sounds of an overplus clip — the well became less monozuke up there. Millie was in her shelf asleep, exhausted for once. The men were repelling all boarders at our entry lock.

A group of Millie's most faithful fans sat under the wall screen, deep in discussion. Is it Functional to call the great over-system intelligent? Surely intelligence is a merely human faculty. The unconnected personify their machine systems: as if humanity were superior to pure operation. They even try to make machines like human beings, a shameful perversion of decent remotics. Oh no. SERVE, which is no more than a local expression of Function's current state, is only the connections, the pervasive and ineluctable connections. The connections are not between all things. *It is* all things . . .

What ingratitude, I thought wryly. We come down here, we put everything right, we run their whole planet for them at great personal expense and inconvenience, and then the Subs tell us, 'Oh, you were going to do it anyway. You're just a current state of the circuitry of the universe.' I had been naïve in my appraisal of the monozuke attitude to VENTUR. Our SERVE was not Function by another name. It was more like Function scratching its nose.

I had never invaded a small group like this before. But the fans showed no guilty consciousness. Occasionally one of them smiled at me encouragingly, as if inviting me to join in. I pretended to watch PEC, hoping I would hear something that would force me to make up my mind. I was mentally rehearsing another interview with Millie. She would not reroute me so easily this time.

Dat's eyes were brilliant. If I was in my own world I'd be careful how I smiled at that girl. She had the look of someone always ready to take things seriously, instantly.

Someone brought in food and they began to rip tabs off the self-heating portions. Saliva gathered in mouth. I had been eating as little as possible. I assumed their rations were wholesome, but the idea wasn't exactly appealing. It was hard to believe that the original genotypes were exactly the same as our food plants in Space. Himem came over to me with a pack full of steaming mess. I declined, and then changed my mind. I felt the need of some protective colouration. I took the portionpack, nicked off the spoon. Here's ALIC, sitting in on a number systems analysis seminar, enjoying a bowl of petfood.

Himem leaned forward, she was kneeling in front of me, and slipped her fingers into my hair.

'Commander Alice,' she remarked. 'There's one thing we're all very curious about. How do you do the processing at SAFE without our alteration?'

To my credit, I did not drop the food. The other women looked no better pleased than I was. Himem scowled defiantly.

So that was that.

I was appalled. UBIQ's eyes seemed to be glaring straight at me. It couldn't be true. If they knew I was a VENTURan, surely they couldn't be plotting sedition in front of me. I grasped despairingly at the lesser evil. Millie shouldn't have told them the secret, but what could you expect from a number? I ought to have made her swear fearful oaths not to boast about who was helping her.

I spoke carefully and slowly. 'Now you are all aware of my desire to assist Millie. I believe the stadium gang took her tag by force and I intended to restore her identifcation. This may not now be possible, though I will aid her in any legal fashion available to me. But I have to tell you that your behaviour has been most irregular and I do not approve of that. It could lead to surveillance conclusions —'

Why were they all staring so blankly? Perhaps I should try SIND.

Dat said, 'I knew you shouldn't Himem. You should have waited for her to come out of it herself.'

She put her sister out of the way, and took my hand. 'Commander Alice, don't you remember? Millie has never had a tag. That's what's so wonderful. Soon we'll none of us have to wear tags. We'll all be like her!'

Millie Mohun's serial tag was not stolen. The SIND boys were not blackmailing her. They wanted Millie to align with them, but she had bigger ideas. She didn't have a tag because she had been born before they were invented. She was now approximately 270 years old — underworld reckoning. For the latter part of her life she had been a legend among the wild numbers, a rumour in north-west centres. Until a talent spotter who believed in her fixed her up with a forged tag so she could come in from the wild. She was the first human being — a Sub, naturally — who would not die. That was why the rebellious basic led people out of the centre. Now that Millie was here, the starships must soon arrive.

Even the Commanders were beginning to hear of Millie. One of them had been so impressed she had decided to leave the meaningless world above and follow Millie into the seriate.

They knew all about me. They supposed that Ram's cousin who was my 'er — companion' had told me about Millie. She was a fan. They knew I had enlisted myself in SAFE. My housekeep at LECM was also a fan: when they read her number on an information burst they knew it was me. And picked me up, and since then everyone had been looking after me. I had been behaving oddly, but they put that down to the new experience of processing, however I managed it. Or perhaps crippling embarrassment over my evil past. The talent spotter? Certainly I could meet him —'

My first reaction was bewildered outrage. I thought they were wired up, but for my convenience not theirs. *They tell each other things!* I was sure basics weren't supposed to do that.

Himem muttered, 'I wish Millie would discourage that bad, silly man —'

'Oh sign off, Himem. She needed the tag.'

They began to argue about the forgery. Himem's contention was that Millie could have lived in the centre with nothing in her ear at all. SERVE would not let her be captured. It would not raise a field against her.

'Don't be plugged. What about the cults?' cut in a practical voice. 'The police have these things called "eyes" —'

'She wears the tag because it was a present! —' exclaimed Dat passionately. 'Don't you understand her at all —?'

I was almost forgotten. I found myself moving away, out of the group. It was involuntary. I wanted, I think, to put a distance between us, even if it was just the breadth of a seriate room. A space across which I could look with pity.

I went to Millie, in her room opposite mine over the square. I had been lying in my shelf unsleeping. Her bunkmate was out, on shift probably. She was awake. She was sitting on the floor by a globall; one of the small luminous globes that you could stick on the lighting in the daytime, to charge them up for the dark. It made steady shadows round her, curves of darkness.

I told her that I knew the truth. I asked her what she'd said to her friends about me. She had been deceiving them, obviously, as well as me.

'I told them you had come down here to help me. And partly for yourself,' answered Millie evenly. No more than that. I felt helpless before such consummate artistry. Wherever did she learn how to play her games?

Outside in the passage a night gang was passing. We could hear distantly the marts booming and the pounding feet and yelling voices. I must have been blind not to have noticed what was happening in this centre. Was it spreading all over the North-West Quadrant? I remembered suddenly, coldly, that my Pia was also a Millie fan.

'Millie. I don't know what you thought I could do for you. Whatever it was, you were wrong. But I'm a VENTURan, of some sort. I know what it means for a person to be in authority. I see that's what you are. Tell the numbers to stop this. Don't murder them! Make it stop —'

She looked at the wall, the blank wall between us and the sounds of that pitiful human storm. Her face was hard and sad.

81

'I wish I could. Oh, I wish I could.'

Her face was sad, but I could still see, or imagined I could see, the ghost of that beckoning smile. I had never felt so strongly there was some mystery about this woman, and I didn't know the whole of it yet.

'Millie won't you tell me who you really are? Won't you tell me what's really happening here?'

For a moment I thought she would. Her eyes met mine directly, thoughtfully.

'I am the connection –'

Connection with what? Was there a bigger criminal behind her?

But nothing more. She changed her mind and decided not to trust me. Silence lengthened, until I got up and went away.

The fact of the conspiracy was enough. The form it took had been chosen with condemning skill. We might hope and believe that the unbridgeable gap between VENTUR and the underworld masses was a matter of intellect, moral stature and all kinds of excellence. But for them, the best argument was the way we lived and they died. If this fantasy was widely believed in even one quadrant of one bloc the effect on the libration must be serious. It was like Millie's coolness, like her nerve, to present herself: instead of a fearful shrunken caricature being dragged about in a carton. Not all impossibilities are equally attractive. Did she realise that she was young as no VENTURan is young? Did she realise the refined insolence of her strong, lovely maturity: which we cannot have and we know it. Which no one can have, unless they accept the rest of that short downhill ride. I thought she did.

Before light change I was on the platform, going back to SAFE. Headshell on, handshake in.

Sabotage is a capital crime. It has to be. It was almost incredible that the fans had been meeting right under the red eyes of UBIQ that clustered over our screen room door, as in every other room, every inhabited space in the centre. Perhaps they thought SERVE had told it not to record Millie's affairs. There would be no warning, there would be no appeal, when the reckoning came. The poor numbers, they wouldn't understand.

82

They would not see that they were condemned by the equations, the balance: by SERVE itself. CHTHON had to write in big letters for the masses to be able to read. There would be no sifting of guilty from semi-innocent. Himem's children. And, here at SAFE. All those Millie-midgets. Did everyone who came to the well know about the seditious part? No one would ask them. UBIQ had recorded them all.

There was only one thing for me to do. I must find Millie's account, have a replacement tag issued and so prove to the fans their story was nonsense. UBIQ must be waiting for a critical development. If I could defuse the situation, the incident-peaking around Millie Mohun would fade away. Millie was doomed anyway, but the surveillance was not vindictive. If there wasn't any proliferation, it wouldn't take any wider action.

After the first shock, I'd tried to question the fans calmly. They explained to me willingly how the tag trick was done. They weren't in the least ashamed of it. Or rather, as they kept assuring me, they would have been ashamed in any other circumstances. They had all the proper respect for VENTUR and for SERVE — but Millie was different. I did not argue. There was no point, in the face of such bright-eyed insanity.

It was well known to CHTHON that 'talent spotters' were a little unscrupulous. The stadiums needed a constant supply of gamesplayers, and many of the best were from the surface. CHTHON assigned quotas to preserve the wild populations, but number entertainment was a high priority. It did not look too hard at individual cases. Naturally, even on the Sub there were corrupt transactions. The wild girls and boys did not always know what was going on. A stadium consortium would understand this. Instead of accessing the subject's account to confirm that she or he had made the statutory voluntary agreement to become a biel, they would purchase from the talent spotter a 'serial x': the transaction to be ratified 'at a more convenient occasion.' Players spent a lot of their time collared and inside the stadium. The irregularity was unlikely to be picked up at once. The gamesplayer was either dead or hooked on glory before she knew she had been bought and sold.

It was the obvious way to get someone into a centre without a valid tag, for a few days. The astonishing thing was that Millie had survived *for years*. A forged tag fitted the immortality story, but I suspected that part was a later gloss. Millie Mohun probably had a sociopathic record. I could see it would be nice for a serious agitator to dump something like that. What did she think I could do? Did she think I could rewrite SERVE for her?

She had enticed me down into the seriate deliberately. She probably arranged that ambush in the Pavilion car park, to arouse my sympathy. What a risk, what a risk she took! But I was to blame, I must have given her the impression that I sympathised.

It was clever of her to pick on immortality. VENTUR had a secret about death, which the numbers were not supposed to guess. They thought we lived 'forever'. The sophisticated would rationalise that to at least a few 100 years: because, over their generations, they saw Rangers still in the bloom of youth. It wasn't so. All we'd discovered in space was the normal human life-span, revealed free of disease, malnutrition and earth gravity. After 100, our reckoning, things were liable to change rather abruptly. 130 was the absolute upper limit, but it was not yet fun to get there. I had always told myself I would route out at my first serious warning. I knew I probably wouldn't. I would retire to a sanatorium. And in my last days I would not be very far from Himem's mother, lying in her shelf waiting for the cleaning grubs. We would be equals then.

We had a massive research budget on the problem, naturally. We lived in hope that someday the random magic of species progression would operate, so long as we made sure all our variants survived. But that was no consolation for any one alive. What kind of mutation was it that could be disseminated among living adults? It had to be pure fantasy. They gave themselves away with the starship element — plugging in to the old story about immortality up in the sky . . .

No, Millie Mohun, you can't hypnotise me. You can't infect me with your absurdity.

Last shift I sat at this console wondering uneasily if Sub serials had the real secret of the nature of the universe. Now I only wished fervently I could wipe the last 4 days. Because I knew what I must do, for the good of the whole stinking seething bacteria colony, and I couldn't do it. I didn't want to see another number face as long as I lived. But I couldn't turn them in.

I felt rather sick. I had been enjoying myself so much, exploring the inner world. I had refused to consider that if Millie's account was to be found I should have had it in 10 minutes. The answer to the puzzle was obvious. There was no error in SHACTI.

I had a sense of unreality. She had been born on the surface where MONSAT was infallible. And if that was a lie, in every centre there was UBIQ. It was impossible for an unlibrated pregnancy to escape the systems' attention. But if the impossible had happened, and Millie was illegitimate: how could I prove that she was not immortal?

SERVE, let me find her. There's nothing else I can do to help them . . .

In desperation I called up the talent-spotter, using information the fans had given me. He was an ex-pet: he'd saved up his tips and bought himself back from the agency. He was still lovely, even in the grainy translation of my SAFE screen. One could imagine how a number with a face like that, watching it fall into swift decay, would clutch at Millie's promise. . .

With a start I realised I was looking at NATENG print and colour pictures. The monitors would go crazy! I escaped —

Something had appeared in my window, uninvited. This happened. The remains of old searches, arbitrary responses to commands I'd cancelled days ago. It was old material, very old. There was no YD, only a patterned band indicating the patchy archives from prerecorded SHACTI, when it was just a Ranger base on the Subcontinent, before CHTHON. Get off my screen you nuisance.

The codes jumped out at me MOHUN.

I was looking at a listing of the population at a soft fruit plant in the north-west hills. The connection between population and plant wasn't clear. They could have been manual labour, things were so chaotic on the underworld in those days. And there she was. Familial details of two xxxx — an obsolete code. They had an adult daughter. Nutritive, non bio: local name, Millie. Here was her portrait. Even worse than the one under Pia's bed. I was never so pleased to see anything in my life. The first thing was to get a fix on this scrap of archive so I could find it again. I managed that quite coolly: and then it was break.

In the locker room people were muttering about the riots. I took no notice. Millie Mohun, adopted daughter of two wild numbers. I didn't like the 'adopted'. It sounded irregular. But at least she was there. I squatted with my back against the partition wall, grinning. Suddenly, the pit of my stomach dropped through the floor, as if SHACTI SAFE had taken off for orbit. I had remembered the pre-CHTHON date band.

I must be temporarily deranged by undereating, and the eerie solipsistic cool of one number criminal. Of course, what I had found was another surface dweller called Millie. Maybe one of Millie's ancestors —.

I sat at the console, the support field held me. I felt the sensors groping in my hair. SAFE didn't learn. I entered my usual H. Nothing happened. I hardly noticed. I was too impatient to reassure myself about that archive screen. I tried another. My screen turned silver all over, cleared and wrote on itself in large bright alpha. UA UA UA. Unauthorised Access. Now why did it do that?

I was wondering, when I realised that the console had started to emit a loud unpleasant bleeping. The girl on one side of me was already plugged. I saw the other's eyes flick sideways briefly in unspecific sympathy, then she was gone. The supers came running.

I sat quiet. There were 4 or 5 of them by the sound. A hand came over my shoulder and touched the board. The bleeping continued, the message kept on flashing.

'My H —'

'It's changed them. On the hour. Didn't you get it on your fax yet? Routine precaution, because of those pisstools in the levels last night.'

Someone who knew her new entry reached down. All at once I understood. I jerked forward, electrified, to see her fingers, for a handshake was invisible on the screen. She barely glanced at me but she did something to the arm of my chair. I couldn't move at all any more.

The alarms stopped. The supers jabbered at each other, and I waited. So the adventure was over. In a moment Millie, the numbers, the desperate sedition, resumed their proper proportions. Well, I would not report them. Leave it to Mission Command, leave it to UBIQ, leave it to SERVE. In the course of nature, numbers claiming to possess eternal youth can only cause a finite amount of trouble. Maybe that was UBIQ's reasoning too. And perhaps I'd frightened them and the conspiracy would die now of its own accord. I knew I was in for a terrible time. I wondered with rueful amusement what Sub SHACTI's Commander would have to say to me.

They took off the headshell. They told each other they had better not meddle with its insides. There was, not unnaturally, a certain amount of excitement when someone casually checked the other part of the equipment and discovered I had no burns. They didn't know what to do about this phenomenon. They released the field, took me out of the chair and led me away. I made no protest. I presumed I'd reach human authority eventually and didn't want my unmasking to be any more undignified than necessary. They took me to a room of violent white surfaces. The light was brilliant, it made me blink after the quiet monochrome of the processing floor. They sat me down again and talked it out over my head.

The SAFE was outside cultural parameters. These supers didn't answer to any Sub enabled. They were not even Subs. Like the ulaux, they'd been brought in from other blocs: it was CHTHON policy. The burns were a mystery to this crew.

'Has the skin somehow regenerated? It's not supposed to do that.'

They poked me.

'There's bone in there! She's never been touched.'

A superior super pulled out my tag and read it on her wrist. She stumbled through a little of housekeep's data, moving her lips —
'She's had the surgery.'

'But there's no sign of it.'

Superior super tried checking my number out on a console that stood against the bright white wall. She used a keyscreen. There was no sound and I couldn't see the display. But I could guess she was being told there was nothing whatever wrong. The women stared at each other in uneasy wonderment. No one spoke to me. I felt like laughing, but I also felt perhaps the joke had gone on long enough. They had not restrained me. I would walk over to that console and put them out of their misery. Then I remembered that I had cancelled myself from the SHACTI register.

'No use asking her anything,' said one woman slowly.

'She'd only talk nonsense.'

I was still waiting to be handed over to the Rangers. The systems are always right. But sometimes, just occasionally, the hardware that interprets the system tells you something that is seriously at odds with observable reality. For these cases, we still need human beings. The women were all looking at each other: at me, away. They were frightened. They felt no curiosity, only alarm. They had rarely seen a Ranger except on the screen. Rangers might be genim of the system for all they knew. It must be an awesome thing for a basic number to work for CHTHON. They were very much afraid of its displeasure.

Something alarmed me. The cunning, utterly unreflecting eyes.

I stood up sharply. 2 of them reacted with professional speed. I threw them off.

I shouted, 'No! You're only numbers —!'

But my voice sounded ludicrous. I was ashamed of it. It seemed to be calling attention to the disgusting fact that these creatures were grabbing me. I fought in silence. *She's tougher than she looks* I heard them gasping, and they got something round my neck. I knew I must not allow this but they did it, and an extraordinary sensation ripped into the base of my skull, a flash of acid yellow.

Once when I was on the transport platform I saw a number-woman in distress. With her hands in front of her she explained something bitterly to the empty air. *Who's she talking to,* I asked And. 'To PEC,' she said, surprised. 'To anyone who's watching. Haven't you ever felt like doing that?' In my ignorance I nodded seriously, while suppressing laughter . . . *Help me, help me! Doesn't anybody see what's happening . . .*

I was conscious, I only knew I must not move, when they

carried me from the bright white room into another furnished with half-familiar metal. A MEDIC room. Of course, if it had to use mutilated numbers, CHTHON wouldn't leave its processers to the Housing MEDIC. It would do the job properly.

It was simple. There was nothing wrong with me except that I wasn't burned.

The MEDIC unit ran test data until it was satisfied. I was conscious all the time, in a way. Then the supers took me back to the floor and plugged me in. My load, which I hadn't been able to reroute this time, had been shared automatically among the shift by SAFE instead; while I was gone. It was routine. Occasionally, although I hadn't seen it happen in my 4 shifts, a processer would have to be taken off for a while. The state they were in sometimes crept over the edge of consciousness and that caused problems.

I should have guessed what it might be like to be a real monozuke. I had seen enabled Subs who had been dedicated for years. A twitching eye, a dropped foot: a selective confusion with words and meanings . . . I might have known the masses would not be paying less of a price for the privilege of being functional. To be a human brain, neither asleep nor unconscious but without self awareness. To have nothing left of yourself but a horrible groping sense of dispossession, that went on and on. To come out of this with no sense of duration: but knowing that a little something had been lost. A little more each time.

The strange thing was, as far as I was aware I didn't know any of this when the supers grabbed me. I thought Sub passive processing slightly gross but harmless. And yet I fought for my life, and knew it.

In the well I crouched in my shelf. The closure opened and one of the fans from the square looked in, the boy with the burned arm. He leaned close and stared at my naked skull: he touched the sealed rims of my burns and the cringing flesh around them.

'You have joined us now,' he whispered.

+

I had a dream. I dreamed that I died. I was climbing what seemed to be a multilevel wall. I fell, and while I was falling I

89

remembered that I was on earth and I knew the ground was racing up to smash me though I seemed to hang suspended. I knew it was such a fall that I couldn't possibly survive. The moment of impact did not come, mercifully I must have lost consciousness. The next thing I knew I was lying in darkness, not exactly darkness but a sensation of darkness, in a pile of other bodies. They were warm and pressed close against me, bare flesh to bare flesh, in every direction. What's happening? I asked. They told me I was dead, which I knew to be true because of the fall. This was what it was like to be dead. How long does it last? I asked. Forever. It can't be, I told myself. My body has been found at the foot of that wall and taken away and atomised. I cannot be experiencing this. There was no answer.

I had heard that death was oblivion. I had heard also the conventional wisdom that says something of us survives, in the unique physical and temporal record that is never erased from SERVE. There are immortals who live on in some real sense in the systems they helped to create: and even for the rest of us a shadowy consciousness may reside. I had always thought I would prefer oblivion but I could tolerate the other. But not this. I couldn't bear this. The systems would have warned me. It would have shown, somehow, through the skin of life — that this was coming. I tried to stop myself from panicking. I knew I was going to start screaming, kicking at the flesh, trying to fight my way out. I forced myself to hold on, second by second, so that afterwards when the ordeal was over I wouldn't be ashamed. The warm bodies of the dead pressed around me, endlessly. There was no escape, no way out, no end. And finally, when I realised it was a dream, I knew that ever afterwards I was not going to be able to forget it. It might be true. How could I prove otherwise? The packed warm bodies might be waiting for me when I really died.

Then I dreamed I was living, as it seemed to be, on earth. But I knew it couldn't be so. This was a complicated dream with an adventurous plot, something like the vics which imitate REM recordings. It had other characters intermittently, in the way of dreams: unspecified friends. Official forces were trying to prevent us (mainly me) from revealing the secret. I kept hiding in the bowels of various places — I think I forgot I was supposed to be on a facsimile planet — and pulling out panels, using a bolt cutter and burning my hands on the hot metal. Finally I tore up the surface somewhere. I peeled back the grass with a thick fibrous layer underneath and there through on the other side was blackness and the stars. I had a great feeling of joy and satisfaction.

Later this radial, which now seemed to be R4, *landed*, an impossible feat. I walked out of it and looked back, and it had metamorphosed itself into an enormous soaring pre-Space earth building, something I had never seen in life. Great dark docking bay doors opened, and all kinds of strange creatures began to walk in, in a stately procession.

Sometimes I saw grey walls and heard voices. Once I found myself standing looking down, feeling coldness strike my face, and that seemed a strange interruption in my vivid dreams when I knew all the time I was safe in my bedroll at home.

'We don't talk about night much, where I come from. We say the quarter, and the YD usually. It is always day you know. The sun doesn't go out when you can't see it. But I'm used to your expressions now —'

I was suddenly alarmed. I had given away my secret! On that sting of alarm, I woke.

The quilt slipped off me and I remembered all that had happened. How horrible. Enough to give anyone nightmares. My closure was open. I saw into my bunkmate's shelf across the room. She wasn't there. I knew I had to go back to the SAFE. It was the only place where I could reach a console, call for help. I looked up at the YD function: numerals ticking over on the wall by the door. With an awful start, I saw it was the middle of my shift. At the same time I noticed there was a girl sitting on the floor.

'It's all right Alice. Your shift's slipped, you don't need to be there yet.'

I didn't recognised her at all.

'How do you know? What's happened — did I make a noise?'

I must have been yelling in my sleep and frightened them. She looked at me with wide eyes, jumped up and ran out of the room.

The others came in. Himem and Dat and the young man called Ram.

'Alice are you awake?' asked Dat gravely.

'Yes, I'm awake.'

'Good. It's been a long time.'

I did not understand her and yet I did. I put my hands up to my head, which had been depilated for the alteration, and felt a thick close growth of hair.

'Where's Millie?'

I wanted her. I couldn't endure all these numbers around me without Millie.

'Alice, you've been ill. It's been — a lot of days.'

Himem took my hand and pressed it. 'Millie went away Alice. She had to do in-persons on the Sub stadium circuit. She was at our capital and there was trouble there. Millie is . . . She was arrested. We're waiting to hear from her now.'

Later, I found out what had happened. I had been out of my mind more or less for nearly 60 days — functioning but never properly surfacing between shifts. The serials had been looking after me. Meantime, unrest in the North-West Quadrant had continued. Millie Mohun had been missing since she disappeared in the course of a riot at the old Sub capital. Only her most infatuated fans refused to accept the truth. She was dead.

# Inside the World

# 1

My console was no use to me. Without an entry code I was helpless. I would never get a chance to fix on the cypher. Before I touched the keys my head was plugged, I was gone. I thought of a plan whereby I would sucker the console and then cause a disturbance. I would have a record, that I could take away, of what the super keyed in to release the alarm. A code-sucker would be a restricted item, but I could ax it on the daysky. While I was out of order my shiftmates had made sure I took my issue. They were worried about me. Processers who had head trouble were sometimes turned off.

I commissioned Ram to access the parasite. He produced a giant, unfathomably primitive box of wires. I threw it in the waste disposal, and there went my slots. SAFE's gates would not accept contraband anyway: not if I swallowed it. I had forgotten that. Daysky was their name for transactions outside the machine – that is, illegal. The reference was to the daytime sky in which 'the Commanders' machines don't show up'. It must be an enabled term. Ram had never seen the open sky.

Pia's cousin had become my ally since I woke up. He wanted to get out of SHACTI too. The young unattached fans, men as well as women, all wanted to transfer to the old capital. They thought they would find Millie there. Himem disapproved. Monozukc don't ask for transfers! And besides, she was afraid he would disappear like the jockey.

I said I would help him. We took the internal transport that carried basics out to the stadium; from the lowest level of the centre, through the Ridge. We got out on to the platform. We were in a cave. The floor/ceiling was not rock, it was terrare-forming laced with cables. I saw light and movement, stepped off the back of the platform and hurried towards it. This was the cultural production area, stowed out of sight and away from accommodation. Ram followed me, scrambling over fat concertina hook-ups.

I stood on the edge of one of SHACTI's sudden little gorges, now a crevasse in the cave floor. The light and movement were of machinery. Compactors were crushing waste into the crevasse floor with a loud monotonous thumping noise.

I thought it was a way out, I muttered.

There were human figures crawling on the moving rubbish, picking it over along with the salvage grubs . . . *This is the way they would cover the earth, if they were let loose.*

Ram coaxed me, with a gentleness that was dimly familiar. 'It's the other way Alice. Come on Alice. There's nothing to look at here . . .'

The 'emart', the global tunnel network laid with electromagnetic thrusters, was constructed and maintained directly by CHTHON . CHTHON and the Sub both agreed that access to facilities in this category had to be outside the Housing. I followed Ram back to the mouth of the cave. On either side of the transport platform were agam units. They faced outwards on to a concourse that funnelled towards the stadium gates; some of them substantial and clearly continuous through the terrareform.

We stood in line, outside the undecorated unit that should have been a symbol of PORT, the system that takes care of travellers. The other transactees were official transfers who had seen their numbers on the screen and come to be processed. Ram had told me that the functionary would demand '1000s of slots'. As he had no income, and the emart was part of CHTHON life support, I knew this was nonsense. I explained to him that it was simple from each/to each for the enabled to pay for their journeys, but his case was different.

Everyone said an active processer couldn't transfer with or without payment. I knew this was right, but I wanted to see the access. The global network didn't carry passengers bloc to bloc. The few enabled who made those journeys had to be shuttled up to LOAX and down again. And my world was up there.

We went into the booth and faced a Sub enabled on a screen.

96

Ram entered his tag. She refused his request in about 10 words, without the slightest pretence of consulting the system. Ram stepped back as his tag was released and looked at me, hopefully. I was at a loss. I had not visualised this scene. There was no board that I could touch, no sensor I could talk to. There was nothing in the booth but a screen, a tag reader and me and Ram. And the next client who had already come in and was sitting on a plastic bench by the door. I asked the woman, politely, how was she able to read PORT's mind like that. She might at least go through the motions.

She said brusquely: 'What are you? Mother, sister? Put your tag in the reader.'

I suddenly, vividly, knew that I could not afford any trouble with the cultural authorities.

I walked, not caring where. The prestadium concourse was garish with variety, compared to level 6 accommodation. I looked at the pets in the open front of a canteen and wondered if I could bribe one of them to carry a message out. But they were collared, and their enabled users did not hire them for conversation. Besides who would believe such a story. A Commander in the seriate . . .

I sat down outside an overplus. Nothing would add up. I could not equate this place with the featureless 'tunnel opening' in the background of my picture of the day I met Millie Mohun. I was in another world. I could go like those SIND boys and lurk below the Pavilion. But I wouldn't see any VENTURan tourists. Unrest had emptied SHACTI. Enabled were not frequent visitors to the basic accommodation, but there ought to be some about. In the last few days I had seen none. Area Command must be restricting access. I rubbed my hand across my face, momentarily dispersing the film of grease. I walked now in a gaseous puddle of eructations, exudations. I had to eat the food. Apparently when I was out of control I had nearly starved myself, but still I had been living on it for 70 days: and I must go on.

A pack of cults went by, the local Sub police. 2 solid gleaming objects flanked the women, menacing even in daylight with all their obstruction handlers retracted. A mobile remote would always come up to you, and say, 'Hello friend.' A station would wait for your touch. There was little practical reason for the salute, it was pure VENTURan sentiment. I watched the big grubs dispassionately, registering my own reaction.

I'd never had the slightest desire to own a DOG. I thought it was poor taste to convert a working piece of hardware for something as meaningless as 'machine companionship'. I never thought I'd be afraid of one. It occurred to me, if I met the louts I had chased away from Millie now, I would be the one to run.

It was clear that the passive processing produced in the brain a state like paradoxical REM sleep. The feeling I called 'dispossession' was caused by conflicting signals. I was in REM paralysis, like someone deeply asleep and dreaming, but I also knew my fingers were moving. Such a small thing. So near to the pleasurable illusion of vic. I had tried to describe the crawling horror to Himem. She knew the sensation I was talking about, but she was bemused: *that's normal isn't it?* The other processers showed no curiosity. Alice had had to have her burns reopened, that was all. Only And knew the truth. But I didn't care about her or any of them. What difference did it make?

The supers had been sticking a tranquilliser strip under my ear at the end of every shift to control my 'overreaction'. My body was so innocent of underworld patent medicines that their dosage completely disoriented me. I was beginning to have patches of recall now. When I remembered my dream of peeling back grass and earth to find the stars, there were hands on me, voices saying, *Alice, there's nothing there, only the utilities. You'll get into trouble* . . . I had never succeeded in lifting a floor panel. My fingernails weren't up to it. Eventually the supers decided I was calm enough to do without 'MEDICation': and I woke up.

I was a serial, listed on a CHTHON interface. SHACTI centre could not transfer me − not that I wanted to go anywhere on this foul planet. It would not let me through its gates. If I tried to reach the mall, I was stopped at the foot of one of the blank ramps that led to the upper gates. Every exit was the same. I had thought of attempting some *intelligent* sabotage hoping UBIQ would notice me and alert Mission Command. But the centres were designed so that numbers couldn't reach anything intelligent. And UBIQ wouldn't alert anyone, it would just react. Sabotage is a capital crime.

If I hung around the exits too much, or otherwise behaved anomalously, I would be punished. They would take me to the EROA access booth on this concourse, where cultural law and order was verified by CHTHON. I would try to tell the functionary I was really a VENTURan, but the systems themselves would assure her I was lying. I would find myself wearing a collar with a sentence written into it confining me to my well: on pain of that acid yellow lightning through the base of the skull. If I tried to burn off the tag, UBIQ would be down on me. If I succeeded and got out on to the surface, I would be on the run. MONSAT tracked, and dragged back for further hideous indignities.

I buried my face in my hands. *I can't get out.*

SETI would not have worried when I disappeared without notice — that was our style. But by this time someone or something had certainly tried to get hold of me. Plaything had probably been discovered. They would know I was lost because I wouldn't have left it behind. The Rangers might even now be scouring the hills frame by MONSAT frame, hunting for me. I could not know. I could not reach them in any way.

The women at the well were trying to get me to go to the cultural hospital because I had no uterine discharge. They were right, I was sick. I felt continually nauseous, debilitated. Passive processing was giving me a headache that seemed to be permanent and I didn't dare take dispenser painkillers without taking reds as well. I had to save my reds. What would I do if the lump under my arm suddenly started growing?

When I first looked at the basic dispensers, I was disgusted at the array of analgesics MEDIC offered. Pain is valuable signal. If something's hurting surely you want to know, so MEDIC can remove the cause . . .

Ram sat down beside me. He smelled worse that I did. He had an overplus chemical concoction, accessed with a few slots scrounged from somewhere. He wore it to cover his body odours, whenever Himem wasn't about. His disappointment was transparent, humiliating.

99

'Well, we are even,' he said nobly. 'I did not help you either.'

None of them could grasp the scale of my catastrophe. They couldn't take on board a helpless VENTURan. The vexed question of Millie's disappearance was far more important.

I put my hands in my hair, shudderingly careful not to touch the mutilations. The heat of Ram's body beside me made me want to scream. I thought of millions, millions of passive processers enduring this existence all over the planet. The Sub version was more grotesque but it was all the same. And all the millions more, useless like Ram. The picture of so much dull mindless uncomprehending misery filled me with such disgust —

Now I'm well punished. This is what happens to people who take liberties with the systems. I had been upset, because my adventure would be recorded but I wouldn't be able to access it. Where was plenum monitoring now? Where it had always been: seeing all but concentrating on the important bits. Not on ALIC.

Suddenly, I thought of the crevasse full of rubbish. Even the simplest processor would be cued to burn out when detached from the cultural plant. But there would be mechanical parts. I'd had phases in my past when I was very keen on handicrafts. I once played 'Asteroid Survivors' for a whole year with 2 lovers of mine. We'd never have come out from under that vic, except that the fights got too bad. I could search my memory. I was sure I could put together a radio transmitter. I'd have to find a way to generate some free power.

It was worth a try. Unless the seriate field acted as an effective horizon . . . I glimpsed the shining walls of the trap and suppressed that thought hurriedly.

'Ram, those rubbish pickers. Is there no routine to stop them? What would happen if I took a carton of that stuff back to my shelf?'

'Well — you'd have to buy yourself in first. But I think there's a waiting list for free patches. People inherit them.'

I stared at him. I felt my face contort and couldn't stop it. A moan of pure frustration finally burst forth.

Ram was very good. They had all been very good, at ignoring my occasional outbursts. They were postively VENTURan in their ability to invent privacy where none existed.

I calmed down, as there was nothing else to do, and sat gazing bleakly at the passing numbers. The significance of what had happened at PORT began to sink in. I had been putting off the humiliating moment when I would go to the Housing, accost a high-ranking Sub over one of those access screens, and scream for help. Now I realised I had no such option. Oh no, this is unbelievable. There *must* be a way. In a little while, I would sneak off home to R4, have my head MEDIC'd and try to forget this nightmare.

Ram sighed.

The commotion startled both of us. A crowd of people had suddenly come running out of the EROA access. It was more than a booth, being also the headquarters of the police. Some of the people were cults, the special Housing kind in green coveralls. But I also saw VENTURan style softsuits. I jumped up. Only the most enabled adopted our formal dress. I might know someone! I forgot instantly about hiding my shame. I ran. Numbers converged eagerly at the hint of some excitement. I elbowed my way through.

'What's going on?'

'It's one of those fans.'

'They've pulled her —'

'She's got a bad tag —'

I pushed and shoved, reaching the front just as a pack of cults hustled the criminal by. I saw my housekeep from the LECM. It was a dreadful shock. I had forgotten all about her. I'd left the poor woman with a 'bad tag' and now she was in trouble. But I couldn't see why she was being hauled through the stadium gates, or how an excited crowd was involved.

The numbers had left me standing. I hurried to catch up, not knowing quite what I meant to do: hoping I had mistaken the face. What was that they were shouting? Millie —?

Millie —?

It was housekeep, certainly. We ran across the permaturf of the racetrack. I heard the name the numbers were yelling. I still didn't understand at all, but I had enough sense to try and extricate myself. Too late. Everyone stood still. The bodies around me congealed into a solid wall. Housekeep was shouting something about Millie Mohun. Housing functionaries in their VENTURan suits were marching up and down with wrists up to their faces, shouting unintelligibly over their PA. We seemed to have stopped because we had run out of ground. We were on the racetrack, on the side with the precipice where there were no stands. There was nothing beyond housekeep now except the seriate field limit. The cults stood back. Housekeep was alone. She kept on shouting. Some of the enabled had climbed out of their suits which lay in an ungainly pile. One of them stepped forward and solemnly gave housekeep a shove.

I almost laughed.

The field bounced her back and someone else shoved her. If she had been a gamesplayer in a collar, she would have gone right over the edge. The limit buzzed her quite hard when she hit it. It was meant to repel sharply, so they didn't fool about with it. She staggered – they pushed her back. After a few minutes, broken blood vessels began to seep through her skin and we saw faint red stains expanding on her pyjamas, on the shoulders and arms and knees.

This was the way they used to do it in the dark ages, when the Subs were the new workforce of the world and security fields a novel invention. If anyone broke their rules they would take her out of the installation and push her against the invisible barrier until it killed her. It was Functional, they said. The system did the killing, no single executioner carried any guilt. But CHTHON had banned this 'limiting'.

Housekeep stopped shouting in the end. She stumbled about, groping and weaving. Whenever she blundered into the wall of cults, standing immovably in a half-circle around her and the functionaries, they pushed her back. She turned away nodding, as if thanking them, and was shoved again.

I thought I had recognised one of the enabled, but I couldn't see her now. The serial press had surged a little, there were bodies in front of me.

'Millie –'

I'd been half aware of Ram, running beside me. The sound of his voice brought me to my senses. I grabbed his sleeve and dragged us both away.

The platform was empty. There was a transport cylinder drawn up to the buffer, but the doors wouldn't open for us. It seemed very quiet. We sat on a bench. Ram drew his knees up to his chin and hugged himself.

He asked me, in a thin unnatural voice, 'Why do they wear those suits? It isn't cold, inside the seriate.'

'I don't know. To copy VENTUR.'

'But why do you? Earth isn't poisonous to you, is it?'

'No. Not around here anyway. It's — a kind of nostalgia. I can't explain Ram. You wouldn't understand.'

A short silence. I drew a deep breath.

'I had no idea it was as bad as that.'

I had gathered that some sections of the community were getting irritated with the Millie fans. I had felt only sympathy for these sections. Millie Mohun had been an unusual person. I could safely say I would not forget her. But it was absurd to go on pretending she was alive.

'They hate us,' said Ram, softly and raptly. 'The functionaries in the Housing, they have turned themselves off to Millie. They will try to pull us all in, saying that we have bad tags. If the Commanders' systems won't kill us, they will kill us themselves. All of us . . .'

He nodded grimly, satisfied at my expression.

Soon the in-platform began to fill up. The event at the stadium must be over. A few faces looked frightened, but UBIQ did not descend in any form. There was no sign of any of the soft-suited enabled. Under the rim of terrareforming I could see a blurred segment of sky and the slopes of the stadium valley. There was the outside world. It was not blue and conifer green now. There had been heavy early snow and there would be more: as far as I could make out through the field. I had not noticed that white on white backdrop while they were limiting housekeep.

I sat still, but I felt panic running through me to my shaking finger ends. A few minutes ago my predicament had been half unreal. I had been more angry than frightened. The shaking was reaction: I had seen a woman brutally killed. But that wasn't all. I knew, though I couldn't get it in focus, that something terrible had happened — to me, not just to housekeep and the fans.

The transport, triggered by weight of numbers opened its doors.

'Ram,' I said. 'What happened to Pia?'

He looked oddly more human now. He gave me a glance that said I was a Commander. He had tried to use me, but I was as much an enemy as housekeep's murderers.

'We don't know.'

'What was her name? My — the woman who was killed?'

'She was called Top.'

We all climbed into the cars. I rocked with my fists between my thighs, a rubbery serial haunch on either side. Ram was opposite. I kept looking at him nervously, but he always turned away. I was wondering — what in the world was my pro-VENTURan acquaintance Yolande T doing, embroiled in such a hideous illegal termination.

# 2

Top (it depressed me unreasonably to think of the woman's comical name) must have been waiting every hour for our duplicate identity to be challenged. Perhaps she went a little mad: at any rate she started accessing Housing functionaries via her LECM console, telling them the good news about the immortal jockey. Millie by then was already dead. On any other bloc the poor number would have been dismissed as a mildly amusing headcrash, but not on the Sub. They waited until my lease ran out and housekeep was between contracts, technically no longer part of LECM. If I had remembered it I would have been desperately hoping for the end of that lease. The Subs examined her account and discovered with glee — so much for my skill — evidence that her tag had been duplicated. But it was no use. When they took her to EROA it returned the judgement that *there was no illegality.* Of course it did. I'm a PIONER. And since I'd cancelled myself elsewhere, at system level there was no duplication. Housekeep had been taken into containment. When EROA refused to co-operate, the Housing functionaries and others dragged her out to the limit.

Top had been on trial in the days since I recovered consciousness. I had noticed nothing. I never read those bursts of green that said xxx had been collared, or xxxx turned off. Out of tact, no one had mentioned the affair: and now the numbers didn't seem to blame me. Perhaps it was only a new morbid sensitivity that made me afraid they would.

Millie's fans were harmless. They had no plans to chop off their tags and run wild. There didn't seem to be any plan at all except to wait for Millie, and gather together to discuss doubtful evidence that she was still alive. Their only crime was to have aroused Sub prejudices. Thanks to Top, the immortality story had gone public. Possibly there were a few recruits, but for the most part the Subs were simply disgusted; basic serials and enabled alike. She was a brain-orgy biel! It was an outrage to suggest Function had elected to keep a creature like that running forever. It did not help that the Millie nucleus was actually orthoprax to excess. Everyone likes an excuse to attack the virtuous.

I thought now the reason I hadn't been able to find her was because she was already under UBIQ investigation. It had finally excised her under cover of riot control. Even if she had been genuinely illegitimate, the scandal was over. But dead, and her secret buried in SERVE forever, Millie Mohun had suddenly become horribly alive to me.

For once we didn't have to wait for stale news to filter down from the enabled world. Several days after Ram and I had seen housekeep limited an overplus clip appeared with a report on 'the Millie fans'. Slots were scraped together guiltily, and our groups accessed a copy. We had to borrow a fourth-floor screen room with a decoder from some non-monozuke, non-Millie well mates. I sat with the fans and learned that the basic levels were being seriously disturbed by a dangerous heteroprax group.

Himem, in front of me, was wearing a patch of MEDIC film above her eye. The night before this, a gang of men had come down our passage desiring to smash up the 'Millie well'. Himem had gone out to reason with them and sustained a nasty cut and several bruises. She studied the generated image of 'rioting Millie fans' patiently, as if she was trying to recognise herself.

There was no mention of the limiting. The clip was not really about Millie fans. It was about the person who had identified the problem and was going to erase it from this and other north-west centres. I recognised with a feeling of helpless disbelief underworld PIONER Yolande Tectonics. The same woman to whom I had made kindly tourist overtures at a SHACTI race meeting.

A clip for the basics did not rate personal attention. We saw Yolande's simplified image, mouthing a machine resumé of the speech she had recorded to network to her equals. She spoke not only of Sub prax but also — as a good underworld PIONER should — of her duty to CHTHON.

The fans whispered. They were hurt and impressed by

106

Yolande's solemn words about Function. As for me. I could have groaned out loud. We were watching, obviously, the promotion of a bold career move.

Yolande expressed her opinion that the trouble would get worse. I believed her. Having gone so far as countenancing outright murder, she'd better make sure this dead jockey scare was convincing.

The SIND boy came in, the one with the burned arm. He began to talk to Himem. He wanted Millie's fans to sign up for violent revolution. Since Millie was dead, and they shared the same enemies . . . I had learned that SINDS were not exclusively anti-VENTURan. Much of their hatred was for their own authorities.

'Yolande T is not my enemy,' said Himem stubbornly, fingering her MEDIC patch. 'I admire a woman like that, who interacts with the Commanders without getting corrupted — sorry Alice.'

'Millie lives!' shouted Dat. 'We'd know if she was dead. It would be written in the codes!'

'There'll be fighting in the passageways,' muttered the SIND boy sullenly. 'You'll find out what it's like now, to be hunted.'

'Is that a threat —?' snapped Dat.

I watched this byplay miserably, and so did UBIQ's eyes. As we all left the screen room, non-Millies came to their room doors and looked after us with suspicion and hostility.

My feeling of doom was soon grimly justified. We had more gangs vandalising 'Millie wells'. We had masked women dragging fans out of their shelves in the night. UBIQ surged, in automatic reaction to the incident level. There were DOGs everywhere: cults wrist-reading tags at almost every junction. This was only a beginning. If UBIQ so desired, it could seal the wells and keep them sealed indefinitely, with the numbers inside living out of their CHTHON dispensers.

On the display screen Yolande's powers were limited. She couldn't have a fan collared unless EROA verified it. But there were the containment shelves where numbers could be kept pending an EROA judgement. There was the *diem:* whereby the cults could apply for access to UBIQ's collection on a specified

107

number subject, and put on a 20-hour human monitoring team. As I knew, CHTHON was already uneasy about unrest in the Sub. Neither the Rangers nor the system would distinguish between Millie and the SINDs, and more incidents, inspired by Yolande, would only strengthen her position.

And besides, housekeep was just as dead as if she had been terminated legally.

I was a Millie, by the well I lived in, by the company I kept. I could not lose that record. If I'd had any chance of escape, it was gone. And now I was in danger of losing my life.

I told the fans I had known Yolande T well, and they had better surrender. She was so violently orthoprax she'd limit them all rather than have anyone connect Function with a brain-orgy biel. Perhaps I exaggerated. But it seemed to me that I did know Yolande T. I thought I could read her mind: I thought she had seen in this Millie fantasy the danger that I once saw. An immortal serial was more essentially threatening — however absurd — than 20 years of SIND excitement. The danger was over. But the woman I remembered would not care about that. She would be interested in punishment, not deterrence.

'Tell me this Alice,' said Himem. 'If Millie is a fake, as you say, why doesn't Yolande T prove it? She has only to display a record of Millie's account.'

I sighed. Yolande would need active co-operation from Area Command to retrieve the account of a dead basic. The Rangers might tacitly approve of this campaign, but they wouldn't go that far. And if Millie had been illegitimate, CHTHON certainly would not admit it now.

'Well, what if they did?'

'I'm afraid it would be falsified data, Alice.'

'Exactly.'

She frowned at me, genuinely puzzled.

We were out in the passage. UBIQ had initiated a full review. People squatted morosely, or leaned on the walls or paced about. There were many unfriendly glances directed our group.

The Millies were still completely confident. Before Millie left for her circuit she had told the inner circle 'they would see her on the screen'. It must have been a joke: monozuke didn't watch

108

racing clips. To the fans, her meaning was now clear. She was in hiding. She would appear in the PEC fragments and give them further instructions.

There were also the Codes. The Subs used a strange kind of exegesis on the random process screens that interrupted PEC. I had watched Dat being trained to be a 'Code Reader' before I was trapped, without realising what I was seeing. I knew of the phenomenon from my burst course but I had no idea basics could be involved. Apparently, however, there were fans who were experts in reading secret messages from the VENTURan oversystem. And they were sure they had not seen Millie's death announced.

Meanwhile, people were beginning to disappear without notice. It seemed being a Millie had become a good way to earn one of those elusive transfers.

The review made me sweat. I was bathed in the acrid smell of my own fear.

'Don't worry Alice,' said Himem. 'Function is still processing us, whatever happens.'

Nothing would convince her that I was not (deep down) a true fan. She respected me — they all did — because I could read the Codes. I tried to tell them any Commander could have done what I did, but they were sceptical.

I wanted to ask if she had news of my Pia. She might know more than Ram. But it was difficult to frame the question. The Subs had such an obdurate attitude towards pets.

'Himem —'

She looked up. We were haunch to haunch, squatting together. I could see her metal through the hair. And she mine. No — it was too incongruous.

'Nothing. Forgot what I was going to say.'

When we moved into the LECM capin, it had a defective bathroom. The replacement arrived from underground balanced on the scrawny muscle-lumped shoulders of 2 male numbers. It was the first time I'd seen that kind of work. The younger half of the operation started to disconnect the failed part. The other one was old, his face seamed, his mouth puckered over a few remaining teeth. Seeing there was a LECM guest present, he carefully resumed his pyjama jacket over a ragged singlet that was darkly stained with sweat. I hovered uneasily.

'You must be hot. Can I get you anything?'

He just stared at me.

Housekeep appeared in her doorway, with an open beaker in her hand. The old creature went and took it from her. The field didn't stop him, he was wearing a collar. He drank without spilling a drop. He looked at Pia, who was ignoring the whole business, her pretty bare bottom tilted disdainfully as she gazed out at the trees.

'I have no daughter,' he said.

Housekeep frowned. But I was touched. I knew even then that for a Sub number this was tragedy.

'I am so sorry.'

'No. I am not sorry.'

He took off his jacket again, tied it round his middle carefully and the two of them shouldered the reject bathroom and carried it away.

I felt quite sick sometimes, remembering myself as a tourist. But it wasn't my fault Pia was a pet. As Millie herself said, it was ridiculous for me to blame myself for the fate of the billions. I could sympathise. I might even do something for them: let people know. But not until I got out of here.

'We are lucky to be processers,' remarked Himem. 'I've been thinking, that is probably what protects you and me. And Get and Ifthen. But I'm worried about Dat.'

A mart started to talk to us from the walls. It told us to begin feeding ourselves back through our entries, back into our shelves. As we shuffled like cars on a parking grid the junction seal at the end of the block opened prematurely. 6 sturdy cults appeared. They took Himem and Dat away.

To everyone's astonishment the sisters returned 60 hours later, unharmed. They had been taken into the President's containment, buried in terrareforming between the prestadium and the Housing. They had not been collared or sentenced, just harangued over a screen. During the second night it suddenly occurred to Himem to enter her tag in the reader in her shelf. She just wanted to commune with Function. The closure opened. She knocked on the one opposite. There was only one human guard in the containment, snoozing in front of her monitors. They walked out. When they were in the prestadium Dat, who had never been there before, suggested a stroll around. She was much taken by the effect of starlight, blurred and glimmering through the field above a world of snow.

Being a Millie fan was not yet illegal in CHTHON. Ways had to be found around that point, because the containment only held numbers charged and pending judgement. Somebody had forgotten to invent a criminal offence. I decided Yolande T must be out of the centre.

When I got back from shift and found the celebration, I was as pleased as anyone. However, I could have wished the sisters had been better frightened. I went to Himem's shelf to remonstrate with her, to tell her it was nothing special. It was only that the system didn't recognise her as a criminal. But I told Dat that, and she just said, 'Yes! Isn't it wonderful!' Himem was on her knees, taking things out of the storage under her cot: a pair of extra pyjamas, a spare quilt, a hairburner, a small plastic and wire model of the logic gates. The vacuum pump for her uterine discharge, worn and well used; with a few clean, elderly stains.

'I am being transferred', she said. 'I don't know what to do Alice. I've never known anywhere but SHACTI.'

I looked at the little heap of objects. You could hardly call them possessions.

*You would call it nothing. But even that nothing which was her everything was taken from her —*

We were informed on our screens that the well was under diem. Our non-Millie neighbours were not at all pleased.

This speeded up my plans. There were things in my storage that would not stand diem. I had a small hoard of dry food, some extra quilts; two spare suits of pyjamas. Nothing was restricted. Until I actually did something criminal UBIQ would let me alone. But the cults would not.

It was illegal for a basic to leave the centre. But Sub SHACTI had a row of gates along the bottom of the scarp. It was different down in the depths but no centre attached to a CHTHON installation went without the equivalent of emergency lifeboats. For humane reasons the field was weak. Sometimes the numbers would take it into their heads to break out, as when they followed the stargazing woman. It had become a fashion, I knew, among the night gangs: to rush out when the cults and DOGs were chasing them. If they didn't come back at once, of course retrieval routines went into action. But it was a hostile world out there: a search was not often needed.

It would be harder for me because I was written into SAFE. But when the young men shoved through, I could take my chance. No use trying to get into the upper centre. I must set out on foot and find the nearest CHTHON node. I would give myself up to the wild number auxiliary in charge, and wait for the Rangers. I had admired the surface of the underworld once, passionately. I had wondered how I could ever bear to return to the blandness of parks and gardens at home. Now I just tried not to think about hypothermia; and charismatic carnivore megavertebrates, lovingly re-established.

We came off shift. It was the day after Himem and Dat had walked out of containment. I meant to return to the well for my cache, and go straight to the bottom gates. If I didn't make it this time, I'd have to try again. It was night. There were cults on the dark platform when we debused. My mind still itchy and vague from the processing trance, I shuffled resignedly. I didn't wake up until I found myself in a small group that had been separated.

I tried the first option: pretend nothing's happened.

'Get back in line, that one.'

I got back in line. One of the cults said to another, 'That's all the deletions. Commanders don't want this lot anymore, we're to have them.'

Second option. Be keen and co-operative.

'Am I being relocated to a cultural interface? OK, where is it? Just tell me what shift and I'll be there —'

Where did I learn these options? I had picked them up out of the air. The other pulled processers stared ahead of them or looked at the floor. I had the impression that they pitied me.

'Am I being transferred? All right. Just let me go home and collect a few things —'

I might as well have been talking to the DOGs. They smiled at each other resignedly, took me by the elbows and turned me around.

'That's all been taken care of, serial.'

We marched away together.

There was a girl. I did not see her, I was too excited. I would not have noticed such a little incident anyway. She came to the platform for the first shift of the day. The gate refused her. She had no recourse, no way of finding out why. She ran home and told her family, 'I've been turned off!' Or perhaps they saw the deletion flashed on an information burst and found out that way. They went to the Housing. No reason given. Function makes these decisions sometimes. The moving parts must accept them. She would have been, as Himem was, the only processer in her family: that was the routine. What was indignity and misery to me was her whole inheritance. The family group would suffer. If they were not monozuke, if they wanted the things slots could access, the girl might put on a collar and become a display ornament on the mall. Or a domestic, trotting where the restraint pulled her . . .

I thought of her as a young girl. They were all young to me, although they didn't know it. Sometimes they seemed like children in masks, playing a grotesque and endless game.

The reallocation sat in an inter centre transport cylinder. The enabled of each bloc leased and customised their own passenger service, but the masses travelled freight. They usually were freight. As I had learned, voluntary transfer was only a hypothetical facility. The masses didn't object, or no one ever heard them. Why should they? One centre is very much like another. Two narrow moulded benches ran down the sides of a dull-lit, windowless compartment, with a dirty strip of metal floor between. I did not recognise any of the other women. They must have come from other shifts, other sectors. We were left in the stationary cylinder for a long, long time.

It was nothing personal. First the SINDs, and then Yolande's Millie fan scare. CHTHON-in-SHACTI had decided to reduce

113

the unreliable human element in its processing. I had not even been identified as a dangerous individual. I was just a number, in a statistical solution to a statistical problem.

When at last we moved I was afraid, for an agonising length of time, that we were heading for the shuttle strip to be shipped to Venus. But then I knew by the pressure change we were going down and down and down. Hours passed, uncountably deadly. At the foot of the hills − apparently − there was a lengthy halt and the cylinder was jolted on to another line. After that, the dispensers beside the per had been replenished, and the water fountain worked for a while.

At some point in the next stage the emart stopped again. The light strips had dimmed and blanked out in trailing patches. Eventually, I freed myself from the weight of my sleeping left-hand partner. A few speedy adaptors were lying sprawled along the floor, in the space they'd claimed. My feet brushed naked flesh where they'd pulled their clothes up to be cool.

Our air supply was very warm and stale. The per stank: its treatment unit had packed up. The door at the end of the car slid away when I touched it, the gate was open. I put out my hand expecting to find tunnel wall, but felt nothing. I knelt and groped. There was a walkway. The air outside was faintly less warm, less stale. When my eyes accustomed themselves I saw red and green dots hovering in the dark, and gradually dim shapes. We had stopped at a freight depot. Further down, a hopper feed had docked with another car and was loading something with a faint rustling sound. It wasn't a walkway, just a contact plate for the maintenance grubs.

I needed a shit badly. I had eaten from the dispenser, and it was a mistake. My bowels were grinding. The number food in SHACTI had probably been of superior quality. It was a model centre, after all, under the care of Area Command. I looked for somewhere to hide, the instinctive gesture; and found by touch a smooth palloy buttress jutting from the wall. I squatted, having no choice. Something moved in the depot plant overhead and a glimmer of light reached me. I saw I was surrounded by little heaps of dried excrement. Human freight must stop here often.

I tried to think of some disgusting ships I had been on. Mineral tugs tramping between the asteroids. No crew, minimal provision for hitch-hitchers. Waking up to find a row of turds bobbing merrily past your nose. This is an adventure, ALIC.

I walked to the end of the cylinder and crouched down. I thought, here is the source of the monozuke ideal. No possessions, no plans, no expectations. A serial is just a moving part in a great process. I had admired that mental discipline. I had even wondered how the Sub had managed to develop such a refined ethic. They were only numbers. How unbelievably stupid can a tourist be?

I had been indignant at the way the enabled treated their masses — no VENTURan society would behave like this! In my world we share everything, I told myself. We don't exploit anyone. I was reassured because I knew VENTUR didn't take anything from the underworld. We gave them all that they had, out of pure pity and generosity.

Oh ALIC, there is only one world. Are you trying to pretend that you didn't know?

I was hurt in a way I could hardly bear to name. Sophisticated people don't use terms like 'womanhood' — not without smiling. But I was not sophisticated, I now discovered. I was terminally naive. Phrases, expressions of my own ran through my head: the sad and lonely destiny of VENTUR, our small population, our almost limitless resources. I believed that we had the right to do what we did to the rest of the human race. I believed CHTHON was a loving, womanly system: firm and nutritive, and only a little corrupt . . . It was so painful to remember what I had accepted; and to know the truth, that I forgot I had been carried to this dark foul place. It seemed I must have come here deliberately, to hide myself and howl.

When I made love to my beautiful Pia, instead of cracking her and snuffing her like a drug, I was afraid I was suffering from bestiality.

Ahead of me, the tunnel disappeared into blackness. A narrow indent for grubs continued, just above the slick curve of the frictionless emart bed. It didn't look wide enough to save me from getting crushed. If I could find my way through the maze of tunnels to an ungated exit — if such a thing existed — I would be lost down in the depths of the underworld, with a tag that said I was an absconding processer.

I might have tried it. Perhaps it was a struggling instinct of self-preservation that stopped me. What I felt was cowardice, misery: a complete failure of morale. I huddled there for a while with my fists pressed against my eyes, trying to shut it all out. Then I went back to the car. Left-hand neighbour and right-hand neighbour had merged. They parted again grudgingly, but I never got back as much room as I'd had before.

# 3

It was about the third quarter of the day. There was a heavy brownish illumination that made no attempt to imitate sunlight. The concourse was large and several levels high. Above the first utility course there were balconies and outside stairways, some closed; others sheathed in clear shell that had turned murky with age. In the background at all points radial passages led away; vertiginous canyons and covered alleys, hoops and slashes of gold in the brown shadows. There were serials passing in all directions. Islands of wall screens stood 10 or 12 standard feet high, flickering constantly with clumsy text and clumsier images. The air was full of sound: and it stank. Not like SHACTI centre, but a fouler and more venerable miasma of endless, endless serial humanity.

So this is the old capital.

We had not been told our destination. The information passed around the car, source unknown. At our final halt we saw glimpses of a big complex tunnel access. As we sat there for hours, the car doors occasionally opened briefly. Nobody tried to escape. I must realise, nobody but myself understood that we were prisoners. We were transferred to the internal transport, and finally debused within the great Housing. In other Sub centres the Housing was a symbolic location, and no more. In the capital it was the place of Function in every sense, many levels deep. Down in the depths crystal was forged through which SERVE carried the systems all over the Subcontinent. Up above was the ax to fax. In between were the Function halls. There was no human processing elsewhere, except what the dedicated did from their home bases.

We were kept in an open dormitory without shelves. In due course, the supers divided us up and we went on shift. We had to

117

strip, be scrubbed and scanned; and then dress in special clothes before we were allowed on the floor. I noted dully there would be no chance of bringing contraband in here. I found out from disjointed coversation in the locker room that this was one of the faces Housing ran for CHTHON. In each bloc culturals were expected to support surface reclamation: among other things they had to maintain the rough tracks our Rovers used in the wild. I was breaking stones.

I thought I would live and die in that dormitory. But after the third shift there was a super handing out parcels to all 'reallocs'. There was one for me. I followed the others until we came to a door at the end of a high wide Housing passageway.

The panel closed behind me. The other processers dispersed. I had made no overtures of friendship and now it was too late. I saw a woman go up to a nearby column and duck her head under an opaque plastic hood. Her lips moved. Centre intercom, I guessed. But I had no one to call.

The print-out parcel contained my souvenir pyjamas and sandals. The grubs that picked up the possessions of realtime transfers obviously ignored anything that came out of a dispenser. I stared at the concourse floor of dirty agam mosaic, wondering how I was supposed to access a shelf. Evidently, serials were expected to know these things. There was a roaring sound in my ears. I faced the millions. Buried alive.

'Alice!'

Two serials came running up, a woman and a girl.

'It is Alice, isn't it? We've been waiting for you. You look surprised. Didn't you expect anyone?'

'We saw your number on our Inserts,' cried the other unintelligibly. 'We have other SHACTIs already. I do hope there are people you network. It's been bad up there, hasn't it −?'

Suddenly the older one laughed. 'Oh what are we processing? You've never seen us before −'

She grasped me by the arm.

'Alice − *Millie sent us!*'

The woman was speaking metaphorically. (She explained quickly, seeing my startled face.) She meant I need not worry any more. She put her arm around my shoulders and told me not to look so frightened. So I tried not to look so frightened. The fans had found me.

'We have a shelf open for you,' she said. 'Come and watch PEC with us, Alice.'

With a shy smile, the young girl gently took possession of my print-out sack.

There was a concourse near my new well, lined with overplus outlets. In the centre stood a dark wall, continuous with the floor/ceilings, over which water flowed, giving off fine spray and a ceaseless hissing sound. It was part of the old capital's cooling plant. A bobbing litter of empty food packs and rotted print-out floated on the pool at its foot. Long-armed cleaner grubs swept the scum vaguely. In a row of grimy walk-in booths, CHTHON's inquiry station stood shining. I approached it warily. I was afraid of everything now.

But it was good to be inside, even if the closed cycle air smelled harshly of sanitisers. Light. Sleek surfaces. This was home. There was a console chair in front of the access screen, with a simple control board.

I entered my tag and signed on. A young man in a coverall looked up and smiled as he resolved.

'Hello friend.'

I grinned. It was wonderful to be talking to a machine again. I told him it was a shame to see CENTRIN dressed up in coveralls. I supposed that was a concession to the Subs' distaste for nudity.

'What can I do for you?'

'Oh, sorry. I'd like to access something from the library please.'

The young man's features shifted, almost imperceptibly.

'We have a fine library here in the — Sub capital —. Just tell me what interests you. I'll give you whatever help you require.'

'I want —'

'Remember, other numbers may wish to use this station. If you need to make a lengthy study, enter your slots in the till and I will process an edited clip for you to take home to your well.'

He smiled. 'We have a fine library here in the — Sub capital —. Just tell me what interests you —'

I began to cry. I didn't mean to. Tears started to run down my face, then I was sobbing . . .

The young man's face flickered.

'Friend, you're upset. We have fine counselling services here in the − Sub capital −. Just tell me the nature of the problem . . .'

My new well was bigger than the one in SHACTI. There were about 100 inhabitants, all Millies. We had an inner and an outer square, each with a dispenser bank that looked as old as CHTHON. Walls and floors were faced with the same yellow-brown agam; stained and cracked with age. The men hung about in the usual way, drifts of litter gathered in corners. The old capital cleaning routines were disgustingly inefficient.

Millie fans in the capital were organised. They watched the green information bursts (Inserts) for new transfers, especially from the the north-west. When they picked up a fan by this method she was questioned closely: added her store of names, numbers and Millie-history to the core. I had very little to offer, but no one was surprised at that. They knew Alice from SHACTI 'had been' a Commander. Naturally I didn't have a Sub's ability to carry information. I could have met the other ex-SHACTI serials, but I didn't want to. I just wanted to be let alone.

I went back, when I was more in control of myself, to the in-station: and came away with the library entry on centre topography: as much as a basic was allowed to see. It was not easy getting screen time. Clip decoders were standard fittings here, but the fans were always watching PEC. Before long everyone seemed to know that I was trying to escape. The serials were puzzled. I was now living in the pulsing heart of human civilisation. Where could I possibly want to go?

Subcapital was a cylinder. It had been enlarged outwards and downwards many times. It had also been reinfrastructured by the CHTHON project so that now basic life support and surveillance ran almost everywhere. There were 14 basic accommodation levels (old style), extending below the crystal furnace, which had once been buried deep under the prerecorded protocentre. The outer sector, or cortex, of each held the physical plant for cultural production. A large bore conduit network throughout carried internal transport, overplus and raw material distribution: another network carried the utilities.

Level 1 had a vic stadium, and the ax to fax part of the Housing. Above the underworld surface was a huge sealed Dome, where there was a Presidential Palace and the most enabled had their homebases, parks and gardens.

The cylinder was double shelled. In between, some of the waste heat from 6 million lives was converted into an auxiliary power supply. My basic-access clip gave only a notional diagram. However, I could make out an archaic but recognisable hazcode. If I could reach them, the walls of my prison held a massive charge of raw electric current, which would kill me.

Subcapital had a CENTRIN of its own. The local information system provided a basic Jam for our screens. It borrowed material from UBIQ: its access was therefore banished, like PORT's, from the precinct of the Housing. The Jam was more informative than my library clip, but not more helpful. All the Subs called CENTRIN 'CENTRIN'. I was grimly amused to find there was one VENTURan system they couldn't bury in Function.

Every off-shift I wandered like a rat in a maze. There were several emart accesses on level 2. The enabled had their own spurs into the tunnel network so they didn't have to mix with basics. The CENTRIN symbal had a huge map of the Sub, where I identified centres with emergency exits to the surface. The PORT symbal had its own cults who dismissed me and told me not to waste Function's time. Processers don't access transfers. Functionaries in the old capital were present in-person behind physical security barriers. I tried 'accosting' them and was forcibly ejected from the Housing ax to fax, with an entry on my tag.

The internal transport was only free for local journeys. It took all my slots, until I became afraid of its tag readers and trudged on foot. I was allowed as far as level 1 with its 'Space style' hologram catalogues and customised accommodation. But the cults did not like to see basics up there, except for the biel decos. It occurred to me that if I had turned myself into a pet instead of a respectable processer, I would have had more chance of escape. I thought this: then I remembered what it was like to wear a collar. I tried to explore the production cortex, but the grubs chased me with a horrible dumb persistence. I was afraid UBIQ had sent them.

I saw cave-ins sometimes, for though life-support was CHTHON's and perfect, the structure was cultural. Grubs cleared away rubbish and any bodies, building plant swarmed over the broken places. I thought of Yolande T's burns, and looked for a way to get into a broken conduit that might take me to the shell. But nothing was ever unguarded.

Tag readers were everywhere: at every door, at every junction. I must use them often enough to satisfy the orthoprax cults who had special access to UBIQ. Sometimes I explored too far. I became unpleasantly familiar with the heart-jarring sensation of running into a gate that was shut.

Up in the sealed Dome, to which I had no access whatever, there was a VENTURan Mission with a staff of Rangers and ulaux. They might as well have been on Mars.

Occasionally when we woke up on the processing floor, they were playing projections of the cold furnace over our walls — not for our benefit but for the glory of it. The Sub capital was the only place in the world where SERVE's crystal was grown/built under full earth gravity; in the artificial micrat of extreme cold. And the Subs were the only human beings anywhere who mediated the process, through the altered brains of a select inner core of functionaries. I was no longer fascinated by the Sub view of reality. I only knew, as images of hugely magnified crystal plant swept over me, that this was the truth. I had become a particle without meaning, taken and crushed by the great machine. It was sentience that bothered me. If I could be mindless nothing all the time, that would be best.

I was so obsessed by the unsolvable maze that I had been in the old capital well a 30x20 before I knew I was living with my Pia. I walked across the outer square one day and saw her. She had grown out her hair and wore a little fringe, but there was no possibility of a mistake. I stood staring: and in a moment everything I had felt towards her, when I treated her like a lovely animal, came flooding back to me. But now she was a human girl.

122

I could have run to her, crying. I had convinced myself she was dead.

Pia saw me too. She gave me a look of cold recognition and disappeared into a doorway.

I had shut myself down. I knew I could not afford to feel anything much. All the panic and astonishment and horror of the first days in SHACTI seemed like a pleasurable orgy now. The relationship between VENTUR and the numbers was a commonplace. I could not believe I had ever not known it. Exploited as waste —. It was horrible. But if I ever got home I would probably manage to live with the guilt, like everybody else.

Pia woke me up. I was in pain again, in the trap again, the bodies of the imprisoned dead pressing around me.

I didn't know what to do. Perhaps I should move out. But how would I survive in the old capital on my own? There were SIND outbreaks, night gangs; and Yolande's campaign was gathering strength. I couldn't lose the Millie record on my tag. At least if I stayed here I would be marginally protected. I decided that the glance Pia gave me had been hostile but not startled. She probably knew my story and had been avoiding me since I arrived. Maybe we could just go on like that.

The next off-shift I was in my shelf: my head full of renewed horrors, unable to force myself out into the maze. In the distance, Sub capital's aged agam could look golden. Close up it was like being walled in with packed, solid shit. My closure was up: bunkmate was off on shift. It made no difference to the air. The old capital had no microclimate, just the same stale warmth day and night, always.

The room door slid open and there stood Pia. She was carrying a steaming food portion.

'Hello Alice.'

She looked at me challengingly. I knew that expression. Pia has made up her mind.

I sat up, confused. There was a rank smell coming from the carton. She put it down.

'Look,' she said. 'I want to talk to you.'

I nodded hurriedly.

'It's like this. The people here know I was a pet, but it's different if they know about — a particular user. Just don't funx me up, OK?'

I nodded again.

It was strange to be face to face with her. I could see that to call myself 'an unpleasant memory' was optimistic. Another user might be that. Not me. I'd gone too far. It was one thing to hire a living human body as a mechanical erotic aid. It was another to try to make that convenient appliance love me.

Things were admitted between us, as economically as if SERVE's light carried them.

'I've brought something for you,' she said.

She ripped the top off the meal portion and handed it to me.

'Eat up. If you're going to live in the Sub capital, you have to try eating earth.'

Something was going on. I couldn't make out what. Why should she bring me overplus food? I had never tried it. I didn't like the idea, and I usually needed all my slots for the current escape plan. Pia stuck the spoon in my hand firmly. She always was a bit of a bully. I knew after a mouthful this was not overplus. Lumps of meat in a nameless stinking gravy, incredibly gristly and fibrous. I chewed and swallowed twice. My palms got wet, saliva rushed threateningly into my mouth . . .

I made it to the per. When I lifted my pasty sweating face Pia was there in the stall with me, watching. She handed me a piece of hygiene tissue to wipe my mouth.

'What was it?'

'Earth.'

I had heard travellers' tales about what the wild numbers ate, beside their CHTHON supplements. Some of the enabled considered 'earth meat' a great delicacy. I had always thought it sounded gross and fascinating: to eat dead wildlife. I would delete 'fascinating'.

The look on Pia's face was an odd compound of frank malice and something more serious. Suddenly she grinned.

'That was a bit childish, wasn't it.'

I shrugged. If she wanted to see me with my head in the toilet, I couldn't honestly blame her.

Pia sighed. She rubbed one hand over her velvet head in a gesture I didn't know. I saw that she had had herself burned, and in the new 'SINDish' way she wasn't trying to hide it.

Then she said something totally unexpected.

'It's really shitty isn't it. Having to live down here.'

Pia's lease had come up at the same time as the capin's. She was repossessed. She was only a pet: no one cared if she was a Millie fan. But few high class erotic toys were wanted at SHACTI at present so the agency had leased her to a shopping mall in the capital. When she arrived, the Millie net captured her as it had captured me. According to the protocols that governed bonded labour she was much better off now. She only wore a collar on shift: and if the pet agency didn't reclaim her she would be free after an Ax30 to renew her mall contract or not, as she chose.

'Are you really a fan now?' she asked me.

I remembered the night when she turned up Millie's face from under her cushions. I was hurt, absurdly.

'Are you?'

Pia gave me a cunning look. 'Oh, they're OK I suppose.'

She had made up the excuse to come to my shelf. I discovered this when Ifthen, the team leader of this community, cornered me to express her approval. She was glad I'd found an interface with my former pet. Function is discrete, she said. If we want unlimited real-life, like Millie, we must be ready to erase past and future. We must live in current state . . . I escaped. Perhaps she was just curious. But it was comforting to know Pia didn't come to see me just to stop our story leaking out.

Pia told me I was dead. I was an unwary tourist, who had taken a Rover up above the snow line and become the victim of a freak systems failure. A body had been located, it would be recovered. The announcement had been on SHACTI Jam shortly before the leases came up. Then Pia was repossessed and housekeep taken off by the cults. I thought of my father, in the sanatorium. I had not seen him for years. My mother was unusual in inviting visits: in VENTUR we considered that part of life to be very private. Probably he would never even know. He had taken an option against bad news. I hoped my desk would remember to send him a present from the underworld. There was no one else — friends. They would be sorry if they noticed.

I noted, without commenting, that CHTHON-in-SHACTI must know perfectly well there was no body under the snow. The system, and the Rangers too, had decided better a tragic accident than a VENTURan gone AWOL, with the Sub in its present state. By implication, I might be in for a certain amount of debriefing, if I ever got out of here. I decided I would really love to have to worry about that.

Jam space was available to the old capital public. It was possible even for basics to put their slots together and buy time. Yolande had not yet convinced the Housing Management to take the drastic action of denying fans ax to fax. And so occasionally a Millie Code Reader would look out of our flat screens self consciously: explaining about the immortal jockey to a potential 6 millions. This was rare. But we could always be on PEC. Whenever possible we must pack ourselves together: to talk about Millie and to watch for her. Subs anywhere might be our audience.

I was there. I had to be there sometimes or in my corridor mates would come, with kindly concern, to fetch me. I wondered always how long it could possibly go on. And wondered also what would Millie have thought of this peculiar half life of hers.

The young men punched each other furtively at the back. The children who had so fascinated Millie were ever present: the babies cried. A group of Code Readers was always muttering, a little apart from the crush. Their fingers stabbed imaginary screens in the air. They didn't need displays from PEC in front of them: they had been trained to achieve near eidetic memory.

Subs believed that any random capture of SERVE code was a hologramic fragment of the complete system. With deep study the whole state of the world could be recovered, from a scrap of production figures for Northern Oceanic's fish farms. Somewhere in that world, the fan Readers would find Millie Mohun.

Sometimes I had the strange idea that I had read that archive screen correctly the first time. I didn't believe in immortal serials. But she was not a normal basic. I had noticed that at our first meeting. There was something incongruously familiar about Millie. VENTURans all look 17, but the adults know each other. We carry our freight of memory and it shows, subtly. Surely in Millie Mohun's eyes I had looked down more years than a serial could know. That was what I felt, that was what drew me. She was non-ephemeral.

What if our research had found that elusive variant, 2 generations ago? For unknown reasons the secretaries decided to raise the baby in secret on the underworld, and somehow she was lost. Even Millie's name was significant. It could be an underworld ID of the same type as 'Alice'. But it could easily be heard as acro. MLE. Maximum Lifespan Experiment?

I had invented part of this story before Millie was unmasked. It added to the romance of my adventure if she was a lost orphan, or a Ranger on a secret mission. The rest had gathered afterwards as I listened to the fans. It might even be the truth, no one would ever know. Poor MLE, if it was. Well, at least her tragedy was over.

The men scuffled, the babies cried. I swallowed a gob of mucus in my throat and thought about Pia. She said it was 'shitty' to live down here. But that was defiance of the people who dared to pity her for her past. She was dazzled. She loved this ancient, splendid, filthy place. She was amazed and envious at how much of its wonders I had explored. An idea would come to me as I squatted there with the fans. I couldn't remember what R4 was like, or why it was different: *I could accept this*. The thought grew so real I could see my seriate life in front of me. And then my mouth dried, my heart began to pound. I fled from the brink in terror. No, no, anything but that. I'll die trying —

+

Shift was over. I sat on the plinth at the base of a talking wall in the concourse outside my gate to the Housing. I was frightened.

Himem's family had arrived in the old capital. Dat had taken the old mother, Himem's partner and the children down to Cav4; the last built and most sordid levels. Perhaps she thought they would be safer there. Ram had moved into our well, to be with

Pia. They were to be married at the next deblocking if Pia was not reclaimed. It had been agreed since they were children, to become effective if and when they were both free. I was glad for them, sincerely. I was extremely grateful that Pia seemed to be my friend, I expected nothing more.

Himem had been taken back to SHACTI from her transfer centre, to the President's containment. That was when her dependants were sent here. The old capital was being used as a sink for undesirables. It was the largest Sub centre, its basic accommodation could swallow a lot of problems. We had just learned from our Inserts that Himem was dead. We could tell by the codes it was not a legal termination. She had been limited.

I couldn't believe Himem was dead. She had been so kind to me. I was frightened out of my wits at the prospect of further escalation. But if I left my Millie well, how would I live? There were SINDs everywhere. The cults were edgy and suspicious. They were very clever at reading tags down here. They might spot something wrong with mine: maybe even connect me with housekeep . . .

I closed my eyes and tried to visualise my garden at home. To be sitting in R4's cool light with the living room wall retracted, scents and a delicate breeze coming in. Dew on my blue grass lawn, and pearling the leaves of my little maples . . .

Without warning, someone grabbed me.

'Alice! I thought I'd missed you. You've got to come. Something terrible's happened!'

It was the girl from Milliefan Command who had met me here when I first arrived.

I tried to run away. She told me there was nothing to be afraid of, but I was not convinced. We scuffled, until I remembered UBIQ and the cults. She forced me to the h&v — horizontal and vertical, the old capital's internal transport. She sat opposite staring at me in hurt astonishment. I had punched her nose.

I had never been to the Millie Command well. When they placed me, the fans explained I couldn't be received by the inner circle — though I had known Millie personally — because I'd been on diem. I had no objection. I assured them I wasn't in the least offended. It was a well in Cav2, on a quiet tidy passage.

Serials were allowed to seal their entry locks in the old capital: from each other, of course UBIQ could override. My escort leaned on the projector to flash a buzzing image of herself into the square. She kept a firm hold on my sleeve.

'Is it Millie?'

She shook her head, lips tight.

Alice is a bit plugged, she whispered when they came to let us in. Faces I didn't know peered at me. Someone explained to someone else about my past in the upper world. Plugged or not, I had to be accessed now.

'They say she knew the Pioneer, intimately . . .'

Several of the faces looked as if they found this difficult to believe. I listened to an extraordinary story. They led me into a 2-shelf room and stood like children, looking down helplessly at their disaster.

After a long, racing moment I turned and said firmly.

'Leave us alone.'

There was nowhere to sit but the end of the open cot so I sat down there and looked at Yolande T. She was wearing pyjamas out of a dispenser, not the superior enabled kind. Her reddish fringe was dirty and unkempt. She appeared to be deeply asleep, breathing quite normally.

Some days ago she had been moving from one centre to another up in the north-east, on her anti-Millie business. She was travelling overground for speed, by special permission from Area Command. Her car's route crashed, dumping Yolande on the surface. As a result of this car crash she suddenly realised the fans' story was true and Millie Mohun the most important thing that had ever happened to the Sub if not the entire world. She resumed her journey and using her vigilante intelligence went straight to the little secret group of Millies in that centre. She announced her new analysis and was promptly despatched to the Millie Command well in the old capital. The anti-Millie campaign had previously been unable to determine its identity.

The fans didn't know what to do. Yolande had brought an escort with her (grandly accessing the transfer). This woman insisted Yolande was absolutely genuine. She was not too popular: they had her somewhere else in the well under guard. It was believed the accident had really happened. There were covert Millie fans in the upper levels of the old capital, who had passed down the news — a few days ago — that Yolande T had been in a route crash. No details.

Nobody had read an event like this in the Codes.

It was Yolande T. Not the cellular image I had seen on seriate screens: but the woman as I remembered her from our meetings, at SHACTI and in the University. I wondered if she would remember me. It hardly mattered. I could soon convince her.

I had never dared give myself up to the vigilantes. I did not trust those orthoprax psychotics to take me to their leader. But here she was. My head was spinning. Suppose she made difficulties, pretended she didn't know me? I didn't need anything more than her wristfax. On which I would find listed all the current Sub handshakes. I could tell the fans I'd confiscated it to stop her calling the cults.

Yolande opened her eyes.

'Had to leave it behind,' she said. 'It wouldn't do, to bring a Pioneer ax to fax down here.'

I dropped her hand, feeling extremely foolish.

'So you're not dead after all, Pioneer Aeleysi.'

I was surprised that she recognised me so easily. I was surprised she could recognise anything at all. For Yolande Tectonics was transfigured. The effect had been masked while she was sleeping. Now I could see her face was hollowed to the bones. She hadn't slept or eaten, obviously, for several days. Her eyes were burning, the pupils dilated far too strongly even for this dull light. I realised with a sinking heart that this was not, as I had assumed, a curiously transparent stratagem for infiltrating the enemy. That route accident had been real. Concussion, I guessed. The nasty kind, with little bits of grey matter sticking to the bone. An expression of irritation crossed the incandescent features. Yolande didn't appreciate my unspoken verdict.

'I hear you got yourself stuck down here. How in the Design did you manage that?'

It had amused me once, that Yolande T didn't seem at all aware of the enormous gulf between us. Now I swallowed her insolence humbly. Oh, the relief of telling my story to someone who would understand: even though she was half off her head. The mention of Millie Mohun didn't seem to excite her, she just looked knowing. I told her how the supers took me and altered me.

'But you're a Pioneer. Why didn't you just ID yourself?

'I couldn't. I'd wiped myself off the SHACTI register, so I'd be properly disguised.'

Yolande was respectfully silent.

Then she laughed, shortly. 'I always thought VENTURans were supposed to be bright.'

'Yolande – You've got to help me!'

'Hmm?'

She was staring at the wall. Wrong approach.

'You had – loss of vision, they said,' I began carefully. 'That's routine with a bad concussion. How is it now? Back to normal?'

'No. It never will be.'

'You ought to get to a decent MEDIC location. You'd better let me take you.'

She gave me a glance of withering scorn. She frowned, pondered; looked at the floor.

I thought I'd lost her completely when she suddenly remarked in a perfectly sane tone: 'Pioneer Aeleysi this doesn't get through the gate. You say you duplicated your housekeep's number. Well, surely that's going to surface somewhere.'

'It might have. But she's dead now.'

'Dead?'

'She was a fan. A batch of enabled took her out on to SHACTI racetrack a few cycles ago, and battered her to death against the limit.'

I spoke with deliberation. Perhaps it was rough therapy but I was desperate. Yolande looked me in the eye, somewhat wearily She said nothing, and I was the one who felt defeated.

'Yolande, you must help me –'

'What a time for it to happen. Right in the middle of this mindless SIND production. If only it had been 30 years ago.'

'Please!'

She returned to me briefly, and smiled; a burst of radiance that made me wince.

131

'Aeleysi, don't you see. It doesn't matter. This world of yours and mine is about to end. Whatever you're doing, wherever you are. It simply doesn't matter any more.'

The Millie Command crew assembled their conference table out of slats of agam, some grades less compacted than the walls or floors: you could get the kit in any overplus. They sat around it on plastic bolsters and stools. I had told them, for what it was worth, that Yolande seemed to be suffering from the effects of a head injury. But she could be bluffing. She could have drugged herself for verisimilitude. Their best plan would be to make some excuse to leave her for a while. Clear this well and don't come back.

So naturally they had decided to settle down to a lengthy conference. In all seriousness, it seemed to them not unlikely that an intelligent woman like Yolande should suddenly have realised the truth.

I couldn't bear to leave. I'd said she was role-playing but I didn't believe it. I was waiting for her to fall down on the floor and get up again returned to sanity. She'd probably be so embarrassed she wouldn't touch the fans. She'd leave *and take me with her*. I sat with the Command crew's dependants, watching PEC at the far end of the room. We were still studying these fragments of plenum, for messages from Millie.

The fans searched the screen gravely. In a grey-walled cubicle a little girl of the Southern1 type sat rocking a baby all alone. Possibly Millie in disguise? Then a huge crowd of possible Millies gathered in a big concourse with walls that seemed to move. No, they were not moving. It was the megatons of seawater outside. I watched the faces round me for my own entertainment. For a long time, looking at serials all the time had been a mean, small part of the torture. I kept imagining them in VENTURan dress; that is, naked. It put me in fits of disgusted laughter. But when the eye is starved enough, it will find beauty in anything.

I owed Yolande an apology. I had always assumed that her motive for the anti-Millie campaign was entirely cynical. I must have been wrong. There must have been intense emotion involved, for trauma to have hauled up such a reversion from her unconscious. She must have been compelled to brutalities like illegal limiting by a belief stronger than anything I could imagine,

132

in the Sub orthoprax. And all the while, guilt and grief were building up inside . . .

The leader of this well, and in effect the Commander of all Millie fans, was an oldish woman: another Himem. Basic Sub serials seemed to have about 6 names they shared between them. I'd heard she was a famous Code Reader. She'd never met an enabled woman of such rank in-person before, but she was standing up to the shock very well.

She explained to Yolande the significance of Millie Mohun. For many years the Sub had been run by alien machines. It was their own fault, they hadn't lived connected enough lives and so they'd lost their privileges. But there was always the hope that the Intersection would come, when Sub culture and Function became integrated again. Millie was the Intersection: the completely connected functional human. And now that she had appeared the Sub would soon be run by Function directly again — *quite peacefully and with no disrespect to VENTUR* —

I hoped UBIQ would be satisfied with the polite disclaimer. Perhaps it was time to go —

Naturally, the perfect human wouldn't break down and die. That was the explanation of Millie's ever-running life.

'That's true in a way' said Yolande, in her clear enabled tones. 'But she's not a Sub. You're in error there.'

In front of PEC our heads all shifted in unison, to see if she was going to lie down and foam at the mouth.

The Command crew looked thoughtful.

Yolande laughed merrily. 'Let's be rational, shall we. A basic number. Not even a number, a biel. An object like that doesn't last 70 years, not processing 270!'

Sensation. I wondered if I could get the poor deranged woman out alive.

'Millie never was a serial. She isn't human, at least not in the terms you know. She is from another world. She is the star traveller. She has arrived at last. That's why she appears eternally young. That's why the VENTURan systems don't know her and can't account for her.'

'Don't you see what this means? There is no need to bother now about who wears a number and who doesn't, or who 'runs' the Sub. Everything — the whole world — is going to be completely different!'

The fans decided to keep her for the moment. They were afraid of what she might do on the loose. I got her to walk with me to the entry lock when I left. We were in the middle of the capital's night. It was dark in the square, except for a few globalls dotted along the galleries.

'Yolande,' I said gently. 'The underworld is always generating "star travellers". It's periodic, like sunspots. It can't be, you know. Don't you think the NET would have picked her up coming in? It's been there for a whole lot longer than old 270 years. Er — Do you remember what the NET is?'

'Near-Space Event Tracer,' murmured Yolande, out of her dream. 'Away beyond the planetary shelf. Waiting, watching — longing.'

'Don't be stupid Pioneer Aeleysi. She was travelling faster than light. Right until her feet hit the ground, I think. It's probably the only way. All these big ships — the whole VENTUR project. All pointless.'

She walked out into the passage with me absentmindedly. Turned and walked back. It was OK to ignore the domiciliary readers, so long as you didn't do it too often. I'd ignored it myself. But I was enough of a Sub now to be shocked when Yolande did the same.

'Yolande —'

'What? Oh that.' She grimaced impatiently. ' That's all garbage now. I've given it up.'

# 4

There was a flood going on as I came out of the h&v. Half-naked
little girls and boys splashed in the grimy wash waving their
trousers over their heads. Knots of adults stood about the concourse staring at the talking walls. Screen displays hiccuped and
flickered: there was a message from CENTRIN. PLEASE
REMAIN IN YOUR HOMES . . . A historic occasion although
I didn't know it. It was the first time I encountered that plea or
threat which was to become so familiar to us all. Every 30x20 the
levels were swept out with water, by night. The SINDs' latest
game was to run around spraying the sensors on passage walls
with waterproof adhesive. The stop cocks didn't know to turn
themselves off. Hence the flood, while old capital's sluggish
maintenance worked out what to do. I rolled up my pyjamas and
paddled.

Above flood level the walls were covered in scribble. I couldn't
read it, presumably it was Synthetic Neo-Dravidian. People were
disgusted by the fact that human excrement and uterine discharge were used to make these scribbles. I didn't feel that way
myself. The whole point, surely, was that we — CHTHON,
VENTUR, the corrupt Housing — had left them no other
medium. No means of communication that was not controlled. I
passed a junction, where sweeper heads bobbed unhappily in a
drain sink, their little red eyes blind and sad in daylight. I had
often thought I should try to contact the SINDs: if they weren't
so dangerous. They must have ways of getting in and out. I could
help them with their marketing technique. *If we could read
SIND, you know, you wouldn't need to scribble your arguments
on the walls. We'd all be converted already.*

Pia said they had completely downed the intercom network

135

now — not that it mattered to me. I never used the things. Those access hoods were a gift to vandalism. I worried about Pia. I would truly be glad when she married Ram. He didn't like VENTURans much, or the Housing Management: but he was a sensible young man.

Yolande T was very bitter about the SINDs. I thought she was overreacting. I said that as a processer at the great Housing I accessed to inform her the heteroprax vandals were quite right. Housing's handshake with SERVE was getting distinctly shaky. She looked positively frightened. 'Don't joke about things like that,' she snapped. 'Not when the Sub's in danger.' But it was only the SINDs who were in danger, surely. I imagined a sharp UBIQ action against them must be coming soon.

Yolande was gone now. The fans, after careful analysis of her input, told her to funx off. They were amazed, I felt, when she meekly obeyed. They were still arguing at Millie Command as to the meaning of that bizarre visitation.

I was early for my appointment. I sat in a little concourse, the junction of 5 narrow, low floor/ceilinged passages. There was nothing it it but a disused heat-ex wall and some damp litter. At least the air was pleasantly cool and humid after the SINDish flood.

She saw Millie Mohun alive, I thought.

Yolande's car hit the ground when its route died under it: reason unknown, possibly an electrical storm. The emergency float tank must have blown. She should have hardly bounced in her seat. But *something hit her.* When she came round, she got out of the car and there was Millie Mohun. How did you know who it was? I asked. She told me, answered Yolande simply. I knew that fans had claimed to see Millie on the PEC screen. In the first cycles after her 'disappearance' whole rooms full of people saw her frequently. She sometimes talked, the way serials did 'talk out' on PEC from time to time. These stories had never disturbed me. It would have been a shame for all that patience to go entirely unrewarded. However, when Yolande T made such a statement it was different. Not more convincing necessarily: but definitely different.

We had talked a good deal in the few days she spent at Millie

Command. None of the Command crew could listen to her without going into strong hysterics, so they needed an interface. I didn't mind. I was curious. And at first I still thought I could persuade her to rescue me.

Millie was not a life form that the searching machines had missed. She didn't belong in our trapped bubble universe: she came from the big outside. Yolande explained this was not impossible. It was a commonplace that at a certain level information quanta could be said to 'move faster than light'. Millie simply found those particles in the information chains that made her; and by a feat of mental agility turned herself into this refined essence of Millie for the duration of the trip.

'But Yolande —' I protested. 'Surely that's not the point. The point is she wouldn't if she could. That's what we know. She couldn't get out again. And what seems to us normal might seem to her — well, maybe just a long slow falling into nothing. Or maybe something like being turned inside out alive, forever. Would *you* care to risk it?'

She looked smug. 'Millie can get out. The event horizon has no power over her.'

'Oh, hasn't it?'

'You see, Aeleysi, no individual connection has a precise location. It inhabits a statistical area. It's obvious, therefore, that some connections overlap the limit of our trapped space wherever that limit is set. And the effect is transferred you see, in a probability tunnel leading outwards . . . or inwards. It's the same principle as your own people have investigated without any results: because they were trying to build inanimate ships. Millie knows the way. As long as she *is consciously* those connections, she's never trapped!'

'You mean she's only probably here?'

Yolande stared me down.

But it was on the broader implications of faster-than-light escapology that she excelled herself. To do the probability tunnel trick, Millie became pure data. When she 'arrived' (we were unclear exactly what this would have looked like to an observer) she equivalated into a human being. And this was the idea that had given Yolande that look of burnt out radiance; which

137

lingered on her until she left though strongly mixed with exasperation and scorn. If whatever Millie was could be pure data, and then human: then human beings could be pure data, and live forever and escape out of this prison.

I queried 'equivalated'.

'Pioneer Aeleysi, don't tell me you have never heard of the principle of equivalence.'

'In spacetime measurement I have. I don't know what it has to do with customised life support for visiting aliens.'

You had to admire the economy of her thinking. I'd been imagining, silly me, she might have difficulty explaining how our visitor happened to resemble the aboriginal fauna so closely.

She stared at her own hand. I had seen serial babies examine themselves in the same way, with blind, unfocused wonder.

'Have you ever felt *trapped* Aeleysi?'

'Is that supposed to be funny?'

One thing puzzled Yolande very much. She took it for granted that Millie Mohun's arrival was a rescue mission. She had come to tell us how to get out. Why then did the star traveller choose to equivalate herself into a basic serial? She must have known what she was doing to herself and the message, by landing down among the numbers . . . (It was part of Millie's repertoire to know what was going on inside a black hole in total detail, before she entered it.)

'I'll have to work on that,' said Yolande.

I was surprised. The answer seemed obvious. I decided not to help too much. After all, it was Yolande's game.

'Maybe it's what you said.'

'What?'

'Death and time being meaningless to Millie. I used to worry about those things a lot. I used to stop in the middle of whatever fun I was having and think "I'm going to die". It upset me. I promise you, I haven't had the same problem at all since I fell in here. Perhaps that's what made Millie feel at home.'

She thought that was very funny.

I accepted soon that whatever Yolande was processing, she wasn't going to get me out. She was refreshingly unsympathetic. I

138

wondered, was she remembering how little Yolande T meant to ALIC once. If so, maybe it was fair. She told me she should have thought a real VENTURan would have found her own way home by now. It was just like one of those brain-orgy games of mine wasn't it. Unless, of course, I secretly wanted to stay.

I thought she might have spared me that. A simple refusal was quite enough revenge.

I had told her frankly I loved her scenario, but I didn't believe a word of it. She was concussed: or she had the weird idea that pretending to have met an alien would further her career. Or someone had slipped her a fundrug of a kind not familiar to a respectable young Sub enabled.

'All right,' said Yolande. 'Think what you please. But I'll tell you something you won't like. This "drug" has made me a mind reader. You thought Millie Mohun was a VENTURan, didn't you.'

She grinned triumphantly at my revealing face.

Some of the young fans were delighted to have Millie turn into a star traveller, but the Command crew was furious. We soon heard from our Jam that Yolande Tectonics' rewire was genuine. Her own vigilantes tried to murder her. After that she vanished from direct CENTRIN, but we found out that she had made an overplus clip all about Millie and was having it distributed. It became clear that she was using her enabled facilities: her freedom of movement and her credit, to promote an entirely imaginary Millie. Millie Command was forced to buy her clips — there had been 3 so far — just to be further outraged. Old Himem and her crew believed Yolande was a cult in pyjamas, trying to destroy Millie fans by driving them all crazy. They talked wildly of 'accessing the Commanders' about her. But the Commanders in the old capital had other concerns.

I remembered my panic the day Yolande arrived. At last, at least, I was no longer a suspicious character. SINDs were so active that lesser anomalies were forgotten by the authorities: and now Yolande had changed sides we no longer had to worry about private enterprise. The fans didn't realise what Yolande had done for them. That dangerous immortal serial was no more. No one could possibly object to an immortal alien life form. It was simply human wish fulfilment . . . even basics had a right to that.

I poked the toe of my scuffed slipper in the litter by the dry pool. Sometimes since Yolande left I had been assailed by a strange temptation to go down to Cav4 and find Dat. She ought to be part of the Millie Command crew, but she was not. She kept out of their way. I'd like to hear her opinion of Yolande's story. Dat remembered the woman who led people out to look for starships, because of Millie. It was a pity she had chosen to live in the worst levels. Why did she do that?

The floor/ceiling had changed tone towards light change, it was time for my rendezvous. I was on my way to negotiate with a daysky dealer. Another move: another route round the maze. I would be ripped again and Pia would laugh at me, or commiserate if she was in the mood. I sighed. I used to think it wouldn't be so bad if only I had a friend. I never guessed it could be worse.

Yolande was wrong. I did not secretly want to stay. I secretly wanted to take someone with me, and I knew this could not be. It was getting to be quite extraordinarily painful.

+

2 shifts later, at a further furtive meeting, I collected my daysky clip. I hurried back to the well, frightened of cults and other roving dangers. Pia was in the screen room on my corridor, alone. I didn't like to ask why she was there. She'd been getting rather irritable with me lately.

'May I?'

'Go ahead.'

She lay propped on one elbow on a long plastic bolster, plucking her eyelashes with a tiny burner, ignoring me.

I pulled our decoder off the wall and stuck its fat little torpedo body on the bottom of the screen. PEC winked out. I dropped my scroll in the receiving slot. What I had bought was a route out of the centre. According to legend, outside the outer shell there were casting bores leading to the surface. Not all of them were filled in. On this clip I would find diagrams of a route, by utility ducts and conduits, right to the shell. The SINDs had found a spot where the raw current could be diverted, and broken through into a casting bore. My daysky dealer swore it was the truth. There was a way, and UBIQ had not detected it. She couldn't tell me how the clip had been made: it had passed through several hands. She thought the SINDs would probably kill me if I tried to use their 'outside line' but that was my risk.

In fact VENTURans did not pluck their eyelashes. The young Subs knew this. Their craze for uncomfortable facial nakedness was satirical. Underworlders often called us 'ballheads' – because of the suit helmets, and the Rangers' traditional headstyle. And, by analogy, *prickheads*.

I had thought Pia might help me to escape. She was a deco, a human decoration in a booth full of hologram images of fancy consumables. She could approach the enabled on level1 – wonderland, as she called it derisively. I couldn't get near them. First contact was the problem: I'd been warned off too often. If Pia would initiate something . . . 'It won't be easy,' she said coolly. 'I only have a few set lines about the cat. I get a jolt if I talk random.'

I remembered a 'jolt'. I had never used that function. But I might have done. My Pia was often naughty. I said I'd find another way. I never asked her for help again.

She was one of the radical Millies, who had instantly accepted Yolande's version. She always knew there was more to Millie than the boring cultural 'put the Code Readers ran on about. Of course she came from the Big Outside. It was funxing read-only, in Pia's opinion. When I asked her why she was a fan, she told me: *'Millie Mohun made me feel like a person. That's all.'* It was enough, I sometimes thought, even to pay for what Millie did to me.

The clip would not play. I tried every combination of the simple controls, ignoring their supposed significance. A blurred frame appeared, and vanished before I could read anything.

'Funx junk it!'

'How much d'you pay?' asked Pia, bored.

I yanked the fat slug of a decoder off the screen, twisting its suckers viciously.

'Pia, lend me your burner, I'm going to teach the little brute to do what it's told —'

'Don't do that. You'll jolt UBIQ.'

She was right. The door would probably seal on us, and we'd get a bad entry on our tags if nothing worse. The decoder's tiny mind would burn out anyway, the moment I attacked it. I knew all this. I had just suffered a sudden craving to torture something small and helpless.

'Sorry.' I smiled sheepishly. 'Momentary aberration.'

But Pia wasn't smiling.

'Alice,' she said. 'I want you to get out.'

'I was just leaving —'

'I mean out of the well.'

'Oh. OK.'

'I can't run it any longer. You don't believe in Millie. You sneer at everything. You're a funxing VENTURan and we don't want you here.'

'I said — OK. I'm going.'

I had known this was coming. Whatever it was that had made her befriend me, she had changed her mind. If she wanted me to leave, I must leave. I would find a new shelf. I would leave the Millies. She was right, it was ridiculous for me to live with them. I got up from my knees, awkwardly; under her hard eyes. A woman in her 80s. Over 90, by their reckoning. Pia knew it if no one else did. If there were nothing else between us, in her world what I felt was ludicruous.

'You'd better take your clip out,' she said coldly. 'It isn't very considerate, leaving daysky in the decoder.'

I took the clip. I was halfway to the door when I realised I had absolutely nothing to lose.

'Pia — *I loved you.* You won't believe me. It sounds — sick, probably. I swear, I hadn't been in the seriate three days: even before I was captured I knew I couldn't treat you like that anymore. But I did love you. I have never been so — out of everything, joyful, as I was with you. I've been wanting to tell you ever since, how ashamed I have been, how sorry. But when we met again I just couldn't find the words. I love you now —'

She looked up at me through this without a flicker of

expression. Then turned her attention to the smooth skin of her wrist, and applied the burner carefully to an invading hair.

'About funxing time,' she said softly.

I found that I was sitting on the end of the plastic roll, as far as I could be from her. I thought, inconsequentially: we could be on PEC.

Pia watched me.

'The Millies told me I shouldn't downrate myself,' she remarked. 'I should just forget having been a pet: because Function's discreet, you know. Only when they told me I mustn't hate you for what you made me do, I knew they didn't know the half of it. When you turned up I was jolted sick. But in the end I thought well — degraded's just a word. So I came to your door.'

Her hands were shaking. So were mine, when I tried to wipe the tears off my face.

'I *am* sick of the way you sneer at Millie.'

'I don't sneer —'

'I was waiting for you to input first,' she explained stubbornly. 'I thought you owed me that.'

She held out her hand. I had been pushed and shoved and handled; and once I'd dragged Ram out of a limit mob. But then I only held his sleeve, and was aware of the distinction. I had never touched one of them, voluntarily. I saw in Pia's eyes that she was ashamed of wanting me, and that turned my heart over. Nothing can be undone. There is only the libration. It has to be enough. I took the hand and followed it into her arms.

We went to my room and shut ourselves in my shelf, I fell with Pia into the starry dark. Still there, still burning, as if we had never left it.

There were streamers by the airvents, coloured print-out littering every concourse. It was deblocking time again. I celebrated my anniversary very quietly. If Pia was aware of it she had the tact not to comment. But probably she was not. One of the young men who went bashfully to the Housing and came back festooned, surrounded by loud and cheerful friends, was Ram. But he still kept a shelf in the long room in the outer square where unattached men lived. He would not take over from Pia's bunkmate until he was a prospective father. She was suspicious. To me, she said, he's all the family I've got. But I know to you he's just a number. In fright, I declared our physical relationship cancelled — unnecessary. I was as happy to be friends. Next off-shift we shared she came to my shelf, looking annoyed with herself.

She said Ram didn't mind.

The Housing Management was in contention with the VENTURan Mission over who should cover the cost of SIND vandalism. Mission insisted the Housing must 'pay', which looked like a bad entry to me. It was the same credit, so why force the culturals to lose face? Sub finance was only nominally independent of CHTHON.

Soon after Pia and I became lovers, or became lovers again, there was an incident on my shift. We were in the scrub: naked bodies wincing in the hot needle water spray. We tried as always not to invade each other, but elbows collided with breasts, buttocks with thighs. Pubic mounds, some bushy, some smooth like mine were jarred by accidental hipbones. We exchanged as always silly smiles and half-drowned apologies. Housing cults, clothed in their coveralls, watched through a tall physical field of glass. They went on watching as we passed through the body search; while we bent over and let the cold metallic fingers probe inside us. There was no need for them to be there. We always muttered about it. We knew we were watched by machine surveillance all the time, but that was different.

Nobody gets dressed.

The other shift was still plugged in. The capital was still served. It was the gesture of responsible processers who did not want to do any harm. Whoever had planned it, the rest of us heard a whisper passed on or just became aware that something was happening. I knew the only option was to go along with the majority. The anomaly is vulnerable. Perhaps there were others making the same decision. I wondered if it had occurred to anyone else that if the cults were really alarmed they could seal the hall, drain it to micrat or flood it with breakdown gas from the cold furnace.

Our elaborate preparations were totally meaningless: a

144

'systematic' memorial of ancient days. But if that was the whole story, the cults wouldn't have been there. This degrading routine was a control tool. I knew that — but I never thought the other processers had worked it out. Much less that they were capable of protesting. I didn't know my shiftmates. Outside, because of Pia, the fans had become real to me. It was better to go blank in here. Now I stood among them looking round me in amazement, exchanging odd, tentative smiles. After about an hour someone went to the dispensers that issued our special suits and punched one out. The event was over.

I was afraid we'd all be turned off. There was a time when I didn't understand why serials behaved as if being used on an Interface was a privilege. I had not accepted then what it means to have no contact whatever with the systems that run your world. I'd learned to cling to the processing because it was all I had. A recognition, a connection; however painful. But nothing happened. And the women, who hadn't managed to achieve anything at all, went about looking almost triumphant.

I had told Yolande her revered Housing was beginning to decay. It might even be so. I sometimes had a phantom feeling, coming out of the plug trance — of loss of power in there? But what I had meant to tell her was that the human connections were breaking down. The functionaries lived up in the Dome or wonderland. They led rich, complex, luxurious lives. Meanwhile, the basic processers lived like monozuke, intimately connected with Function; and were treated with contempt. It must be the same in other blocs — and I knew where they got the model. But perhaps nowhere else was the virtue of the basics and the corruption of the others so explicitly upheld in the cultural prax. This can't go on, I thought; when I first saw how things were. Of course, it could go on forever. But not if even meek processers were ready to face that fear and contempt from above, and challenge it openly.

I was surprised when Yolande did not use the basics to strengthen her Millie story. To me (in the game) the reason for Millie's choice was obvious. Maybe Yolande was too loyal to VENTUR to see it. The human species is not in Space, nor on the enabled malls. It is here in the seriate. Millie's message was supposed to be that the key to our freedom was not in the elusive hyperdrive which all VENTUR's wealth had failed to build. It was in an untapped potential of the human entity itself. By 'equivalating' as a basic number she expressed that message in direct concrete imagery. In dumb show. Just what you would expect from someone trying to communicate in an alien conceptual framework. She even sought out the monozuke. In their own minds, those eccentrics were pretending to be machine parts. But you couldn't get much nearer to naked unadorned humanity.

Only a little while ago I had been congratulating myself on Millie's change of status. No one could feel threatened by an immortal alien. I had not thought it through. I hadn't listened to Yolande. Had she listened to herself? If this immortal visitor was as specified the threat was terrifying. It would blow our society apart. I would have to look at these SIND stirrings in a completely new light, if Yolande's Millie Mohun was real.

When I was listening to all that insanely coherent nonsense, I didn't say a word about Millie's 'non-ephemeral eyes'. I had processed why I had to think she was a VENTURan. I suppose My Sorrow thought she was a horse, by the same argument. I knew the real explanation had to be that I had noticed she was human, when I was certain that serials were not. But I wondered. I had not told Yolande about the archive screen, either. I had never told anyone about that.

I kept remembering how Millie was always so interested in the children. To be released, after being locked up alone in the dark for so long. To live forever in a living universe. If you could be persuaded to believe − for more than 6 seconds together − that this possibility was real . . . The only thing left then would be the awful fear that it was too late, and only a little child could be taught to make that transition. And the hope that you had not become too different from that little child.

I let myself imagine: and touched a core of unhappiness in me deeper than anything I'd suffered in the seriate. It was almost frightening just to play with the idea. I hardly knew what I would be, or what the human race might be − without that core.

+

Pia said she would take me to the Gap. It was the place her friends talked about, the ones who discussed 'ballheads' and 'Free Earth' while pulling faces at UBIQ. We left the h. We were down in Cav3 on level 10, in a bleak area of narrow passages and blank walls between the outermost living wells and the industrial plant. It was the fourth quarter, passage light was perfunctory. The hiss and jar and clatter of cultural industry came to us. Red lines of infrastrip glowed down the left-hand turnings where only plant grubs needed to be able to see. Other figures passed us, muttering. I was reminded of the time I had been taken to the little Housing at SHACTI. The simplicity and homeliness of that occasion seemed to belong to another age. We came out of insufficient light into black and white fractured darkness. There was a crowd.

'Look up,' murmured Pia, close against my ear.

We were standing under the mouth of a huge black funnel. It was an accident of the centre's design, a pit 9 levels deep and we were at the bottom of it.

'It's under the Presidential Palace. In wonderland it's a concourse, and the floor/ceiling of the concourse is the President's containment.'

Utility ducts crossed the blackness. Over the lowest and smallest of them cables were slung, dangling transparent sacks full of globalls. Under the centre of the funnel was a skeletal platform built of fragments of plastic and metal stolen from the industrial sector. It was hung with more globalls.

'There's never been any UBIQ here.'

I wondered if that was true.

In the dark we kissed. To the Subs, physical love between partners of the same sex was a wicked waste. But in the Gap, Pia whispered to me, nobody cared what you did. She slipped her thigh between mine and rocked us. Pia was taller than me: something I had only noticed since I met her in the seriate.

'If we're connected,' she whispered. 'I mean connected with the stars and things, the way Millie proves we are. Then anything you want to do is in the Design. That's what I think.'

Once when she was sleeping in my shelf I fell into the worst of my recurrent nightmares. I woke with the horrors, the warm

147

dead smothering me. But the body pressed close to mine was Pia. I lay awake then for a long time, looking at the dim outline of her face. She was true to Ram. I couldn't wish otherwise. She wouldn't have been Pia if she could dump him. I could share, as long as they would let me.

Up on the platform a gang of SINDs − presumably − were making music. I'd never heard hand-made music before. As they could not use any kind of amplifiction without entering the corrupt processes of the capital it remained a mystery. I probably wouldn't have liked it, I always found underworld music too crowded and confused. The noise around us was a loud babble of voices. Everyone was talking. Some seemed to be yelling, shouting, banging on the floor.

We had forgotten that we'd come to see the SINDs. The noise and the dark made a place to stand, a shelter inside which we kissed and touched. Presently I became aware that a single voice was shouting. There was now a savage-looking young woman alone on the platform: no, in front of a group of others. She was shouting under the sound board they'd rigged up, in a voice trained to be its own PA. I had picked up a lot of the old capital's jargon, I spoke it myself now − decoded, bad entry; doesn't get through the gate. But I couldn't understand much of this.

*Black gap,* I heard. *A hole in space. The ballheads allow no light to escape . . . We will drag them in . . . Crush them in our Hole . . .*

The crowd yelled, banged, stamped. A clot of voices began to chant in jagged unison. The tears on our faces. Run in channels burned. By the Design. It sounded horribly unlike the way granny used to sing it. The shouting woman, whose legs were bare under her pyjama shirt, produced something that looked very like a VENTURan suit helmet. She laid it systematically on the platform, spread her legs and pissed, to tumultuous applause. Ballheads! Ballheads!

Pia and I had been standing at the back. Now somehow we were in the middle of the crowd, jammed tight. There were waves of hatred coming at me −

We fled. We sat on the floor outside the h&v, under one dim light strip. Pia gasped with laughter, still out of breath.

'You shouldn't have run like that Alice. They might have come after you!'

I was shaken. However much I sympathised with the SINDs, that had been an unpleasant experience.

'Pia — Those women are dangerous!''

She grinned at me tenderly, and squeezed my hand in her own.

'Don't worry Alice. You're with me.'

A hot breath of industrial air wafted over us, leaving behind an acrid chemical stink.

'I wish you believed in Millie.'

I thought of the world split open. If it was true, then even the SINDs would have to be satisfied. Their light would escape. We would all escape and walk between the stars.

'Alice!'

She let go of my hand. I saw her frowning.

'Alice. In wonderland there's a cat that sells game replays. It's always empty. No one seems to want that stuff at the moment. In the back they've got a printer. It's running all the time, giving out stadium info from all over the place. Every so often there's a header, with little 6 codes. I think they're like the ones on SHACTI Jam. I don't think anyone's ever noticed. The source must have the error that that printer's up in the Dome.'

My heart began to thump. Pia was watching my face.

'I calc you could use codes like that to get you out.'

'How long have you known?

She turned away. 'Oh,' she said casually, 'a while.'

I could not trust myself to speak.

# And Then She Turned to the Eternal Fountain

# 1

The Mission sent DOGs into wonderland, to control a SIND outbreak. In Threshold centres like SHACTI, DOGs were accepted. Not in the Sub capital! The Rangers' metalloy friends were supposed to be used for their own protection in dire emergency. The reason for this unprecedented move was that the Mission had UBIQ advice that sectors of the Housing Management had organised the SINDs this time, in retaliation for the vandalism levy. I extracted this information from our censored Jam, without much difficulty. The serials too knew exactly what was going on. And even the least 'SINDish' were more indignant than frightened. A Mission Commander makes her own decisions to a great extent: execs have their pride. I did not think CHTHON could have advised the DOGs. The systems cannot help us, if we refuse to listen to them.

It was the end of the current cycle. I was going to the Housing to break stones with my brain. It felt, yes it certainly felt as if it had been breaking stones. And the fingers of my left hand stayed numb and tingling often now, through the off-shift. All my fingertips had started to develop, faintly, that calcined dryness I remembered when Himem's mother touched my cheek. In the end it would be nerve-death, and then I would be turned off. I had not dared to think about these things.

I carried a parcel with me to the Housing. It was a plant, a fern in a little hydroponic pot, all wrapped up in permafilm packaging. It was quite real and growing. The cults were dubious, but in the end they let it go through the scrub with me, and the hazard scanner declared it harmless. I thought I'd get it in. Our cults had been very nervous and placatory since the shift when we wouldn't put on our clothes.

I had been to wonderland, and the codes were there. The

153

header also informed me SHACTI was now changing handshakes every 2 quarters. Which was sobering. But it didn't matter any more. It just made me feel my decision was made for me. No pondering, no delays. The games shop held no stock, only display. In the front there was a mixing desk; and a team game I did not recognise ran about on the showplate. It was quarter life-sized and oddly contracted, so the eye winced at impossible conjunctions of view. 2 bored decos made up as gamesplayers glanced at me indifferently and went on polishing their nails. I saw the hydroponic vendors on my way back to the h&v. It had no human attendants, I wouldn't have dared the transaction otherwise. The permafilm alone was a shocking price. I emptied the last slot I possessed into the shop's till and it thanked me distastefully, obviously wishing it was select enough to refuse nasty hard currency. I crept softly through hushed and musical opulence, afraid of so much space. There was no sign in this area of SIND attack, or DOGs on the rampage. I laughed at the thought of what a first-class liner would do to me — on my way home.

I put the fern package on top of my console, astonishingly green and bright, and wondered why I'd risked so much for it. An act of pure bravado. I wanted to show myself how the walls that had been so implacable would melt away, disappear in front of me. It was a present for Pia.

She would not come with me. She wouldn't listen to any argument. She was afraid of missing Millie's return. There was no longer any question of leaving Pia behind. But I had realised in the end I would have to get out myself, and then send for her. And Ram as well since I knew she wouldn't desert him. They must come home with me. Or if I couldn't ax it, or if MEDIC said Ram couldn't survive the culture shock — then we'd stay on the underworld. I imagined somewhere like the capin in LECM. A life in exile. I could envisage that. Never more to see the stars clear, but I would have Pia, and a wraparound full of trees.

The debriefing I might have to face when I reclaimed my identity was a problem. But I would invoke CENTRIN, the real CENTRIN of VENTUR; and give it my story. If you're prepared to sacrifice enough privacy CENTRIN will protect you from anything. It isn't called the most powerful system under SERVE for nothing.

The cults were muttering about riots. It was strange to hear them, as if no time had passed at all and this was the last day of my freedom, at SHACTI. I would never be inside the Sub Housing again. Magnificent, irrational place. I was glad I had seen it, before it fell apart.

I would still admit it was possible that Yolande's story was true. News might be about to break of the greatest event in the history of the human race. The SINDs and their grievances would be forgotten, and the Sub seriate would be absolutely the only place to be. I might be the envy of all my friends. I could resist the temptation. Let it all happen, but let me watch from my own side of the reac: and Pia with me.

There was no need for any anxiety. The codes I needed for my transformation couldn't be affected by anything that happened on the underworld; and I was very certain I had forgotten none of them. The burns on my head were sealed off with adhesive from the overplus. It was probably the same kind the SINDs had used for the trick they played on our sanitation. Sensors groped in my hair — after an odd pause, during which we processers eyed each other covertly. Don't let there be any incidents today, I begged . . .

I looked at my screen. I am ALIC, I thought. I am free. The adhesive was working. I put my H code in the board.

And then, on either side of me, there was a ripple of bodies stirring.

My eyes were open. No sense of duration. Only the thoughts that had been running through my mind a second ago. I felt sick, sick. It must have been hours since, that I put my H in the board. And it didn't work.

I heard a voice beside me muttering, 'What's going on?'

Relief rushed over me. The H was OK. We were just being kept off line. At that moment something went through the Housing. Something palpable, invisible; pulsed through us and was gone.

A processer whimpered in fright, down the row. Then we all heard running feet. We all heard the shouting.

SERVE IS DOWN!
SERVE IS DOWN!

What a dreadful idea, I thought. Of course it can't be true. I freed myself from the chair and headshell, on my feet in a strange complete silence. Rational light makes no sound, but there were all the ancilliaries. The hums and murmurs; and a constant dull resonance from the cold furnace plant at work. They were all still.

The lights went out. Suddenly, there was an enormous rush of air from somewhere. The slick floor picked itself up under me and threw me at my console. I scrambled to my feet in the middle of a huge roar of sound, and was immediately thrust down again. The sound of the first explosion, a few minutes ago, mustn't have reached us: only its muted shock wave muffled by the massive partitions. There was screaming and shouting. My eyes adjusted. I could see lighting panels in the walls fading to an eerie grey glow. The processers who had still been in their headshells when the rush came were sprawled unconscious. I saw blood coming out of one woman's ears. Someone had better take charge, I thought − which shows how peculiar one's reactions can be under shock. I was holding on to the console, my whole body vibrating wildly. I noticed with astonishment that the fern was still standing there.

Before I could quiet myself enough to start behaving like a space cadet, the massive ceramic door of the hall flew open and in poured a pack of people, most in pyjamas, a few in Housing coveralls. Some were swinging bags of globalls, others were armed with explosive bullet rifles, a kind of weapon only known on the underworld: and firmly outlawed by CHTHON.

They fanned out, threatening. But our cults − if they weren't in on the plot − had only batons and offered no resistance. Invaders took over our consoles, flinging aside unconscious or terrified processers. About half of them were in the chairs, others seemed to be attending on them. A woman dressed only in a shirt, with a long matted fringe to her shoulders, was presiding.

We waited.

On the instant of a major sabotage, the whole Sub capital had been stripped of its systems by the Mission and every gate sealed in a security crash. But in a state of emergency life support should immediately return, on an override straight from SERVE. The lights came up. The hall was alive again. I let out my breath with a gasp along with all the people around me, and only then realised we'd been waiting for the air to fail.

'Oh, what a relief!' cried someone, confused.

The attendants on the new processers flung themselves at the boards. The Rangers were accessing VENTUR for the secretaries' permission to cut off life support. CHTHON was not enabled to do this on its own. But it could be done, or at least sincerely threatened. It was an ultimatum no one could refuse. There was an hour's air, perhaps, in a centre like this. I breathed normally. One might as well. I wondered just how crazy the SINDs were. 2 minutes passed, 3 minutes.

And the lights stayed on.

I stared, at the SINDs who were plugged into our consoles. Amazed, awed . . .

'What about these?'

A girl in a Housing coverall, with a shining crop like my Pia's and a bronzed, enabled looking face, gestured with her firearm.

The woman with the matted fringe looked round.

'They are corrupt,' she said dismissively. 'Wipe them out.'

I did not wait to be told twice, I grabbed my fern and ran.

I burst into what seemed to be a supers' locker room. The walls were drab and dead, bare of the usual projected displays. 2 or 3 tubes rolled on a moulded table, hiccuping wetness, a baton lay abandoned. The empty chairs rising out of the floor looked curiously unconcerned. Down the length of the room I watched a woman picking up something. She fastened it around her waist: a bandolier of chemical charges for a hand-held beam weapon. It was bright earth blue. As she stood admiring herself in the mirror wall I recognised her face. She had been, a few minutes ago, a processer on my shift.

There were charging bodies everywhere, cannoning into each other. The lights kept flickering ominously. I couldn't find my way out. With a crowd of other people I looked down from a huge glass gallery and saw a wedge of blue forcing its way up into one of the main inner concourses. The wall display was still running here but it had come adrift: playing over them enormous shadows of the crystal furnace. The *ulaux*, the underworld local auxiliaries, whose chief characteristic was they they were never local. SINDish bodies creased in two and lost their heads, in a net of ruby that magically appeared and vanished in the twists and turns of battle. It was fascinating, but ragged. There were a lot of creases where they should not be, in the walls and in hapless ulaux too, because they weren't keeping formation. It was wrong, I thought, to use ulaux in the Housing where UBIQ was limited. The Mission couldn't follow events clearly enough for efficient remote control.

The crowd carried me. I wasn't aware of leaving the Housing but suddenly found myself in a seriate concourse, and the lights went down again. We who were running away from the fighting found ourselves engulfed by another crowd hurrying towards it. This terrified me at the time, it was so irrational. I understood later that the Subs had been acting on deep impulse. They didn't know where the trouble was that had such fearful effects: putting out the lights, blanking the screens. So they rushed, if they were near enough, straight to the centre of centres: hoping for reassurance.

They found none. As for me, I didn't know how frightened I was until the explosions started again and I dropped to the floor, clutching my plant with one hand and fumbling with the other for a safety grip. I thought the rotation must be about to cut out.

Eventually, some lights came up. I stumbled into the entrance of an h&v and found out I was in Cav1 on level 4, but in my own quadrant. The inner gate display scrolled over and over: IN ANY CENTRE EMERGENCY DO NOT ATTEMPT TO UTILISE THE INTERNAL TRANSPORT. IN ANY CENTRE EMERGENCY . . . It was good to see something still running as it should. I thought of 6 million people. Was this eruption affecting all of them? Or was it an item on CENTRIN: SIND vandalism at the Housing brought down autonomics in areas of Cav1 . . .

Other people joined me. After a while there were 10 of us, sitting on a bench and on the floor. We wondered what time it

158

was and guessed at the second quarter. The serials whispered to each other. Several of them asked me what was happening. The wonderland fern fooled them, giving me a spurious air of influence and substance.

It's the SINDs (said someone). They've taken over the Housing. And CENTRIN.

I had a strange feeling. Could it be elation?

We sat for hours in the murky brown light, presumably waiting for the hazard message to clear and the gate to open. The air was warm, though no warmer (I assured myself) than was routine. The light failed altogether a few times, and once when it came up again we smelt the fumes of burnt agam and saw smoke drifting at a distant junction. There was no sound. I was afraid the SINDs would come along and spot me in my processing suit. But they didn't.

A light approached, an arc of brilliant white accompanied by the sound of booted feet. We all stirred and looked at each other nervously. It was one lone ulaux, with a patch indicating she was a super: a microg lamp in one hand, a lasarm in the other. There was a moment of uncertainty.

'Go to your homes.'

I said, 'Did they do a lot of damage?'

'Don't you understand English?' she shouted. 'Go to your homes and stay there!'

On my way down the levels, searching in the gloom for little used ramps and stairs, I saw a talking wall that was active. Instead of the usual overplus catalogue and snippets of Jam it was saying: THIS IS DAY THIRTY, THIS IS THE CAPITAL OF FREE SIND . . . There were a few people standing looking at it, they all scurried away when they heard me coming. I too hid whenever I heard anyone; murmuring a few words of comfort to my fern.

The well entry was shut. I stood there leaning on the projector for what seemed a very long time. I could see a back view of ALIC buzzing and buzzing but no one was paying any attention. At last one of the young men crossed the outer square and saw me. I could make out his frightened face, vague and distant through the semi-opaque panels.

'It's Alice!'

The idiot ran off squealing, 'It's Alice!' and forgot to let me in. I was left admiring the state of our passage. There were smears of melted black along the walls, great patches of raw underface. Bits of fallen casing littered the floor. So it had happened here as well, whatever it was. Someone let me in. People came pouring into the square, half the inhabitants of the well it seemed. I was hugged, exclaimed over.

Pia must have laid claim to me publicly in a way she'd never done before, because everybody melted away and left us alone.

'We thought you were dead,' she explained.

'I couldn't use my handshake Pia.'

She nodded. 'I thought of that.'

She looked me over, scowling, counting my arms and legs; about to berate me fiercely if anything was missing. Then I gave her the fern. She held it in her arms and began to smile. It was such a beautiful thing in our murky entry, so bright and glowing with life.

For 4 days we stayed in the well. There was no light except globalls which naturally didn't last long, and a few random strips that came and went in the screen rooms and on the corridors. We used hair-burners to ignite bits of cloth and furniture covering, making very smoky, messy torches. The main dispenser and the other autonomics kept going, patchily. PLS (air and gravity) we never lost. We had no way of knowing whether only our part of the centre was still paralysed, or the whole mass. On our screens we saw only occasional glimpses of a passage somewhere, unearthly bright with microg lamps: fuzzy figures in blue hardsuits talking to their wrists or creeping along clutching weapons. We presumed this was in the old capital. The source was not PEC. It might have been CENTRIN.

I had plenty of time to reflect on the fact that there were no lifeboats in this rotation. The serials were remarkably stoical, inured by several 100 years of living underground. Occasionally 2 or 3 of us would make a sortie. We would grope our way as far as the h&v, find it was still flashing the haz message and grope our way back. We never saw anyone, except a few equally

160

bewildered neighbours. Whatever was going on, the centre was far away from our part of Cav3.

Pia had not been in wonderland when the trouble began. She had arrived for her shift and found that a warning was being passed around by people who were dressed like customers: 'Go home.' So she left. The well had some anxious moments because a gang who had managed to acquire weapons decided to attack 'the Millies'. No one was sure whether it was because we were supposed to be proSIND, or the opposite. They went away after a while. But the thought of more of that kind of reaction was something else to worry us.

On the fifth day, about the second quarter, I was in the screen room on Pia's corridor. The fans were discussing, I think, the possibility of accessing the Mission for mass transfer on compassionate grounds, if SIND unrest continued. In the present circumstances I was impressed by their optimism. Suddenly the wall screen cleared. A face appeared on it: the head and shoulders of a human woman, not a generated image. She wore a grimy pyjama jacket, dispenser issue.

'This is the capital of free SIND,' she said.

Nobody dragged her off. The viewpoint changed. Now we saw a big hall: an in-depth projection of the Subcontinent's surface along one wall with all the centres and the emart network winking. Adjacent to it, a cylinder of moving lights rotated slowly, a scaled down holo of this centre. It was CENTRIN, or the information access location, as the Subs should say. There were people walking about. They were all wearing pyjamas, some of them were armed. They smiled at us.

'Inhabitants of the capital,' she said. 'We are free.' She glanced to one side, we saw her smile and nod. 'We are in charge. If you don't believe me, here's the proof.'

She lifted her hand. Her sleeve was torn, her forearm a raw mess wrapped in shiny MEDICal film. She pointed her finger at us with a proud joyful gesture, and our lighting at that moment, leapt up in a flood of white-gold sunshine.

# 2

CHTHON had pulled the plug on the old capital. Whatever the Subs claimed about their relationship with the circuitry of the universe, their systems were VENTURan systems. Nothing ever came back on line: no industry, no commerce, no contact with the outside world. The dedicated still had their burned brains, but they had no ADAPT signal, no industrial power, no movement of raw materials or products. Enabled personal stations would live on for a while on their residuals and then everything would be gone. DAY THIRTY must have seemed like the end of the world to wonderland and the Dome. The wonderlanders were lucky CHTHON always insisted on running its utilities even through enabled levels.

The SINDs had life support. While the Mission called VENTUR to ratify an 'LS sanction' SERVE returned vital processing into the heads on the interfaces: the air, the water, the food; the sanitation. We processers took this information into our brains every shift. But there was an instruction in what we carried which ensured that at the end of shift we were wiped, and normal consciousness returned to the usurped synapses. The SINDs had found a way to negate that final instruction. What the volunteers took into their heads stayed there. They became 'read only'. They would have to be tended constantly if they were to be kept alive. But what they had instead of minds could not be taken away. When the ratifying decision came back from VENTUR it was too late. SERVE was stolen. CHTHON had been ROBbed. Understanding we were in an emergency SERVE had made no distinction between locations in the Housing. Wherever it found a head, it loaded process. The SINDs had even managed to set up a redundancy. They had enough read only processers, covering enough vital areas, to run them in shifts.

Air and water and food would not have been enough. But free movement, optical monitoring, communication and evacuation could be as vital as air in a closed environment. The SINDs must have decoded that information and transport would come back on the override. Women who were either enabled or had some level of machine knowledge were waiting, at CENTRIN hall. They used their enabled access and the CENTRIN functionaries' stations to take active control of the stolen processing. They got into UBIQ through the Jam link. CHTHON had no security guards to prevent this. How could it have envisaged that anyone would ever steal SERVE? It was the SINDs who plunged us in darkness. They were fighting passage to passage in some places. The Mission couldn't deploy DOGs, because SIND captured gate fields were closed against them. Only ulaux could get through, with their emission blocking obedience collars and shaky suit relays. That was VENTUR in the Reroute: stumbling about, half mindless and half blind.

We learned, from CENTRIN hall, that we had not rerouted alone. Nearly all the Sub centres had been involved: a majority of them were successful — about 3 quarters of the bloc population. Loyal Subs (the SINDs didn't use that description) had fled to the Presidential Palace. In an arrangement the Subs had always resented, it was part of the independent environment of the VENTURan Mission. Sub Capital Rangers were not communicating with the Reroute. Presumably they were discussing moves with SHACTI.

The shuttle strip (we heard) had been vandalised by crypto-SINDs with the enabled rank to enter it. But this was irrelevant. There would be no hordes of ulaux pouring in via orbital. They'd have to be levied first. The whole of CHTHON did not run enough auxiliaries or weaponry to retake even one major centre by brute force. Recovery by harassment would not be easy either. If the Rangers attempted to cut supply lines outside the centres: diverting water and power, or disenabling surface food plant — our Life Support would counter as it was meant to do in any natural emergency, by drawing on other blocs. It would be

163

CHTHON against SERVE. They could easily set up a degrading loop that would unravel the whole structure of the underworld. The more I considered their options, the more helpless VENTUR appeared. It seemed as if an enormous bluff had been called.

If I was dazed, I could imagine how the Sub capital Rangers were feeling. These rerouters were only numbers! I thought of Yolande T's Millie science. Her terms were strange but she was still operating on a level I would once have thought inconceivable. Perhaps it was nonsense, but I was still struggling to keep up. I had told her how impressed I was. But it was impossible to matronise Yolande. 'I've done my Code Reading of course,' she said distantly. 'You used to make up games, didn't you, Pioneer Aeleysi . . .' Now VENTUR was rewarded, for treating the most machine-old culture in our one world like a batch of ignorant plugheads.

I would not be breaking stones again. But Pia went back to her fancy-goods catalogue in wonderland, out of curiosity. She found SIND girls breaking wrap on some of the solid consumables. They were going to destroy what they considered 'corrupt'. Soft currency had died on DAY THIRTY, but tills that would accept slots were non-systematic. They would last as long as the stock. Once it was cleaned up, the overplus was to be allowed to die a natural death. The girls offered to look the other way while she picked over the 'corrupt' items. I would have expected my Pia to come home loaded with loot. She brought a silly mechanical toy for me, and a small VENTURan ceramic flacon of expensive cologne for Ram.

'They're not very good presents,' she apologised. 'My head just crashed. I couldn't think of anything we wanted. It's a pity, it'll all be gone by now.'

Pia had not started her shift on DAY THIRTY. Serials who'd been collared at the crash were also free. Some wore the dead things defiantly; most found ways to cut them off. There were no more biels in the old capital.

Parts of wonderland were damaged in the fighting. But if it had survived, I could be sure that games catalogue was no longer printing SHACTI access codes. I did not even bother to check it out. The women in CENTRIN hall radiated joy and pride over our screens. I could not help being caught up in the euphoria. It was such a time that anything seemed possible. Even Millie Mohun the alien and her rescue mission. Why shouldn't the SINDs have their chance? CHTHON might already be obsolete. The age of containment might be over.

The more excitable fans claimed that Millie had described DAY THIRTY in detail, a year and a half ago when she was here on her in-person tour. How all the lights went out and SERVE was down. They'll tell you to go to your homes, said Millie. But don't you go. Not if you can help it . . . Obviously this meant that Millie verified the Reroute. She was probably running it! The Command crew was more cautious. It might be so, but meanwhile we'd better behave as if VENTUR was about to come back on line. The only thing I ever heard Millie Mohun say about SINDs was that she wished she could stop them. But possibly she only meant she was sorry that the violence was necessary −

The Rerouters had decided to make monozuke of us. We had our dispensers, and on our screens we had PEC and information bursts. That ought to be enough for functional Subs. It soon became obvious there was going to be a flourishing daysky market in information. The CENTRIN machinery was still processing Jam: we just weren't allowed to see it. It was extremely unnerving not knowing what was going on 2 levels away. There were still ulaux in the centre, nobody knew just how many or where. And the fervid Reroute atmosphere might turn against Millies next.

Clips of centre news could be bought − copied on personal stations in wonderland or the Dome. Unfortunately, Millie fans didn't have anything to trade. The Command crew's contacts in the upper levels had always been elusive, now they'd disappeared entirely.

Yolande T timed her reappearance neatly. She brought with her a print-out sheet on which several enabled serials (tag signatures embossed) committed themselves to a credit transfer in favour of the Subcapital Millie fans. It was payable on the current underworld exchange rate at whatever time FUNDS came back on Line. Millie Command was dubious about using daysky processing. But they took it and we had news again: copied clips that we passed round from well to well. I thought the printed currency was ingenious if rather against the flow of the Reroute. Hmph, said Yolande. Give us time, we'll reinvent the cowrie shell.

When she turned up, I knew I had been expecting her. But she had not seen Millie again. She was still waiting, like the rest of us.

For a while there was peace. But it didn't last long. Yolande said it was a 'pathetic inversion' to decode Millie as the culmination of Sub Culture. It was the other way round! It was *the effect of Millie's arrival now*, a ripple running 'backwards' down the world line, that had initiated the whole Sub idea. Without Millie — until Millie, the idea that Subs were connected to the universal circuitry was absurd. Yolande said the monozuke obssession with tag readers and dispenser food was a value-empty analog. No one could achieve connection like that. Connection could only be achieved by Millie transition.

She allowed her enabled fans to remain enabled. Millie Command here had insisted they become basic serials (which explained why we couldn't get hold of any). But worst of all, she was actually letting non-Subs: unburned, unconnected aliens, call themselves fans.

They came to me and told me: Yolande has been interfacing with aliens! Surely, I demurred, we knew that. One alien anyway. She hasn't exactly kept it a secret.

No, no you don't understand, they cried. This is *horrible*.

There were enclaves of Northern1 and Panasian serials in many Sub centres, relics of CHTHON attempts to dilute the overpowering cultural flavour. Of course, they had been attracted by Yolande's promo. Northern1s especially always loved a new starship story. Once again I was summoned to Millie Command for a Yolande debriefing. I was prepared to try and conciliate. I should have known better.

'Alice! Is it true you have accepted these non-Sub contacts.?'

I had visited Yolande in the Millie well where she was staying. It was true I had noticed that at least one of the friends she'd bought back with her was not burned. It was hard to miss. The young woman favoured a 'VENTURan' headstyle.

'I didn't know —'

'You did!' snarled Yolande, glaring at me from across the overplus conference table.

'I didn't know it was going to cause a problem.'

'Would you be one of us, Alice, if your head was not opened to Function?'

Yolande glared and glared. But what did she expect me to say?

Dat was there too, they'd dragged her up from Cav4. But she was no help to either party. She sat looking as uncomfortable as I felt, smiling nervously. I think she would have input for the unfortunate aliens, but Himem intimidated her.

'Any Sub,' intoned the famous Code Reader. 'Who would degrade Millie like that. Is no Sub to me.'

'Funx it — I AM A SUB. I'm as good a Sub as any of you.'

Yolande parted her hair savagely and thrust her mutilated skull at Himem.

'Look at that!

The burns sat in little cushions of half-healed pressure sores. Since her family froze her access to the Tectonics income she'd been financing herself by doing passive plastics processing, until the Reroute ended that career. I wondered how she'd liked it. She'd been 'dedicated' as a rich little girl, but I doubted if she'd been near a processing console since.

Himem was not impressed. 'That would have cleared up,' she said coldly, 'after a few more cycles.'

'If you're going to talk about human interfaces,' I began. 'Why don't we talk seriously? After the Reroute's been settled, the Millies could try to get in on designing a new package. Don't you see the burden, if it has to be there, could be shared out much more evenly —'

They all turned, Yolande included, and stared at me blankly.

An acrimonious discussion followed about a token mutilation for non-Sub fans. Yolande had my sympathy. It was hard to reconcile the stunning possibility of contact from outside, with these mean trivialities. I said as much to her when we had been dismissed.

'As you said — it's just an accident that Millie landed on the Sub. If she "landed" at all, I mean' (I added hurriedly).

'I did not say that. None of you ever funxing listens to me. *I said they had the causation flow inverted.* That doesn't make any difference to the fact that Millie chose the Sub. But we're going to lose all the credit that's rightfully ours, if we don't start promoting —'

She stalked off muttering viciously. She'd like to see Commander Himem wearing the burns on a more sensitive part of her anatomy.

Yolande was non-committal if not cynical towards the Reroute. Possibly she was envious of the achievements of those 'mindless SINDs'. I wanted to believe in it, but I was shaken by an ominous incident. It was 2 cycles after DAY THIRTY. There had been no communication between Free SIND and the VENTURan Mission. Then suddenly we learned that the Rangers were going to evacuate. They had accessed CENTRIN hall to explain that their spur into the transport tunnels had been crippled in the security crash. They wanted safe conduct into the public emart network. CENTRIN had no hope of penetrating the reac to find out if the story were true, but they agreed. It was not. The VENTURans and ulaux were escorted to an emart access, and PORT was instructed to open its platform for transport from SHACTI. Cars crashed in and out poured hordes of new levied troops . . .

The attempt failed. The SINDs weren't entirely stupid, they'd been prepared. They had played at passage fighting before, and the ulaux didn't know the first move. I couldn't feel much sympathy. You wouldn't have lasted long in any battle scenario of mine with a feeble ruse like that. But 4 Rangers, it was said, had failed to get back to the Mission. They lay on the emart platform with holes smashed in them by explosive bullets, left to die cerebral death.

That part was not confirmed on our illicit news clip, automatic censorship was still running. But I was alarmed. I saw how ugly this situation could become. There was now evidence also that the former 'corrupt and degraded' Housing Management had decoded to secure a piece of the Reroute: which could only mean trouble.

I wasn't afraid for myself. I was afraid for my Pia. I was secretly most alarmed when she came home empty-handed from her plunder sortie. I wasn't fooled. She was still my greedy girl, she'd just switched her attention to more dangerous sweeties. Not everlasting life or star travel, they seemed safe enough. But courage, loyalty and cultural pride.

Ram and I would never be friends. He showed no resentment over my affair with his partner. Subs did not expect 'marriage' to be a romance. His dislike of me was deeper and better justified. We coexisted with the aid of that famous masculine aphasia. Ram had no courageous feminine desire to 'talk out' his distrust of the reformed VENTURan. But he was still mine now; my responsibility. He told me, in a rare expansive moment, that he would never forget the stories I used to tell.

'What stories?'

'About space and stars. Don't you remember?'

When I was drugged at SHACTI, babbling in my sleep, I didn't know the young men were hanging on to every word, storing it all in their memories like treasure. The stars, murmured Ram. The stars . . . And he recounted my dreams to me: peeling back the earth and finding on the other side the dazzling bright and dark eternal —

'Do you think we'll go there Alice, really?'

He forgot I was a Commander then, briefly. He was so young, and so hungry . . .

I decided I must find a way to get the 3 of us out. My scheme for breaking through the shell into a casting tunnel might not be so absurd, now that the industrial sector was derelict and waste-energy exchange down to a minimum. We must get hold of some cutting tools. Yolande had with her some of those print-out sheets, embossed with her tag signature. I had an idea she would give me one. She was out of FUNDS, but the daysky dealers would probably accept a Tectonics emboss at face value.

I explained the plan. Pia's room mate came in, and looked interested to see the 3 of us crouched there on one cot. My love for Pia was no secret. By a natural progression of ideas, a lot of strange freedoms were being tried out by the 'radical' Millies now. She left with a grin: remarking we could spread on to her shelf if it was more convenient.

'The trouble is, this really needs 3 people to make it work.'
'3?'
'Definitely,' I muttered.
'Take Ram.'
'No,' he said, never one to waste output.
'Pia, the SINDs have nothing to do with Millie. If she's from outside, the whole world will know about it. We might as well be at SHACTI. We might as well be on Mars —'
'Alice — I can't leave now. If you think you can —'
She broke off, her eyes smouldering: jumped up from her cot and left the room. Ram followed her with exasperating meekness. I could understand their resistance, but not this stupid refusal to discuss things. I hated to even think it, but they were just behaving like basics.

+

Pia had friends in a well that was on our level but out near the cortex. The area had been industrial in the second excavation. The structure was irregular even by old capital standards, with unexpected ramps and gaps in the passage walls where whole wells had been excised and never replaced. Everywhere there was old SIND scribble, smeared and blurred by perfunctory sweepers. We sat in the square while the friends produced an old 'black box' projector of the kind used for interior decoration up in wonderland. They covered the floor with a 2D map of the Subcontinent and discussed new centres that would be built. SIND was going to spread over the surface under a clear canopy like the Dome. At last we'll find out if the sky's really supposed to be shit coloured . . .

I pointed out tentatively that these new centres were encroaching on recreated forest.

They all laughed. Who is this funxing ballhead? said someone. Pia pinched me.

But I wasn't afraid of being discovered as a VENTURan. I scarcely looked the part. And if I was 'found out' they could see I was on their side now.

Two of the girls had torn ear lobes. I was careful not to show

170

that I was shocked. Junking tags was not a part of the original Reroute: the tag had too many strands into Sub culture, not to mention into Life Support. But there were extremists. They were fed and clothed by their friends while they waited for CHTHON to be utterly wiped out. They wouldn't last long if things ended differently. It was the final defiance, a gate of no return. I consoled myself: at least this mad gesture didn't tempt my Pia. She said it would be 'like trying to be better than Millic.'

I knew why I'd been brought here. Pia was educating me. I listened, trying honestly to be fair, but I was not impressed. They were out to destroy the biosphere all over again, the very reason they had to be shut up in the first place. I felt old and wise and exasperated. If this was SIND policy, they could forget about coming to terms with CHTHON –

Suddenly the entry lock started buzzing. We saw a bunch of figures, heard someone crying. The newcomers spilled into the square. The map vanished. I retreated. One of the torn ear girls was beside me – I asked her what had happened.

'It was a rescue,' she said. 'The ulaux up in wonderland captured Input. They didn't know if she was still alive, but a few of her friends went into the prickheads' territory to find out.'

She spoke casually, as a desperate Rerouter should. I was badly startled. I had realised we were with active SINDs but I didn't know we'd come to the front line. In our well we never thought about the ulaux. Life seemed so normal most of the time.

The rescued woman knelt on the floor, her fists between her bare thighs. Her dark face was grey, she was shivering. A young man touched her and she jerked away: he was the one I had heard crying.

My desperado told me: 'The ulaux had her for 2 days.' She swallowed hard. 'The man crying is her husband.'

Someone was banging at the MEDIC dispenser. I tried not to look at the grey-faced woman. I could no longer doubt that the Rangers used ulaux in this way deliberately, encouraging their nasty little urges. It was bad enough for the men to be raped. The women were assaulted at once in their bodies and in their tenuous feeling of superiority over the useless sex.

I wondered what it felt like. The idea had meant nothing to me

171

once. But I knew about humiliation now. The fingers flicking out your tag; thumb in muscle to keep you still. Oh, that intimate gesture . . . The young Subs tried to comfort their friend, but they were looking at each other covertly, bleakly. Their pride and bravery was so thin and new: under it the utter physical helplessness of all their lives. I wanted to leave. I looked at Pia, meaning to signal that we should go. I found that Pia was looking at me.

We sat on the h&v in silence.

I said. 'The ulaux are running wild. No one knows what they're doing.'

Pia gave me a pitying glance. 'They're wearing collars Alice.'

*Pia, not wearing a collar but knowing where it was kept, giving those shuddering little cries she knew I liked.*

She came to my door. Silence. She stared at me. Then she started to cry, put out her arms and held me fiercely, as if every force in the universe was trying to pull us apart.

+

The Code Readers met in the screen room on my corridor to 'Read' one of Yolande's clips. I seemed to have become official Yolande-watcher to the Millie movement. These were still the 3 clips she had made on her pre-Reroute promotion tour, but the fans hadn't finished with them. They gave Yolande the same exegesis they gave SERVE's code: every phrase disassembled, every gate tested.

I told her, one of her problems was that nobody could understand this stuff. It was all right for excitable Northerns, they didn't care. But to watch Sub Code Readers trying to process Yolande into coherent integrated argument was painful.

She laughed me to scorn. I loaded a clip and played to her her own words on the subject of Millie's syntactical relationship with absolute Function: Yolande's grainy image waving its arms about and scowling raptly . . . We sat and looked at each other in the rather solemn silence generated by the utterly unintelligible.

'Oh, well. That's deliberate.' said Yolande quickly. 'They

won't take it on board at once, but they'll internalise it, unconsciously.'

In a moment of weakness I had mentioned my MLE idea to Yolande. She immediately decided that Manifest Life Entity was an excellent description of Millie; and Millie's global rescue naturally accepted the Commanders and their language. The fans were so bemused, they didn't even revolt at this.

We didn't use the screen. The Subs had all the material in their memories (even to her *eye movements*). Yolande used a VENTURan term: 'co-presence'. They wanted it explained by a VENTURan.

A long time ago, I said, there was a lab assistant called EAROM. That's a highly skilled science Code Reader. She was working on a project to librate the mass of the universe. As you know, that's impossible. The equations just won't stabilise. For a while after we discovered we were in a trapped region, this was looked on as a hopeful line of research. EAROM imagined an esoteric particle with a property she called co-presence. A difficult concept.

'Connection,' murmured Dat.

'Sorry. An esoteric connection. The 4-dimensional mass of these particles, I mean connections — or this connection — would make up the balance. EAROM said if these particles existed they must exist in the whole universe. If you see what I mean. Not just in our area. But she never found them. Nor did anyone else. I suppose Yolande thinks Millie has co-present particles in her. We have them too. We "find" them, and that's the way it's done.'

Himem frowned.

Dat smiled.

'You've described the Intersection, Alice. The solution that all Subs hope for. One one level, here and now, it may be a political solution. But there is deeper analysis. In the beginning light and matter were one. Something tore them apart, and in that event we were trapped here. The Intersection is what closes the gap again. Between time and the timeless, between being and Nothing . . . And Millie says it is in all of us. In the pattern of data that informs brain and body: just as SERVE/Function informs our world . . .'

Her eyes were as big as they used to be at SHACTI, and as wild. I wondered, at what point did Millie tell Dat she was from the big outside. Or did Dat just decide that she liked Yolande's version? And if I asked her, the answer wouldn't help me much. I had tried asking Yolande: 'PIONER Yolande. No gaming − is this *real?*' She looked surprised. 'Of course it is Aeleysi. This and nothing else.'

The Code Readers went on, their voices slipping into a time-smoothed mnemonic drone, their fingers stabbing the air. Yolande was getting a good poking. I looked around the room. It was a familiar scene: the serials in front of PEC, the men fidgeting, the babies crying; a group of Code Readers off in a corner. I experienced a sudden shock. Perhaps I ought to feel more sympathy for those women with the torn ears. Pia was not in sight. I hoped she was with Ram, not out doing something dangerous.

It was ironic that everyone thought I had signed up for the Millie project at last. Particularly ironic, because whatever I believed or did not believe for me it all began and ended with one serial girl. Not even a number, a *biel*.

The PEC watchers were studying humanity with the patient loving attention that was Millie's legacy. They had an additional incentive now. In the first days of the Reroute CENTRIN had accepted and transmitted a reproachful address recorded by the Sub President. The Presidential family had been tactfully absent in a trans alt resort on DAY THIRTY; they had then returned to SHACTI. She pointed out the error of our ways, and begged us to return to normality. Needless to say, this did the SINDs no harm at all.

But she was the last we saw of the world outside. We knew PEC was censored. Quite possibly the rest of the underworld didn't know our Reroute had happened. But something might have slipped through. And if they were aware of what we had done, PEC was the only way they could try to signal back to us. The SINDs now claimed they had routed a message through the blockade, to Panasia CENTRIN. They expected a covert reply today: an expression of solidarity.

It never came.

# 3

Pia was pregnant. She had no normalcy implant. She had been ignoring her number on the Inserts, she'd have been captured and given a bad entry except for the Reroute. I understood why she didn't want that protection. If her chance of making the Millie transition had been spoiled, at least the baby would start fair. Close questioning revealed though she and Ram were nominally 'cousins' they were genetically closer than that. Probably there would be no problem, but if there was it might be bad. We had no PRENAT, not even the underworld package for human-body pregnancies. We had lost it on DAY THIRTY.

We had a fight because I tried to help. I was turning out my storage looking for things to give to the torn-ears benefit, and I found a sheet and a half of reds in the pocket of my tourist pyjamas. They'd been there since SHACTI. I had never worn that suit in the old capital. It was too conspicuous: and it was so much stronger than the dispenser issue I thought I was saving it for an escape trek across the surface. I'd forgotten about the reds long ago. I thought briefly of a casual decision – *after all I might eat something.* I gave the pyjamas to the benefit, and the whole sheet and a half to Pia.

She gave them away.

So we fought. She'd saved one strip, in consideration of the lump in my armpit. At my age, she kindly informed me, if I thought it was a cancer sign it probably was. We fought worse than ever. She said I matronised her, that I still thought she was my pet. She called me a ballhead.

Then we made peace, and went to the food dispenser. We chose chili omelet for the fun of seeing egg mix dancing like a mad amoeba behind the wrap. Took it down to the concourse and sat on the rim of the heat exchange pool licking hot orange

175

chili off our fingers. The spray cooled our faces, the passing crowd slapped its slippered feet and muttered and yelled and echoed around us, endlessly. A little girl was idly prying at the back panel of the 'mango juice' overplus booth by the v&h. It still sang, mendaciously:

> sweet mango, fresh mango
> clean cups . . .

and would go on singing until the everlasting powerpack ran down. But there was no juice.

'Here,' said Pia, handing her the strip of film tabs. 'Real Commander drugs. Go off and make your fortune.'

Free SIND was 8x30 days old. I went to see Yolande at her shelf down on 10.Cav3. I proceeded cautiously. We were all getting very dependent on the 'runners' − young girls and adolescent boys who knew which areas in their locality currently belonged to the SINDs, and which to the (ex-Housing Management) Committee of Functionaries. The information could be vital.

She was in a screen room, alone with a carton of wine. She'd sent for me, but she didn't seem to have anything particular to say. We had fallen out since I betrayed her so cravenly at the non-Subs debriefing. We talked about that, and the 'strange freedoms': which Yolande did not approve. She would not interfere, she said, with my depraved personal affairs. But we ought to stop this process of men growing their hair, and sitting in on Millie Code Reading. Men, quite simply, had been dropped by the current of history. It wasn't Yolande's idea. That was the way Function had designed things and no one ought to mess with it. She was convinced it was same even in VENTUR.

'You talk about equality, but show me the male Rangers −'

'Maybe they've got more sense than to want to come down here.'

'Huh.'

'In space you know . . . no one's on top.'

'Ha. We all know you've got artificial gravity.'

For someone so intelligent Yolande had very little sense of humour. I didn't pursue the topic. I was trying to imagine the joy of little arms clinging round my neck. No use − selected right out

176

of me. But I would love this baby (we didn't even know if it was a girl or boy) if it would keep Pia out of danger. She was at present trying to get me to come with her to a peaceful rally in wonderland, in the disused vic stadium. The event had nothing to do with SIND or the Functionaries; and certainly not Millie Command. But we knew the Rangers were monitoring again now, through the dual access to UBIQ. It was hoped that they'd notice this gathering and take it as an expression of good will. I said I couldn't see how it would help for us to be on record as active participants in the Reroute, at this stage. She was by now nearly 90 days pregnant. Surely that was a reason to stay at home. 'You don't know anything about it Alice,' she told me firmly.

The screen, which had been blank without even a holding pattern, suddenly came to life. We saw a piece of CENTRIN hall and some women shouting at each other. A further confused mass of figures charged across the scene and disappeared, there was a sound of shattering wrap. Someone looked straight out at us, glaring and yelling, then ran away. The sound was frightful, completely unintelligible. Another normal third quarter in the Command Module of Free SIND.

'These people,' remarked Yolande dispassionately, 'who insist on dumping the systematically constituted controls. They can't do anything with power once they've got it. They're addicted to opposition. Take some wine Aeleysi, it'll do you good.'

Free SIND wine was dispenser fruit juice, fermented with something from the derelict industrial ring that was probably designed for eating plastic waste. I had once been terrified of the masses' fun drugs. Not that they were poisonous, which they were: but I knew if I once tasted anything that dulled the edge of misery, I wouldn't be able to stop. I would be lost. With a wry smile for that vanished ALIC, I took the carton. I had a headache. I had so many worries now, I was even beginning to miss my 8 hours a day of uneasy oblivion. The wine made me feel much worse.

Beside the bolster where we were sitting, Yolande's good sturdy bedroll was lying on the floor strapped up. I had noticed it when I walked in. It sat and looked at us while we drank, like an unspoken question. *What's happened to Millie?*

'So you're leaving,' I said at last.

'Yes. I have to go. The Subs are after me.'

It was the conservative fans who had lost patience with Yolande and her non-Sub star traveller: about the same time as we all lost hope in the Reroute. Himem talked about the hostility of former vigilantes. She said she couldn't be responsible for what might happen. Which was fair warning.

Yolande sighed. 'The Subs are a euphemism.'

'I know.'

'Yolande — has something gone wrong?'

A superfluous question, if you were considering what we'd just seen on the wall. But she knew what I meant.

'Not at all,' answered Yolande stubbornly. 'There's nothing wrong. Nothing can go wrong now.'

I left her staring gloomily at the empty screen.


The v&h, which didn't take slots any more, was growing unpredictable. Sometimes I thought it was all right, sometimes I felt happier walking. Most people were the same, a random avoidance pattern to counter the random failures. The passages around Yolande's well were very dark, so I took the v. I was alone in the car. It ignored my transact. When the door opened I was on 2. I stepped out to walk back in again, which often worked — and noticed there was a lot of noise somewhere. There was no one in the access but through its entry lock I heard a thunder of running feet, saw some flashes. I went back to the platform and jumped sharply into the car, not in panic just to boot it. One could take it as confirmed then that there was a further major power shift in progress. I felt no grief for the troubles of the SIND rerouters. I'd always known they couldn't achieve anything on their own.

The problems that we were having with the autonomics were far more serious. From the first, from DAY THIRTY itself, we had been managing without certain services. Some of the volunteers had failed to maintain their own autonomics in that rush of input and died physically as well as mentally, so their precious freight was lost. But the success of the others was not complete success. As time passed, against their will, the volunteers' brains began to reject their owners' sacrifice. Individuality started to creep back, corrupting the vital data that had taken its place. And gradually the errors began to proliferate. I should have know that this would happen. But I never imagined the isolation of Free SIND would continue for so long. I thought either they would win or lose: quickly. The Reroute still held the capital environment intact, in spite of its divisions. But meanwhile we were losing the information that fed us, kept us breathing; carried our shit away.

The monozuke of the capital always said the SINDs shouldn't have done it. It was corrupt and disconnected to create ROB processers — to imprison SERVE. Why don't you transfer out then, said the SINDs. Get on to the surface, go and give yourselves up at a netnode. We won't stop you. Attempting to escape from Function's disapproval, answered the monozuke, does not get through the gate.

On the h platform the lights were brighter. A few serials were waiting, looking tired but not particularly anxious. A murmur of conversation — I stood in thought. *She could be in SHACTI. She could be the reason why VENTUR is too busy to do anything about this Reroute. The world could be rocking from the shock of alien contact, and we wouldn't know* . . . Waiting for something that doesn't happen is an odd activity. It has no finite conclusion. You have to impose one, arbitrarily.

I took a drink from a water fountain. Gagged, and spat on the platform. It smelled like, it probably was, pure piss. I'll have to convince Pia. It is definitely time to leave this party.

It was the end of the fourth quarter. The well square was unusually populous for such an hour. They've had a burst about the power shift, I decided. Grey faces in the grey globall light.

'Oh Alice. CENTRIN's gone!'

A few hours later, something appeared on the screen. It was a woman with a strong wise face, dressed in a changing garment of blue and green and brown. She told us to be calm and stay in our wells, go back to them if we were out of location. Her smile flickered. She resolved for a moment into CHTHON's other logo, the rotating earth.

179

The VENTURan Mission had invaded CENTRIN. There was no way to tell if the coup was physical or within the machine.

Once Pia and I went for a walk in one of the hot sectors of wonderland. Pia wanted to see what it was like. I don't know what came over me, I really had no desire for that kind of spectacle. At first it just seemed rather drab for level 1. We were away from the pretty malls. The private gardens and customised living spaces were behind walls much like our own blank walls. The air was a little sweeter and the passing traffic a little thinner. That was all. We walked into a small concourse. There was a charred place in the middle which might formerly have been a live grass plot.

'This is probably as exciting as it gets,' said Pia.

And without warning, without any transition, we were in the middle of a running fight. Every passer-by was scrambling for an open entry, or pitched face down, hands over head. It was a squad of ulaux — hard suits, earth blue; and some SINDs. Impossible to say who was pursuing who. The ulaux patrolled parts of wonderland, not from any hope of capturing the Sub capital piecemeal; but apparently just as a reminder of VENTUR's continued presence. It was hard on the auxiliaries.

There was exchange of fire, both explosive and beam, and choking fumes of seared agam. Cracker strings zipped through the air. The SINDs were hand-processing new weapons now from chemicals and bits and pieces of industrial waste. They had developed a fiendishly simple device, a weighted string of explosive that detonated on impact. If a cracker hit a hard suit across the shoulders or the back of the neck it had a good chance of disabling the LSU. The suit itself would do the rest. Ulaux equipment did not stand up to test. It was embarrassingly obvious that no one had thought much about their survival in combat.

This is why, I thought (face in hands), the SINDs can't be retaken. Any major escalation of these stray bullets and laser cuts zapping our conduits and even SERVE couldn't keep up with the damage. What a vulnerable thing a centre is!

180

When the noise had passed I stood up cautiously. An ulaux was lying on the blackened centre plot a few yards away. As I watched, the safety telltale on the blue shell of his arm shifted out of red, into white. Nobody else around knew what it meant! I ran across, went down on my knees; broke the chest seals, stripped away the faceplate. There was a rim of vomit around his mouth but he didn't seem to have inhaled any. And a powerful smell of shit, but I ignored that. Cerebral death is not a party game. I began to inflate and compress urgently. The suit had checked no life signs for 4 minutes.

Why, oh why seal them in hard suits where there was air to breathe? As if the SINDs could void any part of a centre teeming with their own population. As if SERVE would let them. The boy had choked and drowned inside his armour. I felt bad knowing if it had been my suit, that soft suit I wore for decoration in the pure air of LECM, it would not have let him die. But he was only an ulaux. His collar was still round his neck, carrying the commands that controlled him. A bulky doll, designed to frighten the other serials. And now he might be brain damaged for life . . .

I went on working for several minutes before I remembered where I was. Poor boy, he was dead and dead he would stay. Wonderland had nothing that he needed, and no one seemed to be coming back for him. The passers-by had pulled themselves together and were melting away. If there were any other casualties they had disappeared.

One woman glanced at me and asked another — 'Why did she do that?'

'A Millie, maybe.'

The word had become a synonym for slightly crazy altruism. Millies, people gathered, were against death and violence because they wanted to prove serials could live to be 300 years old. Or else because dead bodies in the passages might scare off an approaching starship.

I was annoyed. I had no desire to be credited for virtues I didn't possess. I had imagined I was back at school doing adventure training. I thought I would get a hiscore for my vic simulated First Aid, that was all.

Pia knelt beside me. She put her arm around my shoulder. 'Hush,' she murmured. 'Don't cry. You did your best.'

I had played and written so many war games: from the moment it started I saw the Reroute as a scenario. I didn't understand the deaths were permanent . . .

No! I did nothing. It's nothing to do with me. I'm a spectator. The vic dream went on, it seemed to go on for a long, long time. I became involved, the way one does in an absorbing story. The terror was real, the pity was real. But still I knew (it was my best kept secret) that in the end I would take my headset off, and walk away.

Get out. It must be possible.

Eventually one of the Functionary party — not a SIND — reappeared in CENTRIN hall. She told us the VENTURan Mission had made an *unsuccessful* attempt to overrun the upper levels. We should stay in our homes for the time being. Then the screen blanked out.

Pia stood in the door of my room. 'We're going up to the stadium now,' she said. 'Are you coming?'

I made a hopeless attempt to retreat into the wall of my shelf. I had the privilege of a room to myself now. My bunkmate must be stranded somewhere, she had not come home since CENTRIN first went down.

'You mean the rally's still on?' I asked weakly.

'It is.'

'How do you know?'

'Don't be a plughead Alice. Because I'm going and Ram's going and you're going and that's what's happening all through the centre.'

There didn't seem to me to be any further need to break the 'long silence'. But Pia had made up her mind.

I sighed. 'Ram and I'll go. You stay here.'

'Stop funxing about and come on. It's a long way to walk.'

As we crossed the outer square I looked back into the open doorway of a screen room. The Millies were sitting and kneeling huddled together, waiting for instructions. On the screen PEC was running, some fragment of routine serial life far away.

I had never been to the vic stadium. Before I arrived in the old

182

capital SIND problems had put an end to mass attendance at the games. We travelled to wonderland on foot, for the v&h was out of action. It wasn't even telling us we must not use it. We could see a lot of new damage. Passing by the Housing annexes I stopped and looked at the burnt out shell of PORT, where I had waited in line once to request a transfer and to be refused. Overhead the wonderland floor/ceiling was split, dripping a solidified black ooze of melted agam. Grubs crawled among the torn conduits. I felt disoriented for a moment, remembering one of my old dreams. SERVE would rebuild. It still held the paradigm. But no one would open a route into the tunnels from here for a while. Pia hauled on my arm and told me to stop acting like a tourist. So on we went.

By this time we were not alone. We'd joined a trail of other serials, trickling like liquid. The inhabitants of wonderland were not about, unless there were any with us; but there were no signs of immediate danger. Everyone was very cheerful. The general opinion was that ulaux forces had been pushed back to the Mission again. We met Val, a friend of Pia's. With her was 'the VENTURan', the Northern1 girl who had defected from Yolande's party and become an honorary Sub. Her bare head looked most odd in the seriate, especially now she'd had herself given a hand made 'token' mutilation. The trickle became a flow. Val's partner was fooling about, pretending to be very triumphant because he'd finally got her to come to the stadium — his favourite entertainment.

There were going to be speeches. We would talk out to VENTUR, the way people talked to PEC. I saw some young men with a great bundle of plastic sheeting. They'd glued bolster covers together to carry a message burned out of pieces of pyjama textile and stuck on the plastic: SORRY ABOUT THE 4 RANGERS! They were laughing a lot, and being lectured by more serious persons. But I was touched. There was something so endearing about the antics of the young serial male.

The flow stopped. Pia explained we were now close to the stadium, which must be slowing things down. She was pleased to think there was a big crowd ahead, she'd been eyecounting our trickle and flow with concern. Though I couldn't, even now, imagine how anyone could look at a pack like this and think *not enough people.*

We looked around for dispensers. A few hopeful youths tried entry locks, but this being wonderland their tags wouldn't have got in, even if anyone inside was disposed to answer the projecter. A scatter of warmish cartons appeared, carried up from below. The provident few succumbed grumpily to social pressure and handed things around. We talked about the status of the Reroute, pooling our ignorance. The Millies' credit for copied clips had run out, and by this time the homebase copying stations had all run down anyway. Behind their walls, the wonderlanders were as helpless as the rest of us, humiliatingly dependent on the CHTHON dispensers discreetly hidden in their lobbies.

There was a strong rumour that most of the luxury residences in the Dome were empty. The enabled were using their private emart spurs. Accessing a car would only take them into some other part of the Reroute: and the SHACTI line was blocked. So they escaped up the tunnels on foot, and got to the surface by clambering through the freight depots. SIND CENTRIN let them go. It wasn't interested in sneaky exits: only entries.

'They won't be doing that any more,' remarked the crowd cheerfully. 'We're all together now.'

When PORT was burned out, all the old capital's emart accesses, private and public, would have sealed off. All but the Mission access that was supposed to be out of action anyway. The basics laughed. They weren't afraid of being contained. They were used to it. VENTUR would have to try harder than that! I kept silent. I did not want to think what I was thinking.

To my surprise I caught sight of a face I recognised. It was Ajoy, Himem's partner from SHACTI. I hurried over, shouting his name. He told me Dat was with him. We peered around for Dat, and Himem's little girl who'd been my friend. I saw Pia, standing beside the group I'd just left. She was looking away from me, smiling, in the middle of a solid mass of sweaty flesh and dispenser pyjamas. I felt a shudder run through me. I couldn't imagine what it was. An earthquake?

In a moment of curious stillness I thought: there's something fundamentally wrong with this. The Mission's screens will show

them an undulating heap of numbers, nothing else . . . I dropped
Ajoy's hand. I began to run. But at the same time, the wave that
was travelling back through the standing flow reached me in
strength, and lifted me off my feet. I turned head over heels. A
crushing, formless weight tried to drive my face into the agam
floor. It shoved me up again. I shouted. I saw the VENTURan's
stippled head and tried to grab her. But it was too late.

+

We walked into the stadium at last down a short tunnel with high
featureless walls, which might once have been covered with
sporting projections. We walked 4 by 4 our wrists linked behind
us in twists of plastic alloy. A blue bowl of simulated sky curved
overhead, traced with delicate cirrus. It must have been holding
that pattern since DAY THIRTY. This big ellipse would be for
track and team. There would be other halls in the complex, for
smaller scale pursuits. I looked up at the empty stands, and
wondered when they had last been filled. The floor was under
permaturf. Cleaning grubs moved about quietly, just as they
would after a vic meeting.

A woman sat down. Many of us had walked for hours to get to
wonderland and after the violence we were exhausted. The ulaux
didn't react. Soon we'd all collapsed.

'Ram. Is it you Ram?'

The people between us were too dazed to get out of the way, or
maybe they couldn't see anyone of their own and felt resentful.
But we managed to reach each other. His pyjama shirt was torn,
his face smeared all over with agam smoke, it was no wonder I'd
hardly recognised him.

'Where's Pia?'

Ram shook his head. He began to cry, trying awkwardly to
hide his face in his shoulder.

I saw a hard suit with a super's patch, walking by beyond the
line that guarded us. She was carrying in her gauntleted hands an
open food carton. There was a reddish crust like dried chili sauce
down one side of the box. Another ulaux stopped her. They
seemed to confer. A blue hand dipped clumsily into the carton
and came up full of tiny dark objects that ran back through her

185

fingers. A good haul — they might be saying. The ulaux must have been using the stadium as a forward base. No one knew that. Or how many ulaux there were. SHACTI must have been sending down new levies — so much for the Mission's crippled emart. They had killed a lot of people, not noticing perhaps that the crowd was unarmed and docile. Then an instruction must have reached them and they began to round us up instead.

The ulaux hemmed us in. There was a silence over the crowd, like the silence in SHACTI Pavilion the moment after a vic. Talk to VENTUR? We must have been dreaming. But now for us at least the dream of the great Reroute was over. We were numbers again.

There was a long delay. Once, I woke up out of a doze and Ram was pushing himself against me, his face burrowed into the front of my shirt, nuzzling my breasts. I tipped him off in unthinking revulsion. A minute later I realised he was only asking; offering, a little comfort. I turned in remorse, but he was gone. I clambered to my feet and began to look for him, along with a few other stumbling figures, peering into faces, calling out names.

I gave up in the end.

If only Pia hadn't been my pet. We could have escaped, but she made it a point of self respect to stay and I couldn't talk to Pia about self respect. But still I had not learned my lesson. I even tried to stop her coming here, for the sake of her pregnancy . . . How could she have a baby if she wasn't brave and strong? Not like a pet but like a human woman.

I knew now as if I could hear her crying that Pia had been frightened all the time — frightened even of this rally. And all I did was make things harder for her. I remembered the capin in LECM. My cedars in the mist. Pia curled on her cushions. I was as happy there as ever in my life: but I kept suffering bleak mood-plunges and I didn't know why. Now the capin and this place seemed to run together and become one, and I understood. Because Pia piled somewhere for disposal in a heap of burned and broken limbs, was Pia my pet in LECM. Can't have one without the other.

It's what Yolande said. We have those co-present particles

streaming through us. They collide with consciousness occasionally and then we are haunted: knowing the whole of what we do, without time's protection.

It was very uncomfortable, crying with no hands to wipe the tears.

I decided to try again to find Ram. But as I struggled upright other people began to move as well. The ulaux had received new commands. We were to form into lines.

Millie Mohun is dead too, I thought. She died just like this. Poor Millie, tag or no tag she was only a number.

Or if she was what they said she was, then the rescue mission failed. She fell into the abyss but she couldn't get out again. She became such a good imitation of a human being she was trapped here like the rest of us. And when she realised what she'd done to herself, she was in this stadium. Under this blue synthetic sky, with a twist of plastic holding her wrists together. Breath behind me, shoulders in front of me. The woman on my left was softly reciting in a firm voice − that is, a voice that tried hard not to shake − *by the Design, by the Design.*

I saw, from the corner of my eye, a figure sleekly covered in blue of a different order coming briskly across the turf. The ulaux super ran to her Ranger, happily, trustingly. She pulled off her clumsy blue ballhead and cried. 'Hello friend!' with pleasure and relief. Was that a real person, or a projection from inside the reac? At this distance I couldn't tell.

We passed under one of the big arches that punctuated the stands. There was a broad tunnel inside lined with hangars where the stadium kept animals or equipment. A cold dank air came from somewhere, reminding us how warm it had been getting in the levels. At last our tags were checked. I had a brief flash of hope: perhaps they'd stop when they reached me. I'd hear a puzzled ulaux voice, her wrist up to her mouth: 'Commander − there's a funny sort of anomaly here −' But that was only a reflex beyond my control, and it didn't happen anyway.

It was gloomy in there. My eyes blurred. I could see nothing but Pia, looking away from me, smiling at something she could see and I could not. In a moment I would know . . .

# How –

But we were not terminated. It would have been a breach of CHTHON protocol. There could never be any reason to punish numbers: they were not responsible. Action was only taken to stop trouble from spreading, and as easy-to-read instructions for the rest. There could be no benefit to the libration in killing us when the whole capital was in reroute. I was in a hangar with about 100 others. After some hours we were moved out and hustled away through the underbase of the stadium. I finally lost hope of finding Ram.

Our wrists were freed, we were scrubbed, collared, detached from our dirty pyjamas. People guessed we must be in the President's containment because of these facilities. We were obviously inside the Mission environment: everything that was failing in Free SIND had started to run as it should. We did not see the rest of the crowd again.

We were in a room under a low floor/ceiling: about the size of a standard seriate concourse. Down one side there were undivided plastic latrine trays; at a hygienic distance water and food dispensers were set in a wall. The nutrient cake was the same as the stuff I'd tried to make Pia eat in our capin. On the other side of the space lay several undivided palliasses, fixed to the floor. The light changed in what seemed to be our usual rhythm. Periodically our collars prodded us towards a gap that opened in the slick wall. We passed through a scrub tube and back into the room. Unless you forestalled it, after you ate your collar would urge you to the latrine trays. There was no question, needless to say, of any kind of resistance.

I thought of the SINDs, waiting hopefully for VENTUR to open independence negotiations with a colony of basic numbers. But none of it worried me very much, not even the latrines. I didn't pay attention. As Pia said once: degraded's just a word.

We were not the only occupants of the room. When we arrived, there were serials in it already. I thought they were SINDs who'd been captured in the attack on wonderland, because they had the matted fringes and terrible eyes of DAY THIRTY volunteers. But as soon as they moved, as soon as they

191

looked at us, I knew they had been living in this room; naked, collared, for a very long time.

Before DAY THIRTY, CHTHON had elected to make a study of the SIND phenomenon. It had taken a sample, including both SINDs and common bad-entries, and isolated them for special monitoring. It was for this purpose that the room had been prepared. CHTHON did not have facilities for holding numbers in confinement, so it took over and adapted part of the cultural containment.

The sample remained isolated. They shared one palliasse, as it seemed they had always done, and guarded a piece of floor in front of it jealously. They took no notice of the rest of us, except to express resentment at our invasion of their private world. But mostly they were too busy to care. They were reading the codes. It did not matter that they had not seen a screen since before the Reroute. They managed with the ones in their memories. Perhaps they'd had some contact with the ulaux. They knew, anyway. They knew SERVE had been stolen; that we had life support. They knew that the ROBed brains were beginning to fight back, disastrously. It was all in the codes. They had seen from its inception that the Reroute was a fatal error. What they were decoding now was the final destruction of the Sub.

They said this destruction was imminent. They also said that the VENTURan Mission was at present preparing to retire to SHACTI in earnest. People jeered at this. Those 2 statements couldn't get through the same gate. It was hardly likely the Commanders would quit while they were winning. The only question was whether we ourselves would be killed when CHTHON had finished its recovery, or just left in here forever.

But I looked at the Code Readers and they looked at me. I was afraid they could read my mind.

Time passed. I lay on my strip of palliasse, idly watching the mad women. The result of isolation was interesting. Whatever they had been before, they were all monozuke now. Their only purpose in life was to read the codes. To go deeper and deeper into SERVE's rational light, to find the world mirrored there. If I'd been a Sub, I thought I would have reacted rather differently. They believed SERVE/Function had told them Subs were special, and taught them how to enter into its processes. If that was true, it was a dirty trick. It only led to this. One of them broke away from the decoding. She looked down at me.

'Stop watching us.'

I shrugged, without rising. She knelt, peered into my face.

'You're a Millie aren't you?'

I knew how she'd feel about anything unorthoprax. I didn't want to get beaten up.

'No I'm not.'

This was ignored. Her knees were on the edge of my bed, there was a mean calculating look in her eye. My heart sank. I had a partial treaty with my left-hand neighbour, but she wouldn't back me up in a fight. The Code Readers could be vicious.

'Millie is alive.'

At least it was going to be only verbal. Another shrug seemed safest.

'We have seen her in the codes.'

'Huh. Plenty of people have tried.'

She smirked triumphantly. I'd given myself away.

'No one has ever read the codes as we have read them. She is there. The Commanders have her in a *study centre*. They are experimenting on her.'

'Study centre,' was an expression of horror, something to frighten children. And adults.

'I don't believe you.'

A cold smile.

'They have her in the hills near SHACTI, beside the alt wall. If you could read code I could show you. But you can't.'

I lay there for a while, and then I strolled over to the dispensers for a piece of cake, taking care to hand half of it to the cake-eaters: a group who imagined they controlled our food supply. The woman meant to make me suffer. I wouldn't let her see I felt anything. It was true that I watched them. I couldn't help it, there was so little to look at in here. I couldn't remember telling anyone I was a Millie. Perhaps they'd read that too in the codes.

I tried not to believe her. But I was so weak and miserable, and it seemed so likely. I couldn't imagine why I'd never considered before that the Rangers would not simply excise a number who claimed to be immortal. However absurd the idea, they would want to investigate. They would hand Millie over to the machines. She might well be alive even now. And though the fans never traced her, that might be because they had never been immersed in code so obsessively as these women. They must have come across Millie by accident. It would have pleased them, to see that presumptuous biel suffering such a fate. The more I tried to argue myself out of it, the more I became convinced. And Pia was dead and Ram was dead. No one could hurt them any more. But poor Millie was still alive, being disassembled slowly and carefully by a CHTHON lab. I couldn't bear it. I had to bear it. There was nothing I could do.

The men in the room became very listless after a few days. There was only a handful of them. They had been a minority in the crowd; many people wouldn't bring men to a serious assembly, they were just too combustible. You would have thought in our nakedness they would have been demanding, and in demand: but there was very little of that. I looked at them, dull eyed and silent, and knew how absurd it was for anyone in this room to hope for anything at all. Men always react more rationally than women. They are naturally realists.

A fight broke out on my palliasse. There was a mysterious object which caused continual squabbles. I'd never seen it, I assumed it was imaginary – we'd all been stripped and searched. I was frightened. Whenever my bedmates turned restless I was always afraid they'd suddenly guess that I was a VENTURan, and turn on me. No one would defend me. My left-hand neighbour's hands wandered, which I tolerated if she waited until the lights went down. But I couldn't call it a bond of affection.

I pretended to be asleep or non-existent while 6 or 8 naked women jumped on their victim. She kicked them off and fell over me, her matted hair flying. I felt something sharp and hard jab me in the neck. I didn't make a sound. I lay there face down and half suffocated until the fight rolled away. When I dared to look up, the victim sat resentfully nursing her scored and bruised breasts. The rest of them were also counting their wounds, muttering sulkily. I looked in the crook of my arm to see what it was that had stabbed me. It was a hair burner.

I put my hand over it very softly and pushed it under the bedding, in the narrow space between the edge of the palliasse and the fixative that held it to the floor. I had no plan: I just did it. Then I lay in terror waiting for the women to start searching for their treasure. I would pretend it had dropped there by accident.

But there was no search. They were still examining their bruises when a cry went up that something had gone wrong with our latrines. The trays ran on tracks out of the wall. Investigation of the slots by which they left the room dirty and came back clean was forbidden by our collars, not that there was much hope of escape through such a tiny gap. Now someone had noticed that the bed of granules had not been renewed. The dirt and piss from last light change was still there.

The Code Readers went on decoding.

We weren't sure when the latrines had stopped moving. We decided it hadn't been getting dark either. We thought we had missed 2 or maybe 3 'days'. It was hard to be sure. But a short while later — perhaps hours? — our dispensers died. We had no food or water. And then the room became very quiet. Quieter than the hangar had been under the stadium. The trouble with basics is that they are not afraid, never afraid enough: not terrified the way I am. Shut in the dark room with the walls closing in they don't scream, they don't kick out and shout for help. They have great faith in death. Or else, if the trapped darkness only goes on, I suppose they think they can bear that too.

I trusted in VENTUR. Whatever was happening, as sure as the Rangers would have briskly terminated us without a qualm if it had been appropriate; so they would not forget us now. They wouldn't leave the poor numbers to needless suffering. I was only afraid we might be despatched in some humane way right here.

We were not. The ulaux came, when it was beginning to get warm and I was beginning to imagine a heavy metallic taste in the air. They took us all out through the scrub into a blank walled corridor.

'Move on.'

We stumbled along. Doors hissed. Doors opened again, and again at the end of a short passage. Suddenly we were out in the open, plunged into sound and colour. The ulaux super walked along the line, passing her wrist over our collar seals and collecting the collars.

'You will be escorted to the access to lower levels of the centre,' she said rapidly. 'Make your way to your locations utilising the emergency ramps. Do not attempt to re-enter the upper level. You will be fired on.'

We did not react at all. We had forgotten that we could be spoken to, we only understood our collars.

We were in a huge hall, astonishingly decorated. The tall screens and pillars that elegantly arranged its space, the distant walls, were covered with what seemed to be holo projections. But they were not. It was all head-woven textile. Forests and clouds, stars, rainbows, flower gardens. Everywhere the exact rich piquancy of *gengra* – line and depth that is not of this world, that only lives in dreams.

I knew this place, though I'd never been in it. It was the Presidential concourse in the middle of wonderland: where the President would come to make her rare in-person appearance for the wonderlanders, in the basement of her palace. The hall was full of people. Hard suits chivvying groups of culturals, children crying, ulaux marching. A running figure in soft blue, talking to herself (apparently) and brushing off hands that tried to grab her. Trolley grubs piled high with bags and cartons tracked the floor, singing out their warning tones. The air was full of voices: cool, terse relays from inside the Mission overlaying the babble of the crowd.

So the Code Readers were right. But I had already accepted that. It was my only chance.

The wall beside me was a river shore. Low sunlight of evening fell glancing through small leaves. The water rippled, a deer had come down to drink. She raised her head and gazed at me with mild dark eyes. She was deformed. No ear, only half a jaw on the left-hand side. I looked up. I saw that everywhere the gengra was decaying. Colours degrading, outlines unravelling. 'Loyal Subs' hurried unheeding through the dissolution. So much of the stuff, it needed close packed light flow nearby to keep it alive.

*The systems are leaving this place.*

The naked prisoners stopped moving. They stared around. The ulaux couldn't shift them. Next moment, their joy was pitiful to see. They wept, they laughed, they hugged each other. They crowded round the Code Readers, who had predicted this wonderful event. The burst of happiness upset me. I wanted to warn them: this couldn't be victory. It couldn't be so simple. But I had no time. My mind was absolutely, extraordinarily clear. No room in my head for any thought but one. A train of grubs nosed through our disrupted line. I stepped behind it, crouched double and ran along. The head grub butted open a utility flap, invisible under its carefully matched gengra cover . . .

I looked back. The prisoners were hurrying without any escort towards an arch in a distant wall, where discreet UBIQ eyes above indicated a serial gate. Through that arch, listed enabled had entered the reception hall. Basic serials had never been allowed in here.

But the ex-prisoners were not interested in sightseeing. Only the Code Readers lingered. Their stale emaciated bodies very erect, they surveyed the dying splendour with bleak satisfaction. Then they too turned and walked steadily towards the gate. The last grub went through the flap and I went with it.

The noise didn't stop. I was in a narrow utility passage, still surrounded by crying, running feet, shouting and arguing, acronymic dialogue and signal over the top. The luggage train rattled away along the wall. I scrambled through a diaphragm and ran, still bent double, until I saw a cluster of little red sparks beside the faint light coming from the floor track. I crouched down in a bay full of cleaning grubs. I put my face between my knees. To abandon a major underworld Mission was a serious decision. I couldn't remember if a plenum vote would be called for, but all the systems would have to be consulted. The big sortie must have been a failure then. Perhaps the Rangers didn't want to go, they still thought they could find a solution; and that was why things were so confused now at the end. So many 'loyal Subs' to be carried away from the wrath of the SINDs.

The grubs huddled together, shuffling a little, small red sensors glowing low down on their snouts; wondering why today was different from other days. They were intelligent little machines, not like the Sub-cultural sweepers down below. Poor things, they weren't going back to SHACTI.

'Hello friend,' I said softly, as clearly as I could. The grub came to me, checked my hand with its snout. It was puzzled. It recognised the phonemes, but all it sensed was an object.

'Hold still friend.'

The others huddled closer together. I put my hand on its body, and leaned my weight to pin it down saying friend, friend all the time. It struggled uncertainly. I got my fingernail under the side panel and flicked it open easily. When they maintained each other the grubs only used a little suction to move it. I used my nails to lift out the motherboard. And for all I knew something somewhere set up an alarm, sealed me off and moved in to investigate. But I had seen the gengra failing. More likely the whole Presidential Palace would die round me as the Mission pulled in its facilities. I would be suffocated probably: I couldn't remember how the air was supplied.

I laid the board on the grub's dead back and took the little burner out of my hair. I pulled the tag down from my ear and laid it against the minute sliver of crystal that held the grub's comparatively large and clumsy brain. Twisted the hairburner to its finest point and drew a line. It was about as dainty, in microcosm, as the gouge left by a ton of passing meteor. The GRUB in this cleaner was exactly the same as the one in a wristfax: sentenced to a lifetime of devastating underemployment. It had, I hoped, accepted my number as input when my tag touched it; as a wristfax would. Then I smashed a hole through the lobes of its poor brain and now, if I'd judged right, it thought it *was* the input. I replaced the board and the panel. I had probably suffocated the poor thing in grease. Modern crystal repels dirt, but there are limits. Its red eyes brightened. At least I hadn't killed it. Sorry, friend.

First I was a serial. Then I was a thing in a collar, then I became a cleaning grub. So we set out. The Presidential Palace joined the Mission. The structure was continuous, except that the President herself couldn't get through the dividing field. But the grubs passed to and fro, I reckoned. And I believed the field wouldn't

198

stop a grub unless it detected something hazardous planted in it. If it wouldn't stop the grub, it wouldn't stop something with the same emission. Me. There were no location signs on the walls in here. All I could do was try to recall the library maps I'd studied long ago: for what little information they gave about the orientation of this enclave. I followed the faint track, gently driving my alter ego ahead of me. It couldn't resist. It couldn't tell itself apart.

Whenever we came to a diaphragm or a junction, the utilities asked – who goes there? – Me, said the grub, and we got by. My eyes strained at the thin reddish glow. I closed them and managed better in the dark. Sometimes diaphragms started to fold on me, but I managed to wriggle through. Sometimes I imagined I was getting short of breath, and that was very frightening.

The running commentary never stopped. I could identify at least four sources. The Palace, the Mission itself, SHACTI; and another, which I guessed was the Mission emart access.

For so long I had been trying to get out. Out of the centre, out of the processing, out on to the surface. That was my mistake. The problem wasn't getting out, it was getting in. I fell out of VENTUR, fell into the churning peopled void. No one inside knew I had gone. Everything meant for my safety had turned against me. My only chance was if VENTUR, for some reason, was not giving full attention to its defences.

I had climbed up a level. I ought to be in the Dome. I pushed open 2 flaps and found draining light and failing gengra walls on the other side. I crouched at a third, afraid to push it. I pressed gently until I could see through the crack. I saw the junction of 2 sleek undecorated corridors. At eye-level, on the corner, a small green, brown and blue spheroid turned gently, wrapped in white lace.

I had to leave the grub behind, it couldn't come out of the utilities. It was very distressed. I hoped some other little machine would come along and be able to repair what I'd done.

There was no one in sight. Silence haunted by a hustling crying crowd, and short commands taken and given. I followed one of the corridors at random.

CAN NPE UPLINE/we don't want their pee. It's all over the place —

CANDO PEDOWN

The Subs were being told they couldn't take any personal effects.

Recklessly, I was stepping on every doorsill. I almost fell into a long room full of consoles. One wall lined with monitors, another glowing with the Sub in lights, the 3D image alternating between number centres, and surface features. It was just what I wanted. Odd to see this place so deserted, in the middle of the Mission's greatest crisis. First problem. To get myself on an emart car, when the personnel transfer was undoubtedly only set up for listed serials. There were cartons of plastic and metal piled up around the Commander's station on a deck in the middle of the room. I saw a stack of lasarms lying as if they'd been thrown there. I picked one up, it was fully charged. I was shocked. I'd better drain these, or the SINDs will have them . . .

I rubbed my eyes. Mustn't let myself get disoriented. Holding the arm I'd picked up I sat down at a console. It was alive. All the screens in here were alive, but empty. Like children waiting quietly for someone to come and fetch them.

HELLO — I broke off, scanned my memory frantically. What does it call itself here? Oh, stupid: HELLO SUBCAP.

On a cultural interface I needed a coded handshake, to prove I was a person not a number. But I was past that entry level here, just by being inside the reac. The game is getting in.

HELLO FRIEND

SUBCAP. I need a listing for another serial on the SHACTI transfer. If I read you the number can you do that for me?

FRIEND, IM AFRAID I DONT RECOGNISE YOU.

I chewed my fist, ready to run.

BUT I SUPPOSE THATS MY FAULT sang the station cheerily. I'M GETTING A LITTLE CONFUSED BECAUSE OF WHATS HAPPENING HERE› PLEASE USE MY CLUSTERS!

I wrote.

SORRY FRIEND. EVOP SET COMP SUBCAP TT LIMFAX UPTO DISCON.

The lists were closed, and out of my reach. For a moment I stared. *There'll be another way.*

Do you still have the CHTHON gazetteer? I wrote. Yes, it did.

The Code Reader had located Millie in a study centre near SHACTI: and that was when I believed her. There were very few of those installations on the Sub. The culturals hated the idea so much, it was only rational to do most of our research on blocs where the issue wasn't so sensitive. But I knew there was a centre up on the alt wall. Thi SETI had reminded me, when she was explaining why I couldn't go shooting on the wild life preserve. I had made a fool of myself, complaining about it.

For a moment I stood on the golden deck, breathed cedar scented air. There was only one number research centre in the whole north-west. Why did it have to get in my way? . . . There was only one place where Millie could be, if she was still alive.

I had no authority to get direct data on a serial subject. But I could access the entry in the gazetteer, which was interactive. I might then − I shut the sound off. I could bet no one would notice my addition to the general babble on the lightlines, but somebody might walk by the door and hear SUBCAP talking to itself. I made up a little procedure and sent it to sneak about the autonomics. The evidence was conclusive. The SIND crisis must have slowed everything down. This lab had not terminated any of its experimental material in the past 2 years 6x30. I searched no further.

If she's there, she's still alive.

It was only then that I realised what I had been doing. I looked at my hands on the clusters. So this was what it felt like, to be ALIC again. It was nice to know that she could still talk machine.

If SUBCAP had not been dying, it could have carried me to R4. I could have recovered my VENTURan self. I could try it, anyway . . .

I took my hands off. SUBCAP waited, patient and alert. I could hear someone walking up the corridor.

'Goodbye friend,' I said softly. 'I'm glad I had a chance to say goodbye.'

Something landed with a thump on the palloy floor. Without thinking I got up and crouched quietly behind the station. A figure in a Ranger's soft suit was standing by the door. She picked up a lasarm and checked it. Her helmet moved, scanning the piled equipment. The thing she had dropped on the floor was a pair of gas flatpacks, bright blue and beaded with condensation. Lox from an emergency air unit. The weapon and the oxygen made things abundantly clear. She seemed lost in thought. Then I saw that she was looking at the monitor wall: at a screen on which a grotesque naked creature lurked behind a row of clean shining consoles. I scuttled for the door.

All that customised, specialised physical machine. It was no use anywhere else, so there was no point in carrying it away even if they could. I didn't wait for the explosion. It caught me and shook me when I was two floors further down.

Extra ulaux levies had been sleeping in the corridors. I stumbled over bedrolls and half-eaten food. I saw a heap of hard suits at a junction, sprayed with chemical disolvent and greasily smouldering. From under semi-sealed doors white fumes came seeping, the contents inside destroying themselves obediently. Plastic alloy and metalglass fusing, crystal and polymer and ceramics withering into dust. SUBCAP Mission was going by the manual, however little use the SINDs might make of anything left behind.

The emart access was empty and dark. A grub was collecting in white emergency lamps from up and down the platforms. It came back to the head of the line slowly. There were no clumsy shutters here. The access was elegantly naked, glistening curves between the platforms and sheer arches above, melting into deep shadow. The discreet lights of safety fields were winking off one by one. Abandoned bags and cases of serial possessions lay scattered and burst open, the grub nudged them aside apologetically. A single trolley was moving vaguely to and fro near the tunnel mouths, whining a little. They had gone. There was one cylinder left, a blurred silver shape up at the end of platform 3. It seemed strange it should be left behind, but it was no use to me. I had been hiding behind a pile of cartons, below the area where lifts and ramps came down, watching the basic ulaux leaving. I should have lured one of them into the dark, overpowered him, disguised myself in his hard suit. I should have used my lasarm to burn the tag from my ear, fallen on one of the loyal Subs and ripped off her serial . . .

My arms and legs were shaking, I felt lightheaded. The containment ration was not meant to support exertion. The reac field would decompose now. I could find my way back to the levels. How pitiful to think of the whole great centre, all the screens empty and everybody waiting. But there was nothing for me there. The people I loved were dead and whether the Reroute was won or lost, I couldn't do anything for the 6 millions. There was only one thing for me to do. Reach the woman who gave my Pia back her humanity, and help her if I could.

It would be a joke if she really was the star traveller, world rescuer. Who would imagine On ALIC R4 being elected for a job like this? *Can't find anybody, so you'll have to do.'*

I wondered how far grim determination would take me up an emart tunnel towards SHACTI. I knew I would try it. I could keep on going, it was only thinking I couldn't do. The only problem was how long would it take me to make myself start. It must be soon. These tunnels would seal when SUBCAP finally went down.

Someone sighed. I lifted my face, and saw a blue suit stepping down from the end of the ramp above me. I had not heard her boots. She had a grub beside her, carrying her bedroll and a small bright clip case with the CHTHON logo on it. She took off her helmet and turned to look behind her. In a moment I heard footsteps and she was joined by several others. There were no ulaux with them. The supple home built suits were lustre bright, must have been their dress uniform. The little group looked oddly formal, like people going to a funeral. I looked for the Commander or Exec, leaving last in the ancient tradition: but couldn't see their ID. Maybe it was true that they had both been killed in the 'evacuation' abort. The SINDs had always said so. The women talked a little in tired, muted voices. I heard that the last cylinder was not going to SHACTI. SHACTI ax was blocked with ulaux and loyal Subs. These Rangers would go 'up to the wall', and take a surface connection back to the Ridge . . .

I must have made some sound. One of them turned and saw me. At least I was dressed this time. I had been rifling the discarded luggage. I was wearing a thing like a sheer in two pieces, of gengra, with a bunch of extra material down the front, and over it a pair of stylish pyjamas (I thought it might be cold outside). I stood up. I laughed nervously.

A young woman stared at me: black eyes in a haughty white face. Not so young. It was a face like mine, a haggard 17yearold. She looked tired to death, her bare head greasy with sweat; the drag of unrelenting fatigue around her eyes and mouth. She reminded me of Thi SETI. She might be a menarch, she had that custom-built air. I looked for her patch. She had torn it off. Of course. It said 'SUBCAPITAL'.

I used to think about the SubCapital Rangers. I would fantasise, if I could access one of them somehow: I could explain everything, mediate.

To the real woman I said, 'Oh, Ranger I'm glad to see you. I missed my emart —'

She gave me a hard look, motioned me forward; pulled off a gauntlet and took my tag. Which was rude, if I was supposed to be one of her loyal enabled. She saw the collar mark on my throat.

'What's this?'

'Please help me! I didn't do anything. I was captured by mistake. Take me with you — I daren't go back to the levels. The SINDs are killing people down there —'

She had dropped my tag. Suddenly her face distorted. She lunged at me.

'You funxing mindless SIND! You — it's people like you —'

'Commander! Commander!'

They pulled her off. They quieted her, and looked at me with anger and helplessness. They never wanted to see another Sub serial as long as they lived. One of them took hold of me by the shoulder, wincing at the smell of my body. She pulled out my tag and used her teeth to open a channel on her wrist: SHACTI. Ax TR + 1. Sub serial. She took the tag and touched it on the contact.

The first woman's face appeared, thrusting forward.

'D'you get any satisfaction?' she shouted. 'What satisfaction d'you get —?'

I could see the emart cylinder up at the tunnel mouth. I knew I was being crazy but I couldn't help myself. While the Rangers were distracted, I broke and ran. Propelled by terror I jumped the first drive bed, and my head turned all by itself. I saw a woman with her head down, carefully adjusting the setting on her weapon. The furious Commander was struggling for possession of what looked like an underworld rifle.

I slipped and scrambled on to the other side. I ran with my knees pumping and arms flailing, felt a terrible sensation in my right leg. Not pain, a hollow hard core surrounded by needles. I fell on it. I got up again. I ran but then the pain suddenly spurted and my leg seemed to disappear below the knee. I fell down again.

When I opened my eyes I was in the emart cylinder, lying on my back in the aisle between two rows of seats. The seats faced backwards. They all had knee rolls and safety harness. VENTUR. I was alone in the car except for my guard. She was sitting a row or 2 beyond my feet with her hands clasped between her knees and her head hanging. Another junior executive doing her tiresome CHTHON tour. She was probably thinking about her ruined career. And why not. She was really young, this one. Half my age. I studied the curves of her cheek and jaw, the graceful balance of her skull on the stem of the medulla. It was stupid of me to run like that. I hadn't a chance of taking over the emart. And even if I had, I couldn't have left the Rangers behind. A tear crawled out of the corner of my eye. I moved my hand to wipe it, and she looked up briefly with no interest at all. I lost consciousness again. Someone had stunned me humanely while I lay on the platform, but whatever had happened to my leg was another matter.

When I next woke we were still moving, silently, and almost without a sensation of speed. The viewports were not playing any scenery to normalise our sense of travel. They were black. It seemed as if we could go on rocking faintly through the blackness forever. The Ranger was asleep, slumped across 2 seats. I watched her for a short time, then I moved my hands under me and began to inch my way down the aisle. The pain around my knee was bad, but bearable. I took the lasarm from where it was propped against her thigh, and turned off the discharge warning. I drew it down and cradled it on my chest. I rested the chargepack against my sternum, covered my eyes with my free arm and fired it at the roof of the car where the tracking lines ran. I went on firing until the emart carefully brought itself to a halt. The emergency doors released with soft little sighs. I rolled over and got up on my good leg. The guard, reflected in a black porthole, was staggering to her feet. We are sorry for this delay said the emart reassuringly. Please remain in your seats. If exit lights flash, please leave the car and go to the nearest relief bay, following relief bay signlights.

'I'll shoot you —' I cried.

She was between me and the doors. I could have wept. I pitched myself down the aisle and hit out at her in baffled fury, because it was madness not to fire, at least try and disable her. But I couldn't do it. I struggled and fell into empty space, fell on to something, screamed as it hit my knee. I looked up, and saw that the doors had closed. The tunnel sucked its silver missile onwards, I wailed, thinking I was going to be smeared along its side. The cylinder whipped by. I was lying on a grub contact plate, about half a yard wide, up against the curve of the tunnel wall. I slipped and slithered trying to get upright. Using the lasarm for a crutch I dragged myself until space opened against my right hand, and crawled into the hole.

+

My back was against a tunnel wall. There was no light. I groped cautiously down my thigh towards my right knee. A bone seemed to be fractured just below in some messy way, certainly not by a beam weapon. The angry Commander must have used her rifle on me. Someone had wrapped up the break roughly. Was that me? The gengra flourish, I discovered, was gone from the front of my clothes. Yes, I remembered now. I remembered telling Pia she must wait for me to strap it up. We were in the casting bore. Pia hustled me on. She was afraid, something terrible would happen if we didn't hurry. In one hand I clutched the lasarm. Pia had the other, tugging on me. 'Where's Ram? I asked anxiously.

*'He's all right. You'll see him again.'*

Her hand in mine was so light, such a fragile presence. Like holding nothing. I wanted my plant too, the one I rescued on DAY THIRTY, but Pia wouldn't wait . . .

The plant died. We could live on the air and light in the levels but it couldn't manage, not for long. I began to sob weakly. I remembered that I wasn't with Pia in a casting bore. She was dead. I would never see her again.

My apology for a dressing was sticky, but the bleeding seemed to have stopped. I had no idea what I had been doing, what turns I had taken. I was totally lost in the maze of unadopted tunnels off an emart line: a network that CHTHON might need but did not yet. I didn't even know what part of the aft wall the Rangers had been routed for. I wished the hallucinations could have gone on. It wasn't going to be much fun dying in here sober.

Millie, are you satisfied now? The first moment you saw me you set out to destroy me. All that production about breaking through the event horizon and living forever, it was just a lie. It could be true, you were lying anyway. You and I know what you really wanted. You couldn't bear to see me happy, could you. You took it all away from me — so systematically. You started there in the parking lot. You destroyed the world I thought I lived in, dragged me down into the seriate and left me to rot. You took the machines away and wouldn't let them talk to me, you took my own head and hands. You wouldn't let me a VENTURan or a SIND or anything. And I thought you'd done all that to me so I could love Pia and not be ashamed.

Oh no, you had to go on taking and taking. Took Pia and killed her. And now you won't even let me die in peace. What did I ever do to you Millie? I suppose you think if you smiled at me across the room again, I'd still just get up and follow —

I hate you Millie . . .

But all the while I knew. I remembered still the moment that I walked into that cramped box of a room. The bedshelf, the sour stains, the taste and smell of that exhausted air. And a voice in me that whispered *this is what I want*. I didn't understand. I was frightened of Millie because she seemed to know what I was thinking. I was glad when she was gone, but Yolande brought her back again: and I couldn't stop the process. It was like a drug, that goes straight to a centre in the brain you didn't know was there. I had been hungry for this all my life. To be free. To be only human, stripped and bare. Nothing to hold me down . . . Clever Yolande, never said how much it was going to hurt. Never said how much it was going to cost, the thing that burnt her face to light and bones. I hate you Millie. But it's no use hating you, because *this is what I want . . .*

I was lurching along, on the lasarm crutch and my good leg, muttering to myself and cursing Millie Mohun. I noticed that the ground had become very rough underfoot. The tunnel had been unfinished since I woke up, just a flat bottomed bore through rock. But now I was stepping around boulders. They were outlined in a faint bluish-white luminescence like no lighting I could remember. Making an effort to shut off the mumbling (though it was the only thing that was holding me upright), I tried to think what I might be walking into. I stopped and reached out one arm and then the other, but failed to touch a wall. I looked up, and saw the stars.

# Let 100 Flowers Bloom

There was a channel of water flowing in the ground near by. I drank from it, crawled back to the tunnel mouth and collapsed there. After a while a dim haze started to spread away on my right. Another interval, and small bars of bright red appeared, defining an irregular horizon. Colour came in slow waves, each stronger than the last, until the sky was full of light and every star had vanished but for one. I watched all this lying against the rocks in blissful helplessness, detached even from the pain in my leg. Looking down at my hands I noticed with amazement the peculiar greyish ochre colour of my skin. It reminded me of something long dead, frozen in a lab.

Later I tried to reduce the fracture, in a spirit of enlightened self interest. But I had to give up because I was only making myself sick. I thought of splints, but there weren't any convenient slivers of plastic lying around.

The huge open space awed and frightened me and I couldn't remember whether the sun's apparent movement was west to east or the other way round, so I waited for darkness. But I knew I must hurry. I had forgotten for the moment why, I just had a fearful urge to keep moving. I found polaris, made a rough calculation of the precessional. I knew I had to go north, the terrain told me I hadn't crossed the alt wall. What happened next I don't know. I was exhausted, and my natural opiates had dumped me. It was a long time since I'd taken any response enhancer, or had a decent diet. My leg hurt so I couldn't see, I must have been out of my mind or I would never have tried to use it.

Big dark shapes loomed close on either side. The stars in a broad ribbon. I had stumbled into a wild number settlement. The blur cleared a little and I saw in starlight boardwalks lined with slender wooden columns. I could smell people, different and sharper than the smell of the seriate. Everything was still. I reached an ellipse of fused earth, made my way with savage determination to the focus where a lozenge of alloy was set in the ground. It was the conplate, which would open when CHTHON's dumper arrived from below to disgorge MEDICaids and food supplements. I fell against an agam plinth beside it, and read the co-ordinates on the sealed display bar let into the top.

211

I was in SHACTI's hills. A loc points north of the Ridge.

The dark ellipse and the sky began to spin. I put my hand on what I thought was a lump of rock. It started violently and shouted in a hoarse inarticulate voice. I grabbed my laser crutch and tried to run — thinking of weird half-human creatures covered in hair.

But the wild numbers took pity on me when they found me. They carried me to one of their wooden houses and there I lay for 4 days, while those PRENAT bone marrow treatments everybody so resents went to work. How bitterly we could sulk at home over a tiny grievance like PRENAT's share of our taxes. The Reroute had reached these people distantly. They thought the Commanders 'would win', though there was one bright spark who'd torn her ear. She was reviled whenever she appeared and pelted with vegetable litter, but gave back as good as she got. Let CHTHON discount that entry. She didn't understand what she was doing.

The floor I lay on was wood, the passage outside was packed mud and open to the sky. The water I drank was carried from a river. It was so strange. I ate earth. For though they hardly knew anything about the behaviour of the centres, they understood CHTHON wasn't pleased, so they didn't feel they could give me any of their supplement. I didn't mind the grainy mush. I didn't particularly care for the arsenide green vegetable stuff. Like eating hot wet fragments of print-out. There were no celebrations due, so I avoided the worst.

I kept asking them the yearday. At first they looked so blank I decided they didn't measure time at all, then I got a date by the old earth calendar. It was near to 180. I tried to put together my recent past. Had I been in the room under the palace for 30 days? I couldn't work out whether that was too long or too short. But it made me feel better to have some hold on the world again. And now, in the capital, the Subs were rejoicing because they'd driven VENTUR away. They still had life support. The errors were not fatal and might never be. SERVE would repair the ulaux damage. Perhaps the attack from the Mission had even stopped their infighting for a while.

The wild people were unnerved when I got up and started

walking about. When they saw the leg would really carry me, they became very alarmed. They were brave enough to tend a fugitive, but this kind of rebellion was too extreme. I left them doing whatever wild numbers do to placate the ever watchful sky.

They kept the laser's chargepack, which was a blow although I hadn't planned to use it as a weapon. In return I had a kind of flattened out bedroll of greasy brown felt, wrapped around me and fastened up with a lot of cord. It smelt strong but I needed the extra warmth. I never took it off, I wouldn't have known how to get back inside.

I knew my location. I took a heading that ought to lead me to the SHACTI recreation preserve. It was a shock to realise how long this was going to take. If I had been thinking rationally at all when I was trying to get out of the capital, it was in terms of immediately arriving at Millie's prison.

I fell in love with the underworld all over again. The sky, the mountains, the clouds. I followed little footpaths that must have been made by the wild people, though I didn't meet many. I passed through patches of ground where they grew their 'earth'. Sometimes in the distance I saw great stretches of orderly ADAPT food plant, with machines sparkling in the sunlight as they tended it.

It was all so beautiful I was very sad to think I was leaving it. But I had made my choice. I looked for the starship in every fold of the ground. The glow of moonrise was very deceptive, and there could be no other explanation for the flashing lights of dawn. I imagined the great dark docking bay opening and the people walking in. And, my shiftmate from SHACTI. Dat, Ajoy, Himem and her children. Pompous old capital Himem too, and Ram of course. I supposed we'd have to take Yolande. And so many, many other faces. If I could only get to Millie, we would all be safe. We would make our homes in the unimaginable distance. Pia would be there too. This starship wouldn't get the causation flow wrong. Pia had made the transition, I was sure she had . . .

Other times, I wondered what hope I had of doing anything. I didn't know what state Millie would be in, or how the funx I was going to tackle the lab security . . . But the starship mood was better. It covered more ground.

I had to find wild settlements to check my location and beg for food. They were few and scattered and tiny. I was climbing always towards the high altitude wall and the absolute wilderness. They knew less and less about the Reroute, about anything but their own lost little worlds. They were still 'Subs'. Some of the women had gruesome handmade mutilations on their heads, set with gold rings. It was startling to remember that the processing alteration predated CHTHON. This wild natural life was as synthetic as Thi SETI's leopards. But the people themselves seemed to have accepted it completely. Nominally they understood the Function idea. In practice they personified CHTHON and SERVE and whatever other system touched them, in the usual ignorant non-Sub way.

The old women sat around the water pump and the communal 'sun-storer' cookhouse, smoking and spitting and criticising the world. They asked me, 'Are you a Millie?' and I remembered it had all started out on the surface, in these hills. When I said no, they jeered. I must be a Millie. If I was one of those disconnected-corrupted Rerouters I'd have better shoes on my feet, and I'd have more pride than to beg where I could steal. Not me, said I. Never heard of her. It seemed safest. But then I was asked: 'Are you with that other one? That other Millie . . .'

The implication — I tried not to think of it. It was just too good to be true.

Seasonal rain drenched me, the sun steamed me dry. Once I slept in a deserted hovel of stones, but after that I lay in the open if I couldn't find any natural shelter. In the mornings, I would wake out of a dream of terrifying vertigo and find my hands clutching earth. But the fear passed, as I began to feel that vast sky as a secure canopy. At night I watched a netted cluster of silver, brighter than the Pleiades, following in the orbit of the moon. Nostalgia pricked my eyes.

The emptiness was alarming. You heard of meetings in places like this, with strange beautiful humanoid entities: SERVE's *peris* going about their mysterious errands. I wasn't sure I

214

believed in spontaneous projections, but a lot of people claim _d to have seen them.

The watching sky didn't trouble me. There was no sense in trying to hide. If SERVE knew what I was doing, it ought to help me, not turn me in.

+

I was alone, under a soft opalescent floor/ceiling. Fortunately it was summer again for this latitude, but now there were patches of compacted grey crystal in sheltered hollows on either side of my path. Not far away, or rather not far above, there would be little left of the green, or the ochre and rust and blue. But my felt bedroll was still holding a good envelope of bodily warmth. Fine mist condensed against my face and hands. When I looked back, I could see tiny fields of wild apricot trees. I had picked up one of the fallen fruits and kept it for a while. Holding the soft bloom against my cheek was like touching a child. There was a minute settlement down there, too small to have a loc point. I had asked if anyone knew of a Commanders' installation up above. Rephrase that: Does CHTHON have a Housing there? I had learned to understand a few of their expressions. They said yes. It was over the wall, where they were forbidden to go because of the horrific wild animals which only CHTHON could control. What kind of place is it? Oh, frightening, frightening.

They weren't surprised that I wanted to visit CHTHON. It was a thing they would do themselves. They liked to wander about and look at any of the remote installations you could find along the Threshold, even though these generally had nothing to do with number support. To look, and perhaps to feel memories stirring. But though no one admitted the place was a 'study centre', this one they would not approach. That excited me. There was a graded Rover trail going up the pass. I looked at it with misgiving though glad of the confirmation that there was something VENTURan nearby. The wild people showed me their own path. It was a wet perpendicular rock slide: a short cut to another settlement in the next valley. I took it.

I had been climbing about 2 hours from the huts when

disaster struck. A piece of shale slithered. I tripped and fell and lost my left slipper. When I found it the sole was split right across, only the webbing upper holding it together. My benefactors in the first settlement hadn't given me any shoes. I sat on a rock and tried first to chew a piece off the cord that bound my smelly wrapper, then to abrade it on a sharp edge. The stones were cold as ice to my bare foot. The cord defeated me, the brief effort made me feel weak, a reminder of the altitude I'd reached. I mentally contemplated the remains of my enabled costume. I'd lost most of one leg already when the wild people were tending my fracture, and the gengra shirt had been quietly unravelling ever since I pulled its ruffles off.

The slipper was not at fault. It was a tribute to Sub processing that it had lasted so long. A dispenser pressie would have collapsed and died days ago. But how could I get on, barefoot?

Climbing, I'd heard nothing but my own noise. Now in the quietness I became aware of a distant regular sound. I looked across the steep meadow and saw beneath me a diagonal stretch of graded trail. There were several small black shapes moving purposefully to and fro between heaps of irregular rocks. They fed their hoppers with sturdy claws, and trundled out into the roadway munching as they went. There they disgorged even pebbles and rolled the new surface down. They looked very contented. SHACTI interfaces were still processing quite routinely, while I was lost out here and the Rerouters defiant down below. I wondered where my stone breakers had been. Nice to think that all the time I imagined I was trapped and tortured I was really trotting to and fro beside a green alpine meadow.

Down in the huts I'd been asked again if I was with the other Millie. Evidence was growing: there was another stranger wandering in this area, begging her food, perhaps confused or injured. *Could* she have escaped? She might, in extremity, have powers she would use . . .

I thought about how tired I was, and the chilliness of the air on my bare ankles. I knew I wasn't going to rescue anyone, alien or not. I wasn't sure any more whether the Code Reader had really told me Millie was still alive. My memory of the containment was very patchy. It was strange that the wild numbers talked like that though. Perhaps they saw me coming, like the daysky dealers in the old capital: and made up the 'other Millie' for fun.

The meadow was full of flowers. I laid my head back on the steep bank beside the path and turned a cheek against the wet stone. Just by me 3 blue poppies grew in a clump of notched glaucous leaves. Each flower had 4 petals around a core of gold. I had never seen such vivid tender colours. Not even in the President's hall of dreams.

I wondered whether people in VENTUR watched the Reroute at all. UBIQ had never stopped collecting. Anyone with PIONER status could have accessed us. What did they think when they saw the pride and joy in CENTRIN hall? This is good, they thought. The numbers are expressing their feelings. We should arrange these relaxations from time to time: it's a healthy purgative. SERVE was right to let the Reroute happen.

Free SIND had almost hypnotised me sometimes while I was in it. I was even concerned for the fate of the Rangers' new forests. I knew now they had never been in danger. The Rangers had retired to SHACTI, leaving the poor numbers locked in where they had tried to lock VENTUR out. In the end they would have to surrender. CHTHON would never let them go.

And the Subs would go on decoding. Patiently, they would extract and analyse the details of their own defeat. They did not approve. I had heard the Code Readers in containment agreeing sternly (I had to smother my hysterical laughter) *not to verify* Function's atrocious behaviour. But they could not escape. If any of the rest of us had been so shabbily treated we would have pulled the plug on the system concerned and built ourselves another one. The Subs had not left themselves that option. They didn't deal with human constructs, they dealt with the Design. No place to stand outside it.

That was what I wanted from Millie Mohun: another place. Where I could get away from pain and loss and guilt. After the emart tunnels, when I saw the sky again, I thought it was all true. A part of me was still wondering now, why I hadn't vanished off the face of the underworld. But where could I go? It follows, if we can have probability tunnels through the horizon (and I couldn't

217

fault the logic), then there is no 'big outside' where the rules are different. If we had ever managed to escape from the bubble in a VENTURan ship we would not seriously have expected that death would cease to operate when we switched the engines into hyperdrive.

Yet Yolande did not invent the bright promise out of reach, nor did our mythic ancestors. These are the eternal verities: good/evil, life/death. And the knowledge that we live already in a world where time and separation are meaningless concepts, and event horizons don't exist. Where there is no destruction, only a ceaseless diaspora of creation on creation. We suspected its existence somehow when we were children. We found it eventually − in all those zillions of events that make up our own reality. *But we cannot get at it.*

No wonder Yolande used to say − if you're not shocked by what I'm telling you, you haven't understood it. She was claiming that the secret fabric of the universe is human. Human personality isn't something we have to get rid of, to be one with the one system. What we experience as our selves; frail and confused essence, is actually the ceaseless dance in us.

Where Nothing is real, where Nothing ever happens . . .

White mist wraiths chased each other playfully across the green grass: my eyes were closing. I heard myself murmuring sleepily. *It's very nice in this meadow Millie. Let's you and me and Pia just stay here.* I had tried to stop myself having imaginary conversations with Pia. I didn't want to deny what had happened to her. I owed her more respect than that. But sometimes I couldn't help myself: she was with me. In a silence like this, it might even be true.

I sat up. The empty hillside was so quiet I was afraid of it. I stood on top of the bank and looked around: for what, I don't know. I stuffed my broken slipper into the front of my wrapper and began to climb quickly. It was some minutes before I noticed I was climbing on grass. I had left the path. I turned back hurriedly but I couldn't see it. The opal cloud had come down. I couldn't see anything in any direction but a few standard feet of preternaturally green grass and glowing enamelled flowers. I stood listening to a sound that had suddenly materialised. The roar of snow water running off a glacier, booming in the bottom of a deep and narrow hollow space.

I panicked. That is to say, I told myself I must keep going straight up hill, and the noise would warn me if a gorge was about to open underfoot. I hurried, I scrambled. In a few seconds I'd fallen and broken my envelope of warmth. My wrapper was soaked from rolling in the wet grass, my bare foot was going numb. I deserved to break my neck. Instead there loomed, on my eye level horizon, a row of blurred cairns. I pulled myself up over the edge of the trail and stood gasping with relief.

I must have nearly reached the head of the pass. The far side of the track was a thick crusted and yellowed wall of last season's snow, twice as high as my head. A cold, penetrating chill came off it. I thought I would rest and eat a bit of the solid grain mush I'd carried with me from below. I would try to tear off some of my remaining pyjama leg to wrap my foot. I could hear roaring again, like the distant mutter and shuffle of a crowded passageway. I swallowed, shook my head and banged at my ears. The roaring grew louder. A shape began to form in the mist. It looked as big as a block of wells, it glowed with lights −

The rover diminished to its normal size and pulled up. It had to. I was standing in the middle of the track with my mouth open, too close for it to take off. A woman got down, wearing a dark blue coverall, a felted jacket and a curious matted cap with handles like ears. She stared at me then walked up and took the laser crutch. It had no chargepack, it was probably damaged beyond recovery, but it was not entirely unrecognisable.

'Get in.'

The back section of the rover was stripped and bare, with fragments of grade rock rolling about in it. Not much like the vehicles I used to know. I sat on the floor, behind the woman and her driver. There was no partition, everything unnecessary had been removed.

'Where are you taking me?'

'To the lock up.'

We reached the top of the pass. I could see through the wraparound another graded trail leading away into the fearsome and beautiful trans-alt. I craned my neck and saw blue earth logos hovering at the junction. Not far below, on a bare wash of shale, there was a squat black block about the same size as this rover and surrounded by a square of winking field markers. I peered at it around the driver's shoulder until the trail rose up behind and shut off my view.

'Is there a CHTHON installation back there?'

The hat turned round. A flat, brownish-yellow face expressed amazement at all these impertinent questions.

'Yes.'

'What is for?'

'It studies the mag-net-ism.'

She turned back to the road. 'Numbers like to hang things on the field,' she remarked threateningly. 'Little things for the system. But I shoot them if they try. I am not tol-er-ant.'

The trail jack-knifed downwards. In a short time, broad terraces of ADAPT apricot and apple stock grew low on either side. We drove into a surface settlement. It was larger than the others I'd seen. It had a CHTHON node, and I had been captured by the user.

She took me into her office, read my tag and entered it on her worksheet. She added details of my capture in possession of a piece of restricted equipment, with the careful enunciation of someone not entirely happy with machines. Then she escorted me in a small lift up to passage level and beyond.

'Where am I?'

'This is Mohun.'

She put me in an upper room with four battered hardmoulded bunks, agam walls and a square hole in one of them barred with dully gleaming palloy. The bunks had no closures. There was a lumpy mechanical lock on the door. She spoke to a sensor patch beside it.

I understood there was another prisoner who was going to join me. Then she left.

I sat on one of the bunks. My leg ached and I felt dazed. It had been extremely stupid of me to let myself be captured. About 10 days of freedom, as far as I could make out. Was I tired of it already?

I had lost my way. The recreation preserve was north of

SHACTI. This was north-west. I tried to remember the loc points I had been following, but I couldn't. I must have set my course for Mohun unconsciously: as if I knew Millie would head for home. How had she escaped? It didn't matter, she was here. Something had collapsed, I thought. I stared at the walls, finding it difficult to understand them. My head felt as it it was packed with MEDIC film. I was very glad Millie was alive and safe. But now nobody (grief welled up inside) would take me to the stars . . .

The door slid open and snicked shut. I waited, feeling ridiculously uneasy, for the other prisoner to speak. I had forgotten what she looked like. She sighed, with manifest irritation.

'Oh, it's you,' she exclaimed bitterly. 'What in the world are you doing here?'

I looked up startled. It wasn't Millie at all, it was Yolande.

+

She was better dressed than I was. She had a soft suit of enabled make under her felt, and a sturdy pair of boots on her feet. Her face glistened with the grease the wild people used to keep their skin from cracking in the cold. Her crown was growing out in tufts, her fringe locks braided in the wild numbers' style. One side of her face was puffy and darkening under the grease, in fact she looked as if she'd recently been beaten up rather severely.

I made this inventory while Yolande sat down on the opposite bunk and repeated her question. Her voice sounded thin and far away. I tried to speak, without success.

At last I quavered helplessly, 'I was looking for Millie.'

She patted my knee. But her eyes were on the cell door.

It jumped open. Two large male numbers appeared, clothed in an odd mixture of ulaux uniform and local dress. They seemed embarrassed about something, but they overcame their confusion sufficiently to take us both by the arms and hustle us into the lift.

Down in the office my poor mangled lasarm lay on the user's worktop, shedding mud and fragments of grass. At the back of

221

the room a door stood open, revealing another cell like the one up above. On the floor inside lay two quiescent heaps of metal and palloy.

'What have you done to my DOGs!' exclaimed the user.

'Nothing at all.'

Yolande stretched out her hand. 'They are merely sleeping.'

One after the other, the dead heaps came to life, trotted happily to Yolande and touched their sensitive snouts to her hand.

The wild males backed off smartly, rolling their eyes. The user held her ground, but she ran a finger round her collar, and swallowed nervously.

'There must be some natural explanation,' she muttered.

A bench of indeterminate substance, dark and greasy looking, stood against one wall. I went and sat down. I had a sudden intuition as to why Yolande was playing this silly game. But I could hardly believe it.

'Oh, there is.'

'What system are you?' whispered the user. 'Are you FUNDS? Is this because of my ledger? I can explain —'

'I am not a peri-projection, you stupid woman. I am a part of Function just as you are. And I'll thank you to remove that ridiculous hat. Have you forgotten this netnode is a Housing?'

The woman whipped her cap with ears off her head, and stood clutching it while Yolande advanced coolly. The node console stood rooted in the concrete floor, enclosed in a protective field. Here the wild people brought their new babies, here they came on any of those few occasions when their simple lives needed to transact with the systems. The user was very majestic then, summoning SERVE through her voice print sensor. But she had no power outside a small range of routine commands. At Yolande's touch, the field opened. The whole console began to glow impressively.

It sang out in a clear tone: 'HELLO FRIEND!'

Mohun's user made a fearful hissing noise, as if she'd just touched something extremely hot.

'You are a Pioneer!'

'Hello friend,' responded Yolande calmly, ignoring her. 'Will you tell these people who I am, please.'

She stopped the recital, cautiously, before it reached her current relationship with FUNDS.

User stared at her and at me, fingering the confiscated weapon.

'Is this one also a Pioneer of VENTUR?'

'No,' said I, wearily. 'I'm a PIONER of V2ENTUR. There's a slight difference.'

Yolande, even then, managed to give me what we call on the underworld a dirty look.

She forgot about me at once. 'Don't know it is part of your duty to give me all assistance I may require? If CHTHON itself calls me friend, whatever do you think you're doing? Letting those sweeper-brained pisstools mishandle me. Aren't you afraid —?'

The woman, totally cowed, gestured to the one plastic chair: sat on the floor in front of it, gazing up at Yolande humbly.

'Please tell me, Commander. Who *is* this "Millie Mohun" —?'

On my bench against the wall I put my head in my hands and groaned.

She had been out on the surface almost since I last saw her. She had known from the beginning that the Reroute was 'none of our business'. It was possibly a side-effect — a flare up on the worldline where the event of Millie's arrival finally collided with human consciousness. But no more than that. It was clearly impossible to work with Millie Command, their ideas were too pitifully localised. So Yolande took the emart to a small north-east centre where she had useful contacts and was smuggled on to the surface. Then she began her real work, telling the wild numbers that the star traveller had arrived. Explaining to them the extraordinary consequences for our perception of the universe: and the role played by rare trans-virtual particles in faster than light travel . . .

She told me this story when we were back in the upper room. The user, meanwhile, appeared with a tray of the finest food and drink, with pungent layered quilts for our comfort, with a pot of the best skin grease.

The last time I looked at wild number cosmology, they were all convinced that the planet earth revolves around VENTUR — identified with that very bright object in the daytime sky. The various little lights at night were considered a public amenity provided by SERVE. I said this to Yolande. I remarked that she had given herself a tough little project.

'But not quite so absurd,' she returned, 'as restricting the news of what's happened to the world, to a culture that decoded to go to war with VENTUR.'

Silence.

'I got out when the Mission left,' I muttered at last. 'Did you watch about that?'

She nodded.

'What's happening now?'

'No one can tell. Function only knows what's processing now, in the capital or any of the other Reroute centres. All the Missions are evacuated. We can only be glad it won't go on much longer.'

'What do you mean?'

Yolande shook her head, gave me a wry look. She mentioned the libration.

I felt suddenly cold.

I said, 'No.'

Yolande shrugged.

But I had known, from the moment I saw PORT destroyed. I just couldn't bear to face it. CHTHON could not accept surrender. We don't punish numbers, or forgive them. That's not the arrangement. I became furiously angry. I began to shout at Yolande. It was disgusting. Her culture was being destroyed and here she was peddling starships. Anyone could see in a world like this there was no star traveller, no rescue. Millie was a number and now she was dead. Only a complete shit like Yolande would carry on running this cynical make-believe —

I heard myself, I knew I was behaving exactly like the exCommander of SUBCAP, when she met me on the emart platform.

A gentle voice I didn't recognise at all said tenderly, 'Come on, Aeleysi. Lie down. You can rest now. There's nothing more to do.'

I have never thought of Yolande as a kind person, but she was good to me in that lock up. Her compassion was endearingly in character, with subterfuges to protect my ego; which she judged, obviously, to be as irritable as her own. The user was only too eager to send her august visitor on her way without preferring charges. The riot she'd caused, talking about Millie to the wild Subs, would go down on the worksheet as spontaneous combustion. But she couldn't release me even into a Pioneer's custody, because of the lasarm. So Yolande stayed. She said she couldn't let people beat her up and get away with it. She wanted the area LDRs to come and give her an in-person apology.

The user explained everyone was gated at present. Of course, movement restrictions didn't apply to Yolande but all ordinary numbers had to stay in their homes. The instruction had come the morning I arrived: that was how I came to be picked up. She promised us the delay would not be long.

I lay in my bunk — physically and mentally exhausted. I was probably suffering from altitude sickness a little, after so long in the depths. Yolande looked after me and did not laugh when I babbled about the starship that was waiting for us somewhere in these hills. I slept a good deal. Halfway through the second day, node peripherals went off the underworld electrical grid and on to direct photonic. The open-sky passage outside our barred hole was deathly quiet. No one came to our door except silently to deliver meals. We could not tell the time exactly. Yolande's possessions had been restored to her, but she didn't have a wristfax any more.

It was about the end of the first quarter, of another day. Our square hole was just a little paler than the walls. We had no night light. Yolande and I lay on our bunks, talking a little. We had not slept. I was warm in my pungent nest, in my stomach the rough consoling heat of an earth alcohol that had appeared with supper.

It was touching that we had both made straight for Mohun. I must have been nearer than I ever knew to actual sober belief in equivalating aliens. We were sure our rescuer would appear, here where she arrived nearly 300 years ago: just in time to save the Sub and make everything right. Of course, Yolande would

225

never confess (since it hadn't happened) that she'd been hoping Millie would turn up. I wondered how long she would go on with the starship promotion. For me, it was all gone. All I had left was a slight wish that I could have stayed in the snow meadow, thinking about Nothing, for the rest of my life. I was happy there with my two friends.

'How I have envied you,' murmured Yolande. 'All of you. Excuse me, Aeleysi, but it does seem ridiculous that you knew Millie and talked to her, and I didn't. What a waste . . . And yet, you know, I would have been terrified . . .'

I cannot remember, thought I, a feature of the woman's face. The smile I remembered, but only in its effect. I decided that this wouldn't be comforting.

'But you saw her Y. You saw her when your car route crashed.'

Quilts stirred as Yolande shifted position a little on the hard bunk.

'That's different.'

'How different?'

It was unfair, perhaps. But I'd always wanted to know.

The bedding rustled testily. 'I can't explain,' said Yolande. 'If it had happened to you, you'd understand. It's very difficult to describe that sort of experience.'

That was as near as we ever came to complete frankness, as to whether Yolande invented her alien, or discovered her.

She started to tell me about the Northern1 girl 'the VENTURan': a pathetic tale of how Himem had ensnared the poor child and deliberately enticed her away . . .

Something went patter, patter in the open passage. We both got up to look out. The people of the settlement were running. They made no more human sound than scraps of blown litter. They whispered away in a dark stream between the mudbrick and wooden houses, across a steep field and vanished. In the pre-dawn darkness they seemed to run straight into the side of a low hill that stood between us and the big ADAPT orchards. We had been forgotten.

I looked south. The sky was full of purple clouds, made visible and outlined by a milky light reflected from somewhere beyond the horizon. I saw a strange aurora begin to form: great arches

226

and moving towers. I said something, I don't know what. Yolande pulled my sleeve.

'Come on Aeleysi. Away from the window, come on. You know better than that.'

The upper room had not been locked since Yolande demonstrated her status. We went downstairs into the user's office and shut its massive door. The physical protection around a node was always substantial. It was supposed to be a formality, to make numbers take the place seriously. I crouched on the floor. I was surprised to see Yolande, too, was crying.

'Don't worry Aeleysi,' she said. 'All is well, all is well. Nothing can change that now.'

Then she hid her face and I hid mine. Behind the heels of my hands white flowers bloomed in the blackness of space, in the void between earth and VENTUR Beautiful, brilliant white flowers. I couldn't shut them out.

# Envoi: An Ambiguous Life

'And what happens to her in the end?'

'Millie? Oh, she leaves in a starship,' said Yolande firmly.

We were in a viewport in the outer wall of SHACTI seriate. After the Sub Reroute, underworld centres all over the blocs had viewports fitted: and permaturf and bits of sky laid on in some of our concourses. The secretaries had decided basic numbers must be developing break-off — the classic deep space alienation syndrome. They didn't want any more disasters. Yolande's ulaux, sitting on the end of the bench with a polite appearance of being out of earshot, caught my glance and smiled in a friendly way. She was allowed out of LC for visits: the personal escort was in honour of her status.

'Does anybody see it?'

'Certainly. Several high-credibility witnesses. Don't know how specific we're going to be —'

She hesitated, looked slightly shifty and decided not to elaborate.

We were discussing the cannibalisation of Millie Mohun, which was in production and would soon be available from the local overplus. It was being compiled from the UBIQ collection for those years; and some MONSAT material where the action moved on to the surface. Much was untraceable, or too sensitive to be released by CHTHON. The clip production plant would extrapolate — and adjust our clothes, our conversation and our politics to the taste of the present. Yolande was ambivalent about the project. She wanted the thing to sell, but she wouldn't let the machinery recall and reconcile her pre-Reroute clips to the extrapolation: which I thought was mean.

She needn't have worried. As a serial, I had no reality rights. But in any case I wasn't going to complain about a creative adaptation of my past. After half a lifetime in love with vic, I wasn't liable to be deeply attached to one arbitrary version of events. At worst, the remixed story would be dot people and that would have its own charm. At best, I might see my life turned into gengra, the stuff of dreams.

'Where is this exciting finale set?'

'Outside SHACTI. Where Dat the stargazer used to go to watch for the ships.'

231

'Is that what the extrapolation decoded?'

She nodded wisely. 'Of course, we don't know the exact site, since Millie encrypted her realtime departure from us —'

'I must admit. I'd have been happier if they could have waited until Ram and I were dead.'

Yolande frowned sharply. On the few occasions we saw each other, I tried to avoid collisions with the bizarre secret behind her reasonably sane exterior. But sometimes I forgot.

+

The Sub Reroute was cauterised in the space of about half an hour. The lesser rerouting centres were taken out with anti-personnel maser irradiation, leaving the structures intact but few human survivors. But the old capital they burned down to bedrock. The Great Housing, the cold furnace, and that revered cube of empty air; all vanished in an instant. The site became a large crater in the middle of a quarantined zone, to be approached with caution for some time to come. Half a billion numbers died, by underworld reckoning: 1 in 20 of the planet's population.

By the time Yolande secured my release from Mohun, the recovery program had begun. CHTHON was seeding the dust cloud to prevent a catastrophic winter effect. There were more VENTURans in-person in SHACTI than the underworld had ever seen: MEDICaid rovers were scouring the depths for survivors. The hotels on the mall had all been rewritten into shelter camps and hospitals for numbers who'd managed to get out on to the surface before that final dawn. I searched the shelter camps for Pia, because I had never seen her dead. I did not find her, but I did find Ram — with Himem's partner Ajoy.

They had been kept in the stadium hangar on the day we were all rounded up. They were in there for days in horrific conditions: but then the doors released and let them go. Ram and Ajoy knew it was all over. They managed to acquire some explosives: got out to the shell, located a casting bore and blasted through. I told Ram later on, he'd better believe I do sometimes have good ideas. He was very ill for a while, as were most of the 50 or so people who got out with him. But with the temporary full MEDIC we had he pulled through.

I could have recovered my identity then, while there were VENTURans about and shock and compassion had partly dissolved the barriers. I did not. It was an emotional time, perhaps I made an emotional decision. However, I never really regretted it even when the excitement was over. Mission Command moved over the wall to Laka Chih, where an all-weather strip was built at amazing expense. The tourists started to come back to the Ridge almost before the last serial refugee was written out. It was decided by common consent that SHACTI should remain SHACTI. The other place became known as 'LC', or SHACTI2.

I didn't hear anything more about the stolen lasarm. I just went back to processing. CHTHON opened up the reroute centres for new skeleton populations (mostly transfers from other blocs). As it did so it reinfrastructured them with non-invasive interfaces. But in SHACTI we carry on the old way and I hope it lasts my time. The microptic injection is so economical that it does not block consciousness, they say. It just gives you a bit of a sick headache as you sit at the face, gossiping. Yolande is amused when she hears me worrying about modernisation. Didn't I once want human processing abolished? I don't tell her I'm sentimental about my poor old burns. That was when I thought everything was going to change, I say. Now I know it isn't — who wants another 8 hours a day down here?

And so I will live out my life, an unbelieving fanatic surrounded by the antics of a minor seriate aberration — the cedars and pines of LECM above, forever out of reach.

Yolande surprised me. There were immense opportunities in the new Sub for a pro-VENTURan with an account clean of SIND connections. But though she was disgustingly tolerant of what had been done, she went on promoting Millie. For years she would come to SHACTI and try to persuade me to join one of her tours. I always said I couldn't leave my family. Ram had married another SHACTI fan. CHTHON pushed him into it, it was determined to get a quick yield on its demographic amnesty. But they were happy enough. I thought of Ram's children as Pia's: it meant a lot to me to see them grow.

The promotion tours ended when she invoked her PIONER status once too often. She'd been in Laka Chih centre for 2 years now, wearing a collar. The Rangers didn't want her but they couldn't let her go. There was a charge entered against her in EROA. Yolande insisted, as was her right, on a plenum trial. It was totally impractical to set such a thing up on the underworld. Especially since the charge in question was something like 'obstructing a seriate passageway' or maybe 'loitering with intent to say something silly'.

Yolande was quite content. She was getting too old for the freight cars anyway, she said. They let her make Millie clips and keep up all her contacts. But it was a sad waste, by any normal standards. She was so ambitious once; and I never met anyone else with a mind quite like hers. She could have done great things – if only she hadn't fallen out of her car on that long ago vigilante mission.

+

A procession of knobbly subjovian asteroids came lumbering towards us, and someone in a floater bumped into the end of the bench. A Millie fan, or at least her mother must be one. She would have been badly handicapped without that chair. The Millies refused to take normalcy implants; a slightly risky piece of bravado even 20 years after a 'completely safe' maser attack. Since CHTHON was still nervous about its image, this had had the odd effect of improving general basic MEDIC access.

'Do you ever think of going back?' asked Yolande.

Once I had hated VENTUR. When they told us how the Commander of SUBCAP fought to the last, trying to save her people. When the recovery teams were smothering a few 1000 survivors with their maternal care . . . But what happened, happened. Sub Culture died. Nothing can bring it back. Yet the Subs go on decoding in spite of all prohibitions, even though the cold furnace is gone and the *dedication* and head burning forbidden. And something of their practice will survive for a while in Millie fandom if nowhere else: the idea of the one great system, and of the value of each human part. By now I didn't exactly blame VENTUR for anything. Not even the millions dead. It would be grotesque to pretend I could care for them. I cared for Pia, and it was I who hurt Pia, not the secretariat.

'No,' I answered.

I puzzle her I suppose, the same way she puzzles me. But as I've told her, I didn't and don't choose the seriate because I like it, but because I *prefer* it. It isn't much of a choice but if things have to be this way, I'd rather be shit than eat it.

We went on gazing at the asteroids. Yolande had come to tell me that EROA had finally made up its mind. She was to be shipped to VENTUR. She was delighted. Her trial would make magnificent free Millie publicity. I refrained from telling her a plenum trial doesn't mean everybody has to watch. It only means they have to pretend they've watched. People are so lazy: and democracy would be such an exhausting form of government, if anyone took it too seriously. Still I wished her luck. I imagined the inhabitants of Maria or R4, accessing PEC and searching the screen for a 30 years dead serial jockey. It wouldn't do them any harm. It might even be educational.

'I saw Dat,' she remarked. 'On the new screen-intercom: you don't have it at SHACTI yet, do you?'

Dat was supposed to have survived. She'd been redistributed in the recovery and was living with a very 'Sub' group of Millies in one of the small centres of the south. Or so people said.

'D'you know, she looks exactly the same as she did in the old capital days —'

I grinned and shook my head. 'Save it for the Northerns, Yolande.'

The ulaux was playing miniature hockey. He heaved a sigh, cleared his wrist and the little scampering figures vanished from the seat of our bench.

Poor Yolande, she couldn't get away with claiming eternal youth for herself, however fuzzy the screen. Her old-fashioned fringe was grey. Her hands had a permanent shake, not from dedication but from the times the Subs had dragged her out to a limit somewhere and whipped her half to death. I don't suppose I

235

look much better myself, I thought. I was old enough when I came to earth, not to suffer much from the lack of radiation. But my 17yearold face gave up after a very few years of full earth gravity. Some day soon now the interface will turn me off, like Himem's mother. And in due course the serials will have proof that VENTURans are not immortal — if any of them remembers my dubious past.

I realised that Yolande and I had been staring at each other without speaking. We both knew it wasn't likely that we'd meet again, in-person or on a screen.

'Yolande,' I said. 'Be careful. You won't find any limit mobs in space but — just be careful. Millie doesn't need any SIND-type volunteers.'

She was telling people now that Millie (who had returned to the big outside) probably would not come back until the whole human race was ready for transition. Which they would demonstrate by joining Millie fandom. She made me laugh, with her transparent dreams of empire.

Yolande stood up. Her final appraisal of Pioneer Aeleysi became a resigned smile.

'Don't forget to watch PEC, Aeleysi'

It was the fans' salute.

'OK I won't. Don't you forget either.'

She was gone.

+

But what really happened to Millie Mohun? CHTHON would not or could not provide any information, outside fragments of the UBIQ collection for her brief years at SHACTI. If my mad Code Reader traced her, she was the only one who ever did. Millie Mohun came in from the surface. Later, she vanished after a riot at the old capital. That was all that ever could be proved. The fans knew nothing more and neither did Yolande. Even she had to be content with mystery, and an aesthetically satisfying fiction. Nobody ever asked Alice.

Overplus booths warbled, singing of 'pure fruit juice' and new well fittings. The human stream flowed by: and I stared into it, remembering . . .

236

On the day after the masers arrived, Yolande left me alone in the lock-up in Mohun. She went away to the nearest centre, which was SHACTI, to arrange my release. She had offered to try to raise my old identity, but I couldn't stand the idea, just at that time. I was frightened. The local people had come out of their shelter after 20 hours. The user explained cheerfully that SHACTI had promised nothing harmful would reach the Threshold. With modern weapons there was no danger at all. I imagined CHTHON disseminating that soothing story to prevent useless panic. The sky in the south was sealed off by thick ominous red-black cloud.

One night I woke up. The square hole was black, but I was aware that I had been woken by something flashing or glowing. The door of my cell opened and there was the user with a microg lamp, in her cap with ears and a felt wrapper over her blue coverall. She bundled me into a warm jacket and led me out. I looked at my sleeve as the jacket covered it and saw with a start that the gengra was gaining colour, it was moving. Energy — nearby. I was convinced the masers had triggered a geophysical catastrophe.

There were other people waiting for us. No one spoke. We climbed the graded trail by the light of the user's lamp and some bleary plastic lanterns. It could have been earth that was burning in them by the smell. It was a long way. They were hill people, they had forgotten I might get tired. 'You are doing well,' said the user encouragingly. *Do you come from a place where there are hills, in your own country?'*

When we reached our destination the sky above was amber. I saw what we had come to see: a glittering new star, reflecting the sun which was still invisible to us. A ship standing off the station. *No*, I thought, remembering Yolande's reasoning. *You can't have faster-than-light ships. Only people.* I looked around, and the rocks seemed to have changed. So had my hand, when I held it up in front of me.

Millie was saying goodbye to her friends, people she used to know no doubt before she was a jockey. I saw her being hugged and kissed. She was dressed in a good thick wrapper and boots, and someone had given her a lumpy cloth sack which was must be full of food for the journey: grain mush and wild apricots with stones in them. I'm afraid I would have managed to discard these things. They were not picturesque. But Millie was an example to all travellers. She held on to the sack, she was still wrapped in verminous and smelly felt when she stepped into a cone of brightness. The ship's lander appeared to be hovering inside, but I couldn't see it clearly. The light was oddly refractive, it altered everything around it. Too late, I realised what was happening.

Wait! I shouted. I'm coming.

I began to run as if I thought I could fly, and kept on until my lungs were bursting in the thin air of the wall. But the cone of light receded, the earth fell away from it and I was left behind. Two brilliant creatures held me up by the arms — superlucent, integral beings. I fell on my knees on the hard, cold shale. It was the Mohun user, and one of her guards.

The vision faded, the seriate passageway returned. I smiled to myself wryly: that moment still vivid after 30 years; my cold bruised knees and my eyes full of light. She really had me then, in spite of everything. But I should have known. Millie Mohun never gives you anything you can hold on to.

The wild people behaved as if nothing had happened, next day. So I kept quiet. Yolande came back. She wasn't excited about anything. I understood that what I saw had not been captured by MONSAT or the NET. I decided to keep quiet forever.

I know that my memory is hopelessly contaminated by the legend. Did Millie really say to me once, *'I am the connection'?* I can hardly believe it. I wasn't exactly in a normal state of mind at the end of the Sub Reroute. I am almost sure I dreamed that departure. And if not, it doesn't seem to matter. The version they've made up is near enough to my 'truth'. Let it be. Let the story spread and fade, the way starship stories do. Meanwhile, I will disbelieve. I feel I owe it to myself. And besides, somebody has to librate Yolande.

But if it was all true and there was a rescue mission, why was nobody rescued? Maybe it was and we are: time's relative. My decision's the same. Like Millie, I take the view that truth can look after itself. Just smile, and let them invent the rest.

I waited for a few minutes to see if my request would come up on the viewport. I'd entered it before Yolande and I sat down: the same as usual. I always ask for the clear shell effect, so I can look at my cedars. Unfortunately, the stupid serials always vote for dreary spacescape.

What can I say? Something happened to me. It changed my perception of the world. And I have gained, although it looks as though I've lost. I'm down here because I feel that what I do matters: and that is worth a great deal. I find I do not worry any more about the endless night, whether it comes or not. But I don't know if Millie Mohun was responsible for the change, or if it was my Pia. After all this time, I know that in my thoughts I hardly distinguish between those two.

No cedars. I got up and began to stroll down the passage with my weight on my left foot and my right knee bent outwards. How the bones begin to creak! I may be lean enough for the probability tunnel now, but if Millie means to come back and fetch me in-person, she'd better make it soon.

# Glossary of Acronymic
# and Subcontinental Terms

**Acronymic: acro**
The language of Space. A compacted shorthand derived mainly
from Natural English. Generally, pronounce the acronym as if it
were a word (laser). Sometimes, as in formal use of personal
names, the elements are distinct. ALIC (Alice) becomes Ae el ey
si. LECM becomes el ee si um. Not all acronymic expressions are
acronyms: many are abbreviations.

**ADAPT**
Automated Data And Processing Transfer: the machine intelligence system that takes care of industrial production. As in all
VENTURan (and underworld) systems, 'ADAPT' is marginally
personified; seen as the descendant of the supernatural entity in
charge of labour, in a primitive pantheon.

**agam**
Underworld building material.

**biel: BL**
Bonded labour: on the underworld a human servant or house
pet.

**CENTRIN**
The system that takes care of interhuman communications.

**(CH)THON**
Combined Holding Terrestrial Habitats Operational Network:
the system that takes care of the underworld. The CH is silent, as
CHTHON is no longer a commercial enterprise.

**clip**
A cinegraphic print-out scroll: a video-book.

**CONMAG**
Constant Magnitude (of x gravities): the form of propulsion used by VENTURan spaceships.

**daysky**
Sub term for illegal transactions (not recorded by the systems).

**deblocking: deb**
Sub term for the process of reversing a young man's long-term contraceptive treatment: a marriageable young man.

**deco:decoration**
A biel employed as decoration in an upper level shopping mall.

**dedication**
On the Sub: the practice of etching brain tissue to hardwire a human being for some industrial or other process task.

**deeby**
Direct brain access: a communication interface used for fantasy and other games.

**diem**
Domiciliary surveillance: underworld cultural monitoring of suspected criminal activity.

**DOGs**
Distance Order Generators: industrial grub converted for riot control.

**emart**
Electro-magnetic thruster. The underworld underground transport.

**Enabled**
On the underworld, a number (i.e. a member of the underworld population) with inherited right of access to certain VENTURan facilities.

**EROA**
The system that takes care of law and social order.

**fax: wristfax**
A personal access-to-facilities.

**Function:functionary**
The single oversystem acknowledged by the Subs: a Sub enabled to access its facilites for the lower orders.

**FUNDS**
The system that takes care of finance.

**gengra**
Generated graphics: a cinematic textile, speciality of the Subcontinent.

**genim**
A machine-generated image.

**grub:GRUB**
General Remote Utility Board. A single-crystal processor widely used in a range of VENTURan mobile and remote appliances. Loosely any mobile appliance.

**H:handshake**
An access code − a password.

**h&v**
Horizontal and vertical: internal transport in the Sub capital.

**Heteroprax**
Counter to (Sub) local practice with regard to transactions with the system.

**Housing**
The symbolic location (see below) of the Sub's one system.

**Jam:JAM**
Journal And Messages: a news service.

**LDRs**
Headwomen of the surface population (a colloquial acronym from Ranger slang – Local Dignitaries Register).

**LECM**
Local Environment Contained Modules: extra accommodation at a VENTURan base.

**LOAX**
Low Orbit Access: space shuttle platform for access to underworld blocs.

**LUDI**
Leisure Universal Design Institute: the system that takes care of leisure and games.

**Lyear**
A lightyear.

**(LR) clusters**
VENTURan style machine keyboard.

**mart**
Machine articulation.

**menarch**
A VENTURan executive: the 'ruling class' in space.

**monozuke**
(derivation) A mechanical connection: Subs who attempt to live entirely as parts of the great machine.

**MONSAT**
The helix of satellites monitoring earth's surface.

**NA alloy:palloy**
Semi-metallic materials developed in space.

**NATENG**
Natural English: the common language of the underworld.

**NET**
Near-space Event Tracer: a monitoring system deployed outside the planetary shelf.

**Orthoprax**
Accepted local (particularly Subcontinental) practice.

**PEC**
Planetary Entertainment Continuum: a continuous transmission of non-sensitive fragments of life in underworld centres, provided to entertain the masses.

**per**
Personal hygiene: an underworld bathroom.

**PIONER**
Passenger or Inhabitant of Neo-orbital Environment Rotation: a citizen of VENTUR.

**PLS:LS:LSU**
Primary Life Support (air and gravity): Life Support: Life Support Unit.

**PRENAT**
The system that takes care of human reproduction.

**PORT**
The system that takes care of travel.


**reac:Reac**
Restricted access: a security field especially one protecting
VENTURans and their installations on the underworld.


**REDs:reds**
Response Enhancer and Detoxifier: a VENTURan
prophylactic.


**SAFE**
Systems Access Facility Enclosure: VENTURan monitoring of
underworld transactions with the systems.


**SERVE**
'zerv': zero-variation process control, the VENTURan
oversystem.


**SHACTI:AC**
Surface Habitat Area Command Threshold Installation:
VENTURan administrative centre for the Sub bloc: the number
accommodation attached.


**siem**
CEM: Crew Environment Maintenance: in Space a human
monitoring duty, now obsolete.


**SIND:SINDs**
A machine-generated language imitating an ancient
Subcontinental dialect. Adopted by freedom fighters: the
freedom fighters themselves.


**SPA**
Stable Point Area: location of the original space station colonies.

**Subcontinent:Sub**
The smallest of the underworld administrative blocs. Corresponding to the Indian Subcontinent. The inhabitants of the bloc.

**symbal**
Symbolic location: a suite of hardware treated as the imaginary primary 'location' of a particular system. The room or booth containing it.

**SYNCOR:syncor**
Synthetic cortex: VENTURan firmware, substitute for human brain processing.

**V2ENTUR:VENTUR**
Vanguard 2 Experiment in Navigable Travelling Urban Rotations: the federated democracies of Space; specifically their capital city, the seven radially linked giant vessels which were once built as multigeneration starships.

**vic:vicset**
Vicarious experience: popular VENTURan entertainment. The headset carrying a vic signal.

**UBIQ**
Uncontrolled Behaviour Incident Quantifier: surveillance system within underworld population centres.

**ulaux**
Underworld local auxiliary: CHTHON's human troops.

**YD**
Yearday: the date, generally including the time of day.